# NO GOING BACK

## ALSO BY SHEENA KAMAL

*The Lost Ones*

*It All Falls Down*

# NO GOING BACK

A NOVEL

## SHEENA KAMAL

WILLIAM MORROW
*An Imprint of HarperCollinsPublishers*

HarperCollins books may be purchased for educational, business, or sales promotional use. For information, please email the Special Markets Department at SPsales@harpercollins.com.

FIRST EDITION

Designed by Diahann Sturge

Library of Congress Cataloging-in-Publication Data has been applied for.

ISBN 978-0-06-286976-0
ISBN 978-0-06-286977-7 (hardcover library edition)

20 21 22 23 24    LSC    10 9 8 7 6 5 4 3 2 1

*For my mother*

# ONE

# 1

AGENTS SEARCH ME at the Canadian border. Of course they do, those fascists.

What exactly is suspicious about a woman traveling alone by bus from Detroit and into Canada with no luggage, I ask you?

Well, put that way, maybe it's fair, but an entire bus is held up while the border agents in their ill-fitting uniforms conduct a physical search of my person and ask me questions verging on the intimate. Intimacy and I aren't well acquainted, so the questioning stalls for some time.

"How long were you in the United States?" the female agent asks again, starting from the beginning. She's likely doing this for the benefit of her supervisor, who has decided to join the party. Though the woman is older, they both look like poster children for the SS, with their blond good looks and their belief in harassing citizens of the country they're supposed to be guarding.

I tell them what they want to know, even though the information is stamped right there in my passport. My voice breaks from the cold. It's freezing, even inside the checkpoint.

Raindrops spatter the windows, and outside I can see the wind kicking up fallen leaves. Sending them dancing. The damp and the gray remind me of Vancouver, my city, but the biting cold tells me I'm far from home.

"And what was the purpose of your trip?" she asks.

I shake myself back to the present and try to focus. But it's difficult. We've been through all this before. This is how they get you: a constant stream of repetition until you change your story out of sheer boredom.

But I've been questioned by fascists before, and I know their game.

"My father grew up in Detroit. I went to visit his childhood home," I tell them. I don't say that he was a child of the Sixties Scoop, a program where thousands of indigenous children from Canada were adopted out of their communities. I'm not sure if cultural genocide is covered in their cross-border orientation handbooks.

The agent doesn't believe me. Her supervisor is too busy sending me a threatening glare to notice the subtle shift of my body, the tension around my mouth. My patience is at an end. They're either going to do a more thorough physical search or not. The words *strip* and *cavity* come to mind. I have never liked being touched by strangers, and the idea of having my cavities inspected verges on the obscene.

Maybe this is why I try to explain myself, for once.

"My father died a long time ago," I say. "Someone he used

to know showed up on my radar recently, and I had some questions. I thought I'd go to Detroit to learn more about my dad's life." And his death. But that's another story entirely. "I wasn't planning to stay more than a couple days, but the trip took a little longer than I expected."

I hear a door open and feel a blast of icy air on my nape. I look over my shoulder to see who's behind me. Whether or not anyone new has come into the station. It's an unconscious gesture, but a telling one.

One that they've noticed.

They exchange glances. "Looking for someone?" says the woman.

"No." My attention moves from the man in the blue toque who's just walked in, the man who was sitting near the middle of the bus we were both on, and snags on the agent's latex gloves. I begin to imagine where those gloved hands might be going shortly. Which cavity they might start with first. I'm sweating now, despite the chill in the air.

The supervisor steps forward and speaks for the first time. His voice is deep and smooth, like the singer of a forgettable jazz band. He looks over my passport. "Nora Watts," he says, drawing out the syllables. Is he trying to be sexy? If he is, it isn't working. "Did you find what you needed in Detroit, Ms. Watts?"

"I found that my father is as dead as he's ever been. Life moves on, and so should I."

"What's wrong with your voice?" The supervisor notices for the first time how rough it is. How it sounds like it's been scraped up from my diaphragm and shoved through my throat.

"Laryngitis."

"You say you live in Vancouver but you're going to Toronto. Why there instead of back home?" The supervisor takes over the questioning now, which is a plus. He seems more reasonable to me right about now, given the choice between him and the woman with the gloves. And I'm starting to enjoy the jazz voice.

"My daughter," I say. "I'm going to see my daughter."

The real question here is: Will my daughter want to see me?

They step aside to decide my fate. I try to look more like a fine and upstanding citizen, though my wardrobe and shabby appearance are telling a different story. That maybe I'm not so fine, definitely not upstanding, and it's possible I don't even have laryngitis.

I look like a woman on the run from her enemies.

A fair assessment, because that's exactly what I am.

Part of me wants to tell them that my father's bloodline goes back to this land before their ancestors even had the thought to come here, but the other part reminds me that my mother was an immigrant from the Middle East, and I may not want to pull that particular thread right now.

A baby in the waiting room begins to cry, putting everyone on edge. The baby's brother, who looks to be about six, tries to get their mother's attention, but she's too busy searching through her bag for something to distract her crying child. Toque Man gives the maybe six-year-old a chummy smile.

As the infant continues to bawl, I stare at the gloves and the female agent's long, thick fingers. Imagining where they might go if I'm not persuasive enough.

In the end, they let me back through to my country of birth with my cavities intact.

Back on the bus, some of my body heat returns. The bus heaves into motion, and I leave Detroit behind. Finally. With the greatest relief, I watch the scenery fly by outside the window.

Oh, Canada.

I relax, thinking I'm in the clear because the Ambassador Bridge is in the rearview mirror.

The relaxation doesn't last for very long.

Toque Man is sitting directly behind the six-year-old's mother, where he's been ever since we first boarded the bus in America. She and the infant have the seat in front of him. The six-year-old is across the aisle. Whenever the boy turns to look at his mom, he sees Toque Man. With the bus only a quarter full, the man's choice of seating is unthinkable. Nobody wants to travel in such close proximity to a young family. Nobody but this guy. At the border, I was too far away to hear what he was saying when his passport was checked, but I know whatever it was, he wasn't being honest. His posture was relaxed, his smile a little too easy. Practiced.

It was the same way he'd smiled at the little boy.

I don't like it at all.

I'm trying to keep my eyes open, to pay attention to the middle of the bus. We're barely across the border when there's a distraction I hadn't anticipated.

The radio comes on.

It's playing a song I recognize, one that I have sung. The song follows me into Windsor and then past it. I have left Detroit behind, but there's that damn tune in my head—and now it's on the radio, too. Sung by an unsigned soul artist and a former blues singer caught unawares on the airwaves, the song is a tribute to a relationship heading for the rocks. A call and response. It's a good song, maybe even a great one, but it isn't the kind of thing you hear on the radio anymore.

Do people suddenly give a shit about independent artists? I'm as surprised as anyone.

The bus sputters on the highway, and for a moment my fellow passengers are jolted into a collective prayer that we won't break down here, not when we're so close to our destination.

I don't know their reasons for the journey, but mine are pure and decent, for once. I may have lied about the laryngitis, but everything else is depressingly true. I *am* on my way to see the daughter I'd given up for adoption as an infant, Bonnie. She's seventeen now. We have not had much of a relationship up until this point, but I'm hoping to change that. I have made sacrifices to cross the border from America into Toronto to see her and to explain that the decision to let her go was made from a place of hurt. But I want to try to have a relationship now. If she'll let me.

The radio host comes on after the song finishes and informs the listening audience that the man on the record is one Nate Marlowe, a soul singer who is lying in a hospital bed, fighting for his life from a gunshot wound. A bullet struck him in the lung. Various complications have left him in critical condition. Nobody knows if he will make it, but the country seems invested in his recovery.

A young black man lost to senseless violence, says the host.

Far too good-looking to die so young, implies his cohost.

The authorities have apprehended two young gang members who, it is suspected, went to Nate's house with the intention of killing another person. He was a casualty in someone else's vendetta. They think the female singer on the hook and the second verse was the real target of the hit. It annoys me, but they're right to speculate. She *was* the target. Nate Marlowe got in the way of a bullet meant for her heart.

I know this because the mystery woman on the record is me.

I check the urge to look behind me because the instinct is getting ridiculous now. It almost got my cavities inspected back at that station.

Toronto is an ugly city, I think, as we drive through it. Better-looking than Detroit, but it can't compare in any way to Vancouver, which is the city where I parked my dog, Whisper. She's in good hands, but they're not mine, and I can feel her longing for me through the miles that separate us. I can't wait to return to her, even going so far as to imagine our reunion and that silky patch of fur behind her ears.

What I don't imagine is the reunion that I'm about to have with Bonnie.

My daughter.

Jesus.

Here goes.

# 2

A HITCH IN the plan. There's a traffic jam in Toronto that's put us behind schedule. What a surprise.

In addition to the existing afternoon parking lot that is the downtown core, apparently the British royals are in town, where the latest power couple allegedly fell in love. Folks have lost their minds, they're so excited. Crowds gathering just for a glimpse of two people. Attractive people, but still. No amount of beauty is worth the crush of bodies on the street and the general lack of respect for personal space.

Finally, we arrive at the bus station. As I disembark, a group of elderly women walk by wearing the most garish little hats I've ever seen. Someone near me whispers that the hat monstrosities are called fascinators, but that's just ridiculous. I don't see a fascinating thing about them.

Distracting, yes.

It's because of these women in the hats that I lose sight of the mother and her two children.

As I move through the station, I keep an eye out for the young family. For a moment, I think they're gone, but then I see them up ahead. The mom pauses by the door to take a phone call as the crowd surges past them. The baby is in a carrier strapped to the front of her body, and the boy is holding her free hand. The pacifier slips from the baby's mouth, and she lets go of the boy's hand for a moment to put it back in.

It happens so quickly.

The boy moves away, and in a split second, he's out the door. I sprint through those doors and see Toque Man, with his hood up now, pulling the boy across the street. There are so many people around. Now that I'm outside, I shout for help. For the man to stop. People turn and stare, look to where I'm pointing. A few of them catch on and start running toward the boy, too.

The man drops the boy's hand and takes off. He turns a corner and is out of sight. I turn the corner, too, but see nothing but a throng of people in the way. I don't know this city well enough to anticipate where he would have gone, so I head back.

When the first bystanders get to the child, he's crying.

By this time, the mother is outside, too. She's holding the baby and running toward her son. There's a look of intense relief on her face, but even from a distance I can see she's still frightened.

I watch as she's reunited with her child, as some of the other bystanders try to explain to her what they saw. A couple of people remember that I'm the one who sounded the alarm and gesture toward me, but I move back, toward the edge of the crowd.

A jogger in skintight running gear is staring at me. "Aren't you the one who—"

"No," I say.

I'm not sure if she believes me, but thankfully she shrugs and turns back toward the scene unfolding in front of us.

When the first police officers arrive, I feel comfortable enough to slip away. The boy will tell them about the man from the bus. The bystanders will confirm the description, and they will find this man and hopefully put him behind bars, where he belongs. I could stick around and share my side of things, but what's the point? They'll just have more questions, and I've had enough of those for today.

Besides, I don't talk to cops.

As I walk away, I take one last look at the young mother. The police are leading her back to the station. She's clutching both her children to her, and it looks as though she'll never let them go again. Good. Her gaze skips past me, not recognizing me from the bus. That's good, too. I have my own child to deal with.

It's cold and I'm suddenly very hungry. I could eat a steak but settle for a grilled cheese sandwich and a cup of watery coffee from a deli nearby. In the bathroom I wash my face and finger-comb my hair. I wince at the reflection in the mirror. Is this the face an estranged daughter would want to see? Maybe not, but it's the best I can do under the circumstances.

I wait for the streets to thin out and then head for the Queen streetcar. On the streetcar I stop thinking about that boy's near miss and try to focus on Bonnie. Toronto meanders by at a slow crawl. With the past few days I've had, not to mention the adrenaline high and eventual slump after today's events, my body just about shuts down.

I'm so lulled by the movement of the streetcar that I fall asleep and miss my stop. The driver wakes me up at the station and asks me if I'm alright. I would tell him the truth, but he doesn't look like he can handle it. I just nod and say yes. A few minutes later we're on our way back.

It's fall in Toronto, the season only just beginning to turn frigid, which is what may have effected the sudden chill in Bonnie's posture. She's a teenager, but all the self-importance and spitfire that go with that age have momentarily deserted her.

We're standing in front of each other, this girl and I, for the first time in our lives. Face-to-face, and neither of us is unconscious. An improvement.

She's leaner than she'd been a year ago, at least from what I saw in photos. Tougher, too, given the suspicious look she threw in my direction when she first saw me, before she recognized me. Ah, those eyes. There is no denying they are mine, dark and fathomless. I try to read her, but I can't.

This is normally what I'm very good at.

Observing people, seeing what's beneath their surfaces, what they keep buried. But Bonnie remains a mystery. Some people say that you can never know your children, which might be true.

There is so much I want to say to this young woman, this teenager.

"Nora? What are you . . . is this about the tattoo?" Bonnie says, to cover her shock.

"What tattoo?"

She doesn't answer for a moment. Then, her voice low with urgency, she tells me about the tattoo she remembers from the time she was kidnapped over a year ago. "I can't get it out of my head. I draw it all the time. It makes me feel like I did back then, when they took me. Like someone's always watching," she says.

"Have you told your parents about this?"

She shakes her head. "No. It's just a feeling, right? I don't want to freak my mom out." She's scared but doesn't want anyone else to be.

This caution, the instinct for silence . . . I guess there must be some connection between us after all.

All my hopes of what this reunion could be fall away, and now I'm scared, too, though my fear means almost nothing. I have lived with it for far too long. It has made a home inside me, and I have come to expect it.

No, it's *her* fear that is a travesty. I've made a powerful enemy, but it hadn't occurred to me that he would be keeping an eye on Bonnie. But it should have.

I tell her there's nothing to worry about, that I'll look into the origins of this tattoo for her. Then I leave before she can ask any questions.

I stay in Toronto for two days, at a motel on the east end of the city. It's close enough for me to keep an eye on the sleek town house that Bonnie shares with her adoptive mother, Lynn. I watch, but don't see anything suspicious. Yet.

It means I have some time.

I can't stay here if I'm going to look for the man who has made my daughter scared for her life, the one who was behind the attack on Nate Marlowe. She doesn't know that he's after me. And she sure as hell doesn't know that I'm going to find him first.

# 3

THIS IS HOW it started: When Dao was a child, his mother told him he had to be the best at everything to make it in this country that took them in. Their new, very cold home. It was a lot because he was just a child. Turns out he wasn't good at much. And she didn't exactly set a decent example herself. She was always too overworked, too tired to give anything her all. So she wasn't especially good at anything, either. In fact, his first memory, when he was four years old—

No, wait. That's too far back. If he's going to give this a go, collect his thoughts for what they're worth, he should start with more current events.

First, some courage.

He crushes up the last of his oxycodone hydrochloride and snorts it off his dresser. Makes a mental note to buy some more. Down here, the pills are easy to get and cost almost nothing.

Now he's flying. On top of the world. Feeling so good—so euphoric, in fact—that he's ready to think about those current events.

Before he can get started, the call he's been waiting for comes through.

"Is it done?" he asks.

There's a pause on the other end of the line, which worries him. It's always bad news when there's a dramatic pause. What his contact says next confirms it. "Nora Watts got away. I don't know how. And she knows about the hit now."

It takes him a moment to process the sheer incompetence at work here. "I thought the people you hired were professionals. I paid them for a job."

"We thought so, too."

He can feel his euphoria deflating. "Is she still in Detroit?"

"We don't think so. Look, Detroit was a fuckup, and we're obviously not going to give them the other part of the payment."

No shit. He doesn't actually care about the money. It's chump change, and turns out, he's the chump. "Where is she now?"

"She hasn't turned up back in Vancouver yet, but—"

"So you botched it, spooked her, and now she's on the run. That it?"

"We'll find her."

"You sure about that?" Dao asks softly. It's not that he's being unreasonable. This is what he pays them for.

What follows is a series of useless promises and excuses from his guy. Dao hangs up in the middle of it.

He flings open the windows of the bedroom that has become his entire world. A rush of cool sea air blows past him. It's raining, and that's depressing, too.

Rain makes him think of Vancouver, that godforsaken city he's always hated.

He goes down to the gym and works out until he's lathered with sweat. Even that can't help his anger from building.

He showers, and by the time he dresses for the day, the sun has come out.

Good. It gives him energy. Seems people have forgotten how much fear he can invoke and that he has friends in powerful places.

Maybe he should remind them.

A little maid, the newish one, is on her hands and knees in the kitchen, scrubbing the floors. He takes a moment to appreciate the view. When she sees him, she gets up, apologizes, and leaves the room so quickly she could have been a figment of his imagination. Moves with the flight instinct of prey.

She has the right kind of attitude, that one.

He notices that his hand is clenched in a fist but can't place the moment the anger had taken over. But the maid had been aware of it. Of course she had. Scurried away like one of those lizards he so enjoys crushing. He imagines her, the little maid, under his boot. Squirming to get away. Her friends and family:

*Wonder what happened to her?*

*She was crushed.*

*What do you mean, "crushed"?*

*Dead. Smashed into the ground. What else?*

But he's not actually mad about the little maid. It's not her fault he's so angry.

No, the blame lay with someone else entirely.

He calls his guy back. "Double it. Double the money."

"You sure you want this woman so bad?"

Dao doesn't even deign to respond to that idiotic question. Would he have done any of this, *any of it,* if he weren't sure? "Call me when you find her."

He leaves the house, whistling. He's got an appointment with his Humas, his fixer, and this time heads are going to roll.

# 4

STEP ONE OF finding my enemy is to pick up my dog.

Whisper has nothing to do with it, per se, but I can't be expected to embark on an important life journey like this without her. I left her in the care of my mentor, Sebastian Crow, who died while I was in Detroit. After a short, intense battle with cancer, he is now gone. Whisper has been with Seb's ex, Leo Krushnik, ever since, and I'm just about tired of being without her. When Seb died, Leo said he would look after her until I get back.

When I show up in Vancouver at Seb's Kitsilano town house, Leo closes the door on me.

I stuff my hands in my coat pocket and wait for a full minute on the doorstep. I can hear Whisper whining inside.

"Oh, alright," Leo says, admonishing someone. Me or her, I'm not sure. He opens the door again, takes in my tired face, slumped posture, bleary eyes, and lets me in. His reluctance is a new stain on our relationship. We used to be on better terms, Leo and I, and I'm sad it has come to this.

Whisper trots to me as I kneel on the ground with my arms wide open. She's a gray mutt of indeterminate age, with a distinctly feline personality. The personality thaws for a moment as she gives in to her excitement at seeing me, her primary food person.

Maybe her favorite food person?

I can't tell. Her tail whips back and forth, almost of its own volition. Her throaty cries tell me that I'm forgiven for leaving, but my departure will never be forgotten. She hesitates after briefly licking my face, as if deciding whether to take this lovefest any further. She settles for pushing me over and barking for a while in complaint. Then she lays her body on my lap and presses her face into my chest.

"That is a nose," I say, giving it a smacking kiss. The nose in question is as warm as rubber on a summer day. She whines and sneezes off my kiss. She knows it's some nose, has always had a good idea of her own worth. I'm lucky to have this kind of love in my life, I think, as I glance up at Leo. I wonder if the glint in his eye is a look of possession directed toward my dog, but no, on closer examination I see it's a tear.

He goes into the kitchen.

I don't follow immediately, but when I do, I notice for the first time that he's wearing Seb's ratty old plaid bathrobe. When I saw him last, he'd been in a pair of charcoal slacks and a tailored Oxford shirt. We'd both been working at his small PI firm at that time. He was looking a lot better than he does now.

Leo looks at me, really looks, and says: "She's not safe with you."

"What?" It takes real effort to make my voice this clear, and despite the effort, it still sounds like some small animal has attacked my lungs. Leo doesn't notice.

"Whisper. She's better off with me. There are people after you and she's getting on in years. I think she deserves some stability, don't you? You upend her life to nurse Seb; then you run off to Detroit, where you almost got yourself killed."

I look at Whisper, who isn't young—that's true—but is otherwise the picture of health and vitality. Her eyes and ears are as sharp as they have ever been, and her coat is shiny and thick. She's in better shape than I am.

"One person is after me." I think about it for a moment, then add, for clarity: "Right now. Only one person at this time. How did you know about that, anyway?"

"Because it's you, and someone is always trying to murder you for some reason or the other."

He's not wrong and won't get any debate from me on the subject. Leo and I know each other too well to mince words. Back when he and Seb were together, I worked for his fledgling PI firm as an assistant of sorts. Also helped him find missing people because I have a knack for it. Before Seb broke up with Leo and asked me to come help him with his memoirs and freelance reporting, Leo and I had been close.

But things have changed.

I see now that Seb's death hasn't made it alright between us again. Hasn't come close to healing the wounds of Seb's abandonment.

"I can look after my dog," I say.

He sighs. It's nice to see his flair for the dramatic is still in good shape. "Can you look after yourself? You should talk to Brazuca."

Jon Brazuca, my ex-sponsor, who is also an ex-cop turned PI, isn't exactly in my life anymore. Not enough to swap "you'll never guess who's after me now" stories, anyway. We would have nothing to do with each other if he hadn't started at Leo's private investigation company. Which we both, at one time or another, worked for.

"What does Brazuca have to do with it?"

"You don't know? He's been looking for you."

"Yeah, to tell me Seb's de— To tell me about what happened to Seb."

He buries his head in his hands. His bathrobe gapes open at the top and the bottom. "Nora, you're literally the worst. Literally. In case you missed the point, I'm being literal here. Brazuca's been looking for you for weeks now. He thought you were in some kind of danger and that there were people after you in Detroit."

"I don't want to get into what happened in Detroit."

"Tough. Didn't Brazuca warn you? Isn't that why you're even alive?"

"Haven't spoken to him."

"Jesus," he says. "He must be so worried."

Leo does the thing I try to persuade him isn't necessary.

He calls Jon Brazuca.

# 5

BRAZUCA MUST HAVE been sitting at home waiting for this opportunity to limp on over here, because within the hour he's in the kitchen with us, rubbing his bum knee, staring at me like I've just risen from the grave and am haunting him instead of the other way around. The last time I saw him, he was working on his health, but all of that seems to have escaped him because here he is, looking like he hasn't slept in weeks, like he's surviving on coffee and frozen meals. Looking, if I'm being honest, like me and Leo.

"What the hell happened in Detroit?" he asks, as soon as he walks into the kitchen. "Are you alright?"

"No, she's really not," Leo says sadly.

"I'm fine," I insist.

"Nora, your voice . . . it's because of the fire, right? That warehouse that burned down . . . you were in it. Has there been damage to your throat from all the smoke you inhaled?"

Leo stares at me. "You were in a fire? I thought . . ." He's not sure why he hadn't noticed how rough I sound. I can tell it bothers him, that he's missed something this important.

"Have you been to a doctor?" Brazuca asks.

I shake my head.

He doesn't like this. It's one of the reasons I don't enjoy being around cops, or even ex-cops such as Brazuca. They're too used to getting their way, making veiled threats that pass as suggestions.

"She doesn't want to talk about it," Leo says.

"She has to talk about it. There are people trying to kill her."

Leo dislikes this male posturing just as much as I do. He frowns at Brazuca. "She knows that. And it's only one person right now, so you can just chill."

Brazuca stares at me. "Do you have anything to say here?"

"No."

"Goddamn it, you should! Nora, listen. I went to Detroit to look for you. Just got back, actually."

This takes a moment to process. "Why would you do that?"

"Call me crazy, but I was worried. I used to be your sponsor, you know." And he used to be more than that, I think. "I was on an assignment and you came up. I investigated an overdose death for a client and, by chance, discovered that someone connected to the Three Phoenix triad used a biker gang to keep watch on a woman. That woman is you."

"I've heard of Three Phoenix. But they collapsed twenty years ago when their boss, Jimmy Fang, fled the country to escape trial," says Leo. He's incredulous. I don't blame him. It's all a bit hard to swallow.

"Three Phoenix was part of a larger network of criminal

organizations out of Asia; it had connections to larger triads like 14K and the Big Circle Boys. They were fluid and worked well with other crime syndicates. They didn't watch you themselves—didn't have to. They used a gang that operates out of the port. I'm assuming that when they found out you were in Detroit, they decided it was the perfect opportunity to get rid of you. Someone called someone else, and boom."

"Except no boom," says Leo. "She's still here. What's this about, Nora?"

I don't answer. I need a minute to think. Brazuca steps in to fill in the gap. "A couple years ago, Nora's daughter, Bonnie, was kidnapped by a wealthy family. The Zhangs. In rescuing her, Nora made an enemy of Dao, head of their private security, who has links to organized crime. Dao disappeared, but it turns out he's still got a grudge. All the Zhangs died, and only he and Nora survived."

Leo puts the kettle on and foists mugs of instant coffee on us. There's no milk or sugar, so Brazuca and I drink it black while Leo pours a generous shot of whiskey into his. It doesn't aid in his understanding of the matter much, but it does improve his mood. "So Nora crosses this Dao guy. He wants revenge and uses his criminal contacts to keep watch on her in Vancouver and attack her in Detroit."

Brazuca takes a bracing sip. He grimaces and puts down the mug. "Sounds about right."

"People with mononyms are terrifying," says Leo. "Is Dao a nickname? A surname?"

"I don't know. He's a ghost." Brazuca tries the coffee again. From the look on his face, the second attempt is even worse than the first.

"He's not a ghost," I say. "I've seen him in real life, heard his voice. He's real, and there's got to be something we can use to track him down. Everybody's got some paper on them." Even those who do their best to avoid it, like myself. "I just have to find it."

"*We* have to find it," says Leo. "You're not doing this alone, Nora. This man wants to hurt you. We find information on him, prove that he put a hit on you. Build a case against him to take to the cops."

"Or you could let Leo and me figure this out," Brazuca says to me. "Move somewhere else and lay low for a while. Hope Dao forgets about you and this whole thing blows over."

I shrug it off. "Costs money to lay low."

"I have money."

He doesn't give the impression of a man who has come into sudden wealth. There's no Ferrari outside. "Where did you get money?"

"I did a freelance job recently. It paid well. And I have some savings of my own." There is a directness in his gaze that I remember from our shared past.

I have a certain skill that has deserted me in the past year but is coming back quickly. I think my fear for Bonnie has put this ability to discern truth from lies back at the center of my life. Brazuca had been the one person I could never quite figure out, but that block seems to have crumbled. I see him clearly now, and I'm curious.

He's not lying to me, but he's hiding something.

"And you're just going to give me some of this money to disappear?"

He shrugs. "It's an option. It'll be a loan you can pay back whenever you're able to."

"Why would you do that?"

This pisses him off, though I don't understand why he thinks I'll just take money from him without questioning his reasons. "You know what, Nora? I don't actually know why. I just can't believe that this is happening, and it all seems a bit dangerous. And, if I'm being honest, more than a little absurd. Why would this guy Dao hate you so much? Let me guess. You don't want to talk about it."

He pushes away from the table and goes to the window. I follow his gaze, but he's not looking at anything I can make out. Just considering the sky and, perhaps, what he'll do with all his money now that I've decided to let him keep it for himself.

Leo takes offense at Brazuca's tone and glares icicles into his back before turning to me. He puts his hand over mine. I don't love the touch, but this is Leo, and it's impossible to be upset at him. Even though he may have designs on my dog. "Nora, hey, we're with you on this."

That may be true, but even I can see what Leo is really saying is that he needs this right now. Here in this kitchen is the first time he hasn't looked completely bereft since he opened the door to me.

Brazuca looks at our hands on the table, Leo's still covering mine. For a moment I think he's about to add his to the pile, but he thinks better of it. We don't touch, Brazuca and I. Not anymore. Some parts of my past have to stay there, and the line between us is one that neither of us is willing to cross.

Thank God. I'm not sure how much more masculine intervention I can take.

"If we're going to look for Dao, we can work through the only angle I've been able to find," Brazuca says.

"Which is?" Leo asks.

"Before the head of Three Phoenix, Jimmy Fang, fled the country and the case fell apart, there was some suspicion that someone on his side was talking to the cops."

"A snitch?" I ask.

Brazuca frowns. "We prefer to call them 'police agents,' actually. But no, I checked with a police contact and I don't think there was anyone official who went into witness protection. The information never had a chance to come out in trial."

"But you think someone was talking to the cops?"

"I've been a cop, Nora. There's some information you

only get from close sources. I've been over the case time and again, looking through Three Phoenix associates. I narrowed it down to one guy."

In the waning daylight Brazuca talks about what he's unearthed on the Jimmy Fang case, which may give me a lead on Dao's network. Maybe even a way to find him before he finds me. Brazuca tells us about his police source and the criminology reports he's read. The countless articles and interviews.

Rain patters against the windowpanes, turning the little yard behind the kitchen into a pit of sludge. Brazuca and Leo are both animated, both so earnest. I've never been good at reading Brazuca, but, for what it's worth, he seems invested in this. Maybe I'm growing as a person, because I don't immediately discount the instinct to trust him. Even though there still may be a betrayal or two up his sleeve. I fall into the circle forming around us, but carefully. Like a woman with something to lose. Inch by inch, bit by bit.

Finally, Brazuca turns to me. "One last thing, Nora. You can't stay here. The people who've been watching you know this address."

"You can use my apartment in Chinatown," Leo offers. "Whisper will be better off here, though." An argument ensues. There's no way I'm leaving her behind. Finally, Leo agrees to hand his keys over.

After Brazuca leaves, we sit in the kitchen for a long time.

To fill the silence Leo puts on Chopin's nocturnes, which

he believes Seb loved as much as he did. He thought Chopin was "their" composer when in fact the nocturnes were only special to Seb because Leo couldn't get enough of them. Even in this, they didn't understand each other. Or the love they shared. The Chopin is endless, playing from the laptop in Seb's old study on a loop, our own personal dirge.

The rain outside turns to snow, and I am riveted by the sight as it hits me that this is actually happening. Snow in Vancouver and, in order to find the man who's threatened my life, *we* are going to look for a snitch.

# 6

"YOU'VE NEVER REALLY told me about your daughter," Leo says to me, from the foot of the stairs.

I pause midway up. "We're not close."

"But she's the reason you won't get out of town for a while. You're worried about her."

This is what happens when you let people in. They think they know you well enough to question your motives. The trouble with Leo, though, is that he actually does. "Dao knows who she is. He can use her as leverage. The fact that we're not close is a good thing. For her." I try to sound upbeat but fail miserably. There's nothing cheerful about this situation.

"Do you need help packing your things?"

"No. There's not much." Then I ask him something that's been on my mind since he reluctantly opened the door to me. "Why are you living here? Why is it you're the one getting rid of Seb's stuff?"

He looks so miserable, I almost wish I hadn't asked. "Seb left all his assets to his son, who's just a kid. He had no other family. His ex was going to hire a company to pack up the house before she put it on the market. I offered to do it instead." The last part he says while looking down at his bare feet.

I get it. This is closure for him. He's not ready to let go.

It takes me no time at all to gather my meager possessions from the room upstairs where I lived for about a year. There's an envelope waiting for me on the bed with my name scrawled across it. In Seb's handwriting. Tucking the envelope in a duffel, I pile all my belongings and Whisper into my old Corolla, which still starts, and drive over to Leo's Chinatown apartment.

We're quiet as we take the back stairs up to Leo's second-floor unit. Whisper and I, we're used to being stealthy. It comes from the years we spent living in the basement of Leo's small PI company on Hastings Street, back when both Seb and Leo worked there.

Leo's apartment is noisy, a far cry from the sleepy Kits town house. There's a covered balcony from which Whisper and I watch the goings-on beneath us. She's still startled at my sudden reappearance in her life, so we go for a long midnight walk. It's still snowing, lightly now.

I listen as the sounds of the city find me in the darkness. Feel its beating heart.

I let Whisper off-leash because I sense she'll stay by my side tonight, and we walk until my mind clears.

It's not that I don't want help. It's that I don't want the baggage that comes along with it. The responsibility of putting other people in danger.

Brazuca had been nudging me earlier, testing me. He wanted to know my intentions with Dao. I've been thinking about that, too. Protecting Bonnie is number one. Making sure that it doesn't spread any further than it already has is another.

But his safety was on my mind also. His and Leo's.

When I was in Detroit, I was being followed by a gang member or two who'd been hired to kill me. I'd suspected Dao had been behind it, far too late. Brazuca confirmed it tonight. Dao, through his connections, had been having me watched. Biding his time until it was somehow easy. A murder in Detroit? Nobody would blink an eye. He knew that. It's why he set those young men after me.

They found Nate Marlowe instead.

Shot him one morning as he stepped into his kitchen, before I could warn him, or move, or speak. I watched Nate fall to the ground, and I saw the light go out of his eyes. I sat by his hospital bed and told him how sorry I was, but it wasn't enough. He had been the first man I'd let inside me in a very, very long time. It wasn't a decision I'd made lightly, and I made it only because it was him. A musician who saw straight through all my bullshit and wanted me to sing with him anyway. I didn't deserve him, but I didn't need a bullet to take him away from me. Now, according to a new radio update, Nate is recovering at home. But his voice will never be the same.

Dao has taken something beautiful from the world.

The blues song I sang with Nate Marlowe, the one I've been hearing on the radio, is about a woman who is nothing but trouble. As much as I try to run away from it, hide, bury my problems or drown them in a barrel of whiskey or one of its substitutes, it always finds me. I'm caught unawares, with my pants down.

I'm going to have to start paying better attention, taking stock.

By Leo's bedside I find a selection of healing crystals hanging from leather thongs. I take one down and hide it in his bedside table by a half-empty box of condoms, making sure to keep the condoms in front for when Leo goes looking. Safety first. Then I thread the brass key from my pocket through the strip of leather and tie it around my neck.

Taking stock goes badly, worse than I could have anticipated:

Intuition, jacked.

Strength, poor.

Cardio, not impressive but better than your average citizen.

Dark circles, under eyes.

Excessive mucous, nostrils.

Old gunshot wound, shoulder.

Old sprain, ankle.

Fresh scratches, arms and legs.

Fresh purple bruises, ribs.

Fresh scarring from smoke inhalation, lungs and throat.

Spite and vengeance, heart.

Continuous battering, soul.

I heard a stoned hippie say once that a complete body transformation is possible after seven years. We shed dead cells, can repair or erode tissues along with general health and well-being. After seven years it is possible to be a whole new person. Imagine that. But seven years seems like a long time. I might not be alive to experience this new me.

Sleep eludes me after coming up with this impressive list. I flip through one of Leo's old magazines and read about cosmetic solutions for the dark circles. In the bathroom mirror I see a stranger in need of some eye cream staring back at me. This face could scare away any teenager, the hollows beneath my eyes more like shadowy pits, but I don't linger on that thought. I'd caught a glimpse of the price of the cream in the magazine, and there's no way I can afford to do anything about the circles just yet, maybe ever.

Most of the things on the list are unimportant in the grander scheme of things, and I can always start doing something about my strength. My soul is what it is, and there's nothing to help it. As to my heart and the trouble I'm in, that's another story. But not one for tonight.

I've been avoiding the envelope Seb has left for me, but now there's nothing else to do but open it. He has left me a copy of the manuscript for his memoirs and nine thousand, four hundred, and eighty-seven dollars in cash. The manuscript I put aside because I can't bring myself to read it. The money I keep handy.

I think Seb must have known me better than anybody on the planet. The year I spent looking after him coated our bond in steel. I watched him deteriorate, took him to his appointments, picked up his meds, helped him with his syndicated news blog and the freelance assignments that came his way—along with the research and organization of the memoirs. He gave me the money from the blog and assignments. And I guess he stashed some extra as well.

If it had been officially bequeathed, the lawyer wouldn't have been able to find me or I might have even been required to declare it on my taxes, if I ever decided to file them. Seb must have known that. He was likely also aware how far I can stretch money like that. Certainly long enough until I can figure something else out. It isn't a fortune, but it's enough to buy me some time. For what, though? He didn't know about the trouble I've found myself in when he left it for me, but he must have sensed it. That I might need some cash to tide me over.

I don't deserve this kindness.

I miss him suddenly. In our study, where we worked on his memoirs, he sat by the desk or on the couch. We talked everything through before a word was written. He got sicker and sicker as the days went by, but his mind was still lucid. I wonder how he was at the end, but I don't have the right to know that. I wasn't there for him during his last days because I went to Detroit. How alone he must have been.

My phone rings.

I'm tempted to ignore it because I'm depressed and because it's late, but the call is from a Toronto number. That can mean only one thing.

"Are you okay?" I ask Bonnie, as soon as I answer. "Did something happen?"

"Hi . . ." She takes a moment here to think of what to call me, then settles on nothing. "I didn't think you'd answer."

"Why did you call, then?"

She hesitates. "To say goodnight."

I check the clock on the phone. "It's two a.m. there."

"I know."

"Okay . . . goodnight." I can't think of what else to say, but this is clearly the wrong choice because she replies with a curt "'Night" and hangs up.

What was that about? I have no idea, but I know that I handled it—whatever it was—badly. There's no winning with teenagers.

With the brass key around my neck, I sit in the darkness with Whisper at my side and watch the neon pink light of the Szechuan place across the street stream from the open window into the room.

Dawn can't come soon enough.

# 7

*THAT WAS A MESS,* Bonnie thinks, after she hangs up.

She'd called Nora for a reason, and it wasn't to say good-night at two a.m. Like an idiot.

In her room, propped up on her bed with her sketchpad in front of her, Bonnie frowns at the bit of nothing she's drawn, an uneven attempt at sketching Nora's face. She's been at it all night, and it's still the worst drawing she's done in years. The only reason she's even doing it is because she's regretting the way she treated Nora when she'd just showed up out of nowhere.

Bonnie hadn't expected to see her birth mom in front of her all of a sudden.

She'd just gotten off the streetcar and was putting away her headphones because she rarely wore them while walking alone anymore. Then she'd looked up from the knot of wires and there was Nora, looking beyond tired. This woman, this stranger that she didn't immediately recognize as her mother.

She didn't know what to do, so she didn't even say hello. Didn't even ask her inside.

Instead there was some rambling about her nightmares

from the time she'd been kidnapped. It sounded as though she blamed Nora for what had happened to her, but she didn't mean it like that at all. She was scared for Nora. Seeing her there in person did nothing to calm her fears. She's as scared for Nora as she is relieved that her real mom, Lynn, had adopted her. It's a bad thought because Nora isn't a terrible person. She just struggled and was hurt and couldn't look after Bonnie even if she'd wanted to. Bonnie knows all that, she does.

She was just too surprised to remember it all on the phone. The sound of Nora's voice like sand. Empty as the desert.

Bonnie flips through last month's sketchpad and takes a couple of photos of the tattoo she's been drawing, the one she'd seen on her birth father. It's of talons, dripping with blood.

It's these photos she sends to Nora because something tells her that this is what their bond is based on. The time that she was kidnapped, the hurt and the fear, then the hope when she'd learned that her birth mom had come looking for her after all. That she did care.

So what if she couldn't ask Nora inside? At least they had something. They both faced the people who had taken her, both faced that fear. Her mom Lynn had been scared, too, but it wasn't the same. Lynn hadn't gone searching the way Nora had. Lynn thought Bonnie had run away, which was fair because she'd done it so many times before, but it had been Nora who'd tried to rescue her.

And Lynn doesn't know what it's like to feel as though you're being followed.

After hip-hop class this evening Bonnie felt eyes on her the entire streetcar ride home, but she couldn't figure out who'd been looking. It was the same feeling she got some mornings before heading to school.

It was just a feeling, but after she'd been kidnapped, feelings like this were impossible to ignore.

This is what she wanted to talk to Nora about, something she instinctively knows Nora will understand. But she couldn't find the words when it mattered. It hasn't even been two years since she first saw her birth mom. When she'd been younger, she thought they would have so much to talk about. She'd imagined the conversations they'd have. It was stupid, but she always felt that talking to the woman who brought her into the world would be easy.

Easy doesn't even come close.

Every now and then they'd send photos, though, and for a while it had been enough. Images from their days, their lives. It was something. But maybe it's not enough anymore.

Bonnie turns off her light and takes a peek out her bedroom window.

There's no one out there.

Just like the other hundred times she'd looked, waking in the middle of the night with an unsettling feeling, only to peer into the darkness. "Stupid," she mutters to herself.

She doesn't see the car lingering farther down the street, engine off, driver masked in darkness. Hadn't noticed it had been there for a few hours. Doesn't see it pull away several minutes after her light goes off.

No, by then she's fast asleep.

# 8

WHEN BRAZUCA OPENS the door to the Hastings Street office the next morning, the dog lifts her head, assesses him, and finds him unworthy of further contemplation. She puts her head back down. Not surprising. He's never had much luck with females of any species. Why should this be any different?

He finds Nora slumped over Leo's desk, Leo's laptop in front of her. Within a moment of him entering the room, she wakes. A switch that's instantly flipped on.

"Did you come in through the back?" he asks.

"Of course. No one saw me."

He goes into the kitchenette and puts on a pot of coffee. He has spent the past several weeks obsessing over Nora's safety, and here she is, sleeping in the office. Seeing her at Leo's desk gives him a sense of relief that he refuses to analyze too closely. He tells himself that what he feels for Nora could never be sexual, except it had been, once.

He hears Nora leave with Whisper, but they're back in about ten minutes, Nora brushing the snow from her fall jacket. She joins him in the kitchen, somehow knowing the moment when the coffee is finished. They take their mugs of hot coffee back to Leo's office.

"Bonnie sent me photos of the tattoo she remembers. She's been drawing it. It matches the Three Phoenix ink. I also found this."

On the computer screen she shows him an image he's well familiar with. Of Jimmy Fang standing in front of a shrine with his shirt off, the distinctive talon tattoo inked on his chest.

Brazuca nods. "That's the old school of gangsters. I hear some of them are moving on from identifiable tattoos. Which is why Dao must have been upset to see Three Phoenix ink on Kai Zhang. Not only did he not earn it, but it's also not the way some of them do business anymore. Stands out too much."

"I've been catching up on Three Phoenix," Nora says. "There's not a lot about them on the web. They went underground twenty years ago. And, you're right. The last time they were on anyone's radar was when Jimmy Fang was arrested. He jumped bail, disappeared. I was just getting into the charges."

Brazuca sits across the desk from her and rubs the ache out of his bad leg. "The police were looking into money laundering and extortion, but the main case against him was based on a shootout in front of an underground gambling den in Chinatown. He was identified at the scene, and his fingerprints were found on a weapon used at the shooting."

"Who made the ID?"

"Parking lot attendant from a lot across the street."

"I'm guessing that's not the snitch."

"I wish you wouldn't use that term. Police agents are a valuable source of information," he says.

"Sorry, who's the police agent snitch?"

Of course this is a losing battle with Nora. She has never been one for the rule of law. "My best guess is a small-time crook named Joe Nolan. He went to school with Jimmy Fang and was a known associate, but not inner circle. He did some time for assault and was back in the mix as soon as he got out. When Three Phoenix fell apart, Nolan moved out to Port Moody, where his brother lives."

He gets his laptop from the other office, the one he shares with Stevie Warsame, Leo's other partner in the PI business. When he returns, Nora is stretching out a kink in her back. She looks tired, he thinks, tired but alert. Her hair is swept off her shoulders. It's longer than he's used to seeing it. With her thin face and big dark eyes, she looks like a ragged doll someone has left out in the rain.

She spends a moment scrolling through the photos on the social media account he's pulled up.

"This is Nolan?" she asks, somewhat incredulously.

"He your type or something?"

She ignores his sad attempt at humor. Pushes the screen back toward him. The man in the photos is over two hundred pounds of pure muscle.

She gets a look in her eyes sometimes, Nora does. As though he doesn't deserve the air he breathes. He'd been dishonest with her one time, about one thing, and he'll never live it down. "Jimmy Fang had a huge network of associates," he says. "All the cops needed to do was find a pressure point in his network and then exploit a grudge. I think Nolan had the biggest pressure point."

"If he was talking and had this pressure point, as you say, why not go into witness protection?"

"I don't know. But I have a theory. I think the cops turned him because they had something on him and they threatened jail time. His older brother is high on the autism spectrum. After their mother died, Nolan became his primary caregiver. He couldn't afford to not be around for another jail stint, and he didn't want to disrupt his brother's regular routines by relocating. The case hadn't actually progressed to trial."

It all comes back to family.

"I'll go talk to him," Nora says, finishing her coffee and standing. "This Nolan guy."

Two can play that game. Brazuca stands, too. "Look, you can try to find him on your own, if you want, but it'll take time. The other option is to ride with me. I already have his address on my GPS."

He expects her to put up a fight, maybe have a little bit of an argument on their way to his MINI parked out back, but she doesn't. She looks like the fight has gone out of her, which worries him more than he cares to admit. He lets Whisper into the back seat, because Nora insists on taking her, and drives them out of the city.

When they're on the highway, he sneaks a glance at her. No, it's not that the fight has gone out of her. It's there in the hardness in her eyes, the set of her shoulders, her grim expression. It's that she's saving it all up.

And it's a good thing, too, because it has been at least ten minutes since he's noticed the dark sedan a few cars behind them.

He speeds up suddenly, changes lanes, and takes the next exit off the highway. The sedan switches lanes but doesn't take the exit. Maybe it was too close to make, or maybe he was wrong about the tail.

There's a moment of breathless silence, and then Nora looks over at him. She's shaken but trying to hide it. "My enemies or yours?"

He's not sure whether or not she's joking, but she seems to be taking it all in stride. "Could be either, or just my imagination."

"Did you get a license plate?"

"No, they were too far behind for that."

"Okay," she says. "If they've turned around, they'll come back to this exit to look for us. I think we should keep going."

"*If* we were actually being followed, there could have been a second car. I don't want to chance anything. Nolan is our only lead, and I don't want to do anything to spook him. Who's 'they,' anyway? We don't even know." He gets onto the highway heading back to the city. "We'll try again later. Nolan's employed in construction in Port Moody, but he works the door some weekends at a club on Granville. Let's go tomorrow night."

"He goes to a Granville club all the way from Port Moody? That's insane."

"Not if you time the drive right. A lot of people make that commute for work."

"What club?"

"Ha. You'll just have to come with me tomorrow to see. I'm not taking any chances you'll cut me out."

She refuses to meet his eyes, and that's how he knows that's exactly what she was planning to do. He drives her to China-town and trusts her instincts when she asks him to let her off a few blocks away from Leo's place.

"See you tomorrow," she says, opening the back door for Whisper. The dog bounds out, waits patiently for her leash, and then they're both off.

# 9

IN THE PAST I've dreamed that drums are summoning me, but to where? I never figured it out. This is why I've always preferred the guitar. A stringed instrument asks you to sit and stay awhile. Marinate in your depression. It doesn't want you to get to your feet.

Today, drums shake me out of the lethargy I've felt since Brazuca dropped me off. At first, I think it's coming from inside Leo's apartment building—some neighbor from hell—but no, it's happening outside. The drums are prodding me to leave the apartment, even though I've just arrived. To venture outside and be among people. There are voices lifted upward as people chant and talk and shout to a live percussive soundtrack.

I leave Whisper inside to rest when I go. She doesn't like people in this kind of proximity. Neither do I, really, but I can't stop my curiosity.

When I get outside, it feels different from the crowd mucking up traffic for the royal visit. There's a sense of purpose here, and one of discontent. No garish hats in sight, but there are quite a few signs announcing that water is life.

"What's going on?" I ask a young man in horn-rimmed glasses.

He hoists up a stray strap of his backpack. "Oil spill in the Burrard Inlet," he says. "Government backed a new pipeline going from those fuckin' tar sands to the coast and a tanker leaks on the damn water. We've had enough of this shit."

He gives me a fist bump even though I haven't agreed with anything he's said. It's not that I disagree, just that this settler colonial state was built on the exploitation of resources. No matter what friendly, aw-shucks Canadian face they put on it, it's never going to change.

I decline his tempting offer to share a joint and am about to turn back when an indigenous drummer passes by. She's dressed in jeans and a winter coat with the hood up. With her earnestness, her sense of conviction, the fierce expression on her face, and the slope of her high cheekbones, she resembles my sister, Lorelei.

Which makes me wonder if Lorelei is here today.

I follow the drummer, looking for my sister, hoping to catch a glimpse. I'd first moved out to the West Coast after Lorelei had gotten accepted into university here, just to be closer to her. She was so full of conviction, my younger sister. I was proud of her. Despite being put in care after our father died, she had come out of it full of confidence and a belief in her ability to change the world. My aging out of foster care pushed me right into the army. They took one good long look at me and sent me packing, too. Confidence and conviction have eluded me at every turn, but it seems right that Lorelei should have it.

I've never known how to speak to her, but I moved here anyway, to be near her, waiting for a phone call that never came. She's a righteous bitch on most days, and I suppose I'm waiting around for the moment she's not. Maybe today is the day. I live in hope.

The drums pull me deeper into the crowd, but I lose sight of the young drummer. I imagine my sister's face everywhere and allow myself to be swept into a march just for the desire to see her again. Her feelings toward me have never changed mine toward her. I keep away, but that doesn't mean I don't miss the sight of her, as complicated as our relationship is.

It's during this searching that I sense someone's attention on me. A man in a dark green jacket with his hood pulled forward is watching me. Every time I catch a glimpse of him, he disappears. Now the drumbeat speeds up, but I'm not sure if it's in my head. The crowd pulls me too close, and someone is shouting on a megaphone up ahead.

There's a call and response, no less musical than the blues.

"The system isn't broken!" shouts the woman—man? Does it matter?—on the megaphone.

The crowd breathes in, almost collectively.

*"It was built this way!"* they cry back, on the exhalation.

Someone jostles me, and I flinch away. There is a rage here, building. The feeling sweeps over me. I'm not angry, but I feel a peculiar fear that has to do with being surrounded by strangers. I don't want to see my sister anymore. I only want to leave.

"The system isn't broken—"

The crowd is moving, and I'm being sucked toward the center, where the megaphone is. There's an alley opening to my right that I head for now.

*"It was built this way!"*

There's a flash of green in my periphery, but when I look, it's gone again. Someone swears at me as I bump into them. Pushing past the outraged faces, the sharp elbows and wandering hands, I reach the alley. I know where I am. Just through here I can make it to the next street over, and away from the noise and sea of bodies.

"The system isn't broken—"

As I move deeper into the alley, I feel a hand on the back of my jacket pulling me into a doorway. Instinctively I drop to the ground, bracing my hands on the filthy concrete and lashing straight up and back with my right leg. But I slip forward, and the kick is shortened. There's a howl of pain as I catch a man in the knee. My aim had been for the groin.

*"It was built. This. Way."*

"Hey!" someone shouts. I get to my feet and stumble forward, looking for any kind of weapon. There's a broken hockey stick nearby that I just manage to get my hands on when I hear someone behind me.

I turn, the hockey stick raised.

An older woman wearing a vivid red poncho cringes back. Her crooked eyeglasses fall off her face. "Honey, it's okay," she says, bending to look for them. "I saw that man pull you. He's gone, don't you worry. I saw him run away. He can't hurt you anymore."

She's right. The glasses are closer to me than they are to her. I return them to her.

"I can wait here if you want to call the police?"

"No, I'm fine. Thanks."

"Really, it's no trouble. There are predators everywhere, and we need to stick together to catch these bastards! Imagine preying on an innocent woman at a rally! People are . . . I just don't even . . . are you sure you're alright?"

"Yes, thank you," I say, still trying to get over being called an innocent woman.

She insists on giving me her phone number just in case I want to file a report later. "Maybe there's a paramedic around to help you with those hands," she says, looking at the scratches down my palms from when I dropped to the ground.

"No, really, it's nothing."

She wants to be helpful but doesn't know what else to do. I say bye to my good Samaritan to let her off the hook. Then I stand in the entrance of the little alley and scan the crowd, still marching. The green I'm looking for is long gone.

"The system isn't broken—"

"*It was built this way!*"

"Water is life!"

A sea of people wash past me with their drums and chants. I lean a shoulder against a doorway away from the alley, facing out into the street. Searching for a green jacket in the crowd, even as it thins. Waiting for the adrenaline to come down. Besides, I need a moment. I've scratched my palms and had a close call.

Was this some kind of crime of opportunity? A case of mistaken identity? A quick rape down a dark stairwell? It could be your garden-variety downtown eastside mugging.

It didn't feel premeditated. Or careful. It didn't feel like Dao. But, then again, putting a hit on me in Detroit didn't feel like him, either. The cool, calculated man I'd encountered would never be that sloppy. The truth is, he's as much a mystery to me as he has ever been.

# 10

BACK AT THE Hastings office Brazuca finds Stevie Warsame sorting through his store of surveillance equipment and gadgets, putting some in the desk behind him and others in one of the two duffel bags at his feet.

Warsame was a cop, too, before turning to private investigations—though it had been his choice to leave the police department he served in Alberta. He never mentioned why, but Brazuca has a good idea that Warsame's Somali heritage might not have gone down so well in certain circles. Not that you'd know from Warsame himself, who seemed to dwell on nothing but the condition of his surveillance equipment and the various gadgets he kept in what he called "resale ready" shape.

Brazuca sits at his desk and frowns at the opposite wall. He's still trying to process the events of the day. He wants to be alone but can't think of a polite way to ask Warsame to leave.

Warsame, sensing his mood, looks Brazuca over. "What's up with you?"

"You notice anyone watching the office lately?"

"Should I be worried about something?"

"Don't know just yet."

"The way I remember it," says Warsame, slowly, thoughtfully, "you ran into some trouble with a biker—what was his name? Wasn't too long ago, either."

"Curtis Parnell. According to my police guy, there's a warrant out for his arrest, but he's skipped town."

Warsame finishes up with the equipment and zips the black duffel. "Or he's here, just laying low."

"I wouldn't worry about him," Brazuca says.

"Who are you worried about, then?"

"It's nothing. Just a feeling. Probably need to get more sleep, is all."

"Could be a feeling you listen to. You don't mess with the bikers in this town, man. Even I know that." Warsame reaches for his jacket. "You know where Krushnik's been for the past few days? I've been trying to get him to sign off on an account. Been getting nothing but background checks these days. It's been brutal out there."

"He's taking some personal time, I guess. Sign off on it yourself. You're a partner."

"This company is going to shit," Warsame says on his way out, looking harassed. Brazuca doesn't blame him. He's never been one for paperwork, either.

Brazuca looks around the tiny office. He wonders if he should care that the company he's spent the better part of a year working with is falling apart. But finds he doesn't, really. He's got other things to worry about.

Curtis Parnell, the biker, had snapped a photo of his face when Brazuca was looking into a drug case for a wealthy playboy who'd lost the love of his life to an overdose. Because of Brazuca's intervention, Parnell's house had been raided, a selection of drugs and weapons seized, and Parnell went into hiding.

Brazuca really shouldn't be so invested in Nora's hardship now that he's got a fugitive enemy of his own, but there's something about the danger she's in that feels more real to him.

Years ago, back when he was on the force, the shrink they forced him to see after he'd been shot in the leg had told him he had a hero complex. Immediately after the session he went out with his cop buds, got wasted, as they were all borderline alcoholics, and then he chose to forget that unhelpful assessment. He'd been shot at, was an alcoholic with a bum leg. What kind of hero is that?

He logs into his bank account online and stares at the balance. His playboy client who he once thought was a friend, Bernard Lam, had paid him an obscene amount of money to look into the death of his mistress. At first he thought the number was a joke, but Lam had money to burn and this is how he wanted to do it. He could have bought a new yacht or luxury property in the Caribbean, but he chose to give it to Brazuca instead to run down some leads. And, in return, get details about the people involved in smuggling synthetic opiates into Vancouver.

Brazuca got the information, but the price had been high.

If this thing with Nora hadn't cropped up, Brazuca would have left Vancouver weeks ago. Not out of fear of Parnell but because he's tired of being here. He doesn't particularly like this city. It's cold. Not just the weather. The *people* are cold. Distant. Just because you're from a place it doesn't mean you've got to put up with it for the rest of your life. He's stayed out of habit and a concern for a woman who's most definitely in trouble. A woman who, like this city, doesn't even really like him.

There's nothing keeping him here but him and his hero complex.

# 11

THANKFULLY, 544 HASTINGS Street is still in the shitty part of town. It means that there are no upwardly mobile citizens in their business-casual wear to sneer at me while I linger in the back alley of the office, watching the lights inside switch off. Stevie Warsame left a half hour ago, but he's not the one I'm waiting for.

I watch from behind a dumpster, settled next to a young woman with piercings at her brow, one nostril, and both ear-lobes and helices, as well as a single flash of silver at her upper lip. When I saw her here, wrapped up in her sleeping bag, I couldn't hear her breathing. So I put a finger under her pierced nostril and waited until I felt her shallow breath. Satisfied that she was alive, I turned to watch the back of my old office.

It begins to rain.

Brazuca exits the building and pauses in front of his MINI. It's possible he's considering why the hell he even bothers cramming his long limbs in such a tiny space. Eventually, he comes to terms with his poor taste in vehicles and gets in. I watch him leave, even trailing out of the alley afterward to see if anyone's paying close attention to his disappearing tail-lights from the street.

Nothing stands out.

If there's surveillance on him, it's not an amateur job. The downtown eastside is at once derelict and bustling, as it always is, but no one here seems to care about Brazuca's movements.

When I return to the dumpster my friend is stirring. I leave quickly so she doesn't have time to take in any identifying details. People would be surprised at how much a body on the street can observe. I would have asked her if she'd noticed anybody watching the place, but I don't want her to pay any particular attention to me. It could be self-defense, a hunch, evidence of a life lived in the shadows. Whatever it is, I simply don't want anyone to get a good look at my face. There's a man who's made a target of me. No woman in her right mind can shake that.

As I walk back to Chinatown I feel more myself with every step, finally back in a city that has come to be my home. The rain falls in a fine mist, and I'm soothed by the slick of moisture it leaves behind, until it turns to snow again, and my mood changes along with it. Winnipeg, where I grew up, was far, far colder than this. In my youth, I would even consider this to be T-shirt weather. But I am old now, or, at least, older. I am no longer an idiot.

When I get back, I take Whisper on a short walk. Keeping her on-leash, even though it irritates the scratches on my hands. It's only when I close the door to Leo's apartment that I'm finally able to leave Brazuca behind, along with the easy camaraderie we seemed to have fallen into. I took the back alleys through to Leo's apartment, and I was careful to keep a watch out. I make sure to check the cars on the street from the balcony anyway. There are no dark sedans to be seen, but there are quite a few station wagons and beat-up SUVs.

Funny, I'd never imagined that Leo would choose to live in a place like this, this tiny one-bedroom apartment that smells of fried food and marijuana. After their relationship ended, I'd been so concerned with taking care of Seb that Leo disappeared from my life.

He hasn't done well in my absence.

The space itself is clean and relatively tidy, but Leo's upscale wardrobe looks out of place here, crammed, as it is, into makeshift shelving. His artisanal pottery collection is strewn about hodgepodge, and I don't think I've ever seen his shoes in worse shape. His bed looks secondhand, and he hadn't even bothered to make it up before he left.

What in holy hell has Seb's death done to him?

The one thing that's quintessentially Leo is still in place, and I breathe a sigh of relief to find the sleek espresso maker he ordered from Italy a couple of years ago still in working order. Though, he's out of the beans he used to special-order from Portland and is now relying on average grocery-store coffee beans. It's sad how far he's come down in life. A man like Leo doesn't naturally forgo his fair-trade, organic Arabica. The coffee is a reflection of his state of mind, which is so obviously depressed. Leo and I . . . we've been through too much for me to look at his coffee selection and not feel a twinge of concern.

He's been in here while I was out, too, and filled the fridge with gourmet dog food for Whisper and a pitiful selection of cheap frozen pizzas for me.

And there's Chopin playing from somewhere, our own personal dirge.

His note to me begins with a *Hey, Roomie*, so I put it down unread and sit at the kitchen table, which is bare except for a book on dating in one's thirties.

I leave that unread, too.

After I clean off the dirt and traces of blood from my scraped palms, Whisper and I both eat ravenously, as if it's our last meal. I let her out onto the balcony to cool off and close the sliding door to keep the warmth in. I watch her until a kind of peace settles over me. She falls asleep to the sounds of the city, and it's her utter relaxation that guides me to the sofa.

It gets cold after an hour. I pull a blanket over me and wonder just who could have been following me and Brazuca in the car and who tried to grab me at the protest. The protest attack certainly happened, but it was confusing and sloppy, so I file it away.

But it's possible that Brazuca was imagining things on our drive. He'd been looking at me in a way I don't like. As though I'm some sort of fragile thing. Like I can be broken. I don't blame him for being on edge. When I saw him about a month ago, he'd been on a health kick and had even been consuming large quantities of vegetables. This commitment to his well-being seems to have vanished. And his limp is worse than ever.

Earlier today I watched him drink almost an entire pot of coffee on his own. He dropped his car keys on the way to the back lot, and when he bent to grab them, his bad leg seized up. He spent several minutes driving through what must have been excruciating pain. When he jerked the wheel of the car suddenly to get us off the highway, his hands shook. He didn't notice, but I did.

Brazuca's nerves are shot, and he's too damn proud to admit it.

# 12

I CALL SIMONE, my friend from AA, to let her know I'm back in town.

"I know," she says. "Brazuca came to a meeting last night and told me. I shouldn't have to find these things out from him, Nora."

"I've been distracted by Whisper." Somehow I know this is the only answer she'll accept. She has a dog, too, so she knows what a woman's priorities should be.

"Don't give me that," she snaps.

A lot must have changed since I saw her last. She's never been quite this testy with me. "Are you performing tonight? I'll come by to see you." I don't mind her drag club, and it's been a while since I've witnessed the level of coordination she can manage in stiletto heels.

"No, I'm doing pole class tonight, but you can meet me after. I could use someone right now."

Ever since we first got to know each other through our various addictions, Simone has become a fixture in my life. Drag performer by night and cyber security expert also possibly by night (no one who's ever met her seems to know what she does with her days), she is my one constant in this whole city.

She's right. I should have called her a long time ago.

The temperature is dropping by the minute. I shut the balcony door, turn on the heat, and curl up on Leo's couch. I've taken Leo's work computer and now put on some Aretha Franklin because it makes me think of Detroit, Nate, and his famous soul singer of an aunt. The depression and guilt hit me almost immediately. I know he's still alive and recovering at home. But I'm not sure I can reach out to him. I wouldn't know what to say. *Sorry you almost died because of me* doesn't quite cut it. *This guy has a vendetta against me, see. Tell me, what do you know about triads?*

I could also tell him how good our song sounds on the radio, but is a hit record worth it if it comes at the price of his health?

As I watch the sun drop out of sight, my thoughts turn from Nate (who I can't help) to Brazuca (who I might not want to). I think it must have something to do with the fact that Brazuca seems to be having such a hard time getting a grip. But that's ridiculous. I'm not the center of the universe, after all. He must have problems of his own. And now he is trying to avoid dealing with his own shit by taking on my burdens, too.

Well, that's unfair.

I don't want to be responsible for the downward spiral of his life. Which is why, several hours later, I go out without him.

I know where Nolan works. Brazuca must have forgotten

that I've spent the past several years looking for people that others have misplaced or temporarily forgotten. It was almost too easy for me to locate the name of the club from some of Nolan's online posts. And Granville Street isn't too far away.

But first, I have some pole dancing to take in.

# 13

I DON'T FIND Simone at her pole dancing studio in Gastown, and she's not answering her phone, either. People need their space, and some of us need a lot of it, so I don't fault her for not showing up or forgetting to give me a call. Maybe grinding against a metal pole just doesn't seem as attractive a way to spend her evening as she'd thought. Or maybe, like me, the thought of holding her body on said pole in dangerous and unlikely positions is enough to keep her away. It's possible that she's only just started thinking of the hygienic implications of rubbing her bits and pieces against a surface that so many others have rubbed their bits and pieces against.

Whatever it is, she's not here, and I have a feeling she's not planning to drop by anytime soon.

I stick around the pole studio as long as I can without looking like a subway flasher or that I'm interested in a membership, and then I go clubbing.

It's not for me.

I'm wearing far too many clothes, and I refuse to stand in line for the opportunity to have my eardrums blown out. The bouncer working the door ignores me completely. I'm forced to tap him on the shoulder to get his attention. He turns. His ears are pierced on both sides, and he's got tiny genie hoops that glint at me in the dim light outside of the club. "Yeah? I don't got any change on me, lady."

"That's okay," I say. "I have lots of money."

He takes a long look at me now. "Good for you. Save up some of that Welfare Wednesday cash?"

"You know it," I say. I'm used to people casting aspersions based on my general appearance. But have they considered the cost of cosmetics lately? "So much that I want to spread it around. Joe Nolan working tonight?"

"Don't know who that is," he says, lying.

I can tell it's an instinctive reaction, that it's not personal. He's just not used to giving out information for nothing. This is a game I've played many times on the cases I used to work for Leo. "I owe him some and want to give it back. You know, before I spend it all on hookers and blow."

He's interested now. Even laughs a little, making the genie hoops dance. "You could give it to me. I'll make sure he gets it." His expression is telling me there could be hookers and blow for more than just me.

"I like to look a man in the eye when I settle my debts." This comes out harsher than I expected. The techno music inside makes me short-tempered.

"I respect that," he says, though his voice is doubtful that he does. "But I'm not sure if I know where he is, if ya know what I mean."

"Maybe this will help you remember." There's forty dollars

in my wallet. I hand him twenty, in hopes that he comes cheap.

To my delight, he does.

"Joe sometimes works the door at the Van Club, for private events. If you don't find him, come back. You can leave the cash with me."

"Sure thing," I reply, even though I have no intention of leaving any more money with him than I already have.

I look at my phone and think about calling Simone. I don't do it, because if she wants space, that's fine by me. She probably got wrapped up in work, hacking into servers and chatting about her various digital accomplishments with other cyber fanatics the world over. If that's even what they do. I send her a text instead and even try out an emoji, for effect. It looks wrong, coming from me, and I immediately wish I hadn't. Lesson learned.

In truth, I'm relieved that she's ditched me for the night. I'm not sure I'm up for much conversation. My voice, normally deep, is venturing into Tom Waits territory. Traces of the smoke I inhaled during the warehouse fire in Detroit linger in the tissue of my lungs.

As I walk to the Van Club I hum a little to clear it, even though it hurts. I'm in tune, which isn't surprising because it's me, and I always am.

# 14

THE FIRST THING I notice about Joe Nolan is that he has a lopsided, little-boy smile that he directs only at the attractive women entering the Van Club. The smile disappears for the men and the average-looking ladies, even though they have money to spend, too. Nolan's blunt features are softened by the smile, but nobody looks at him long enough to notice.

The club is a members-only affair and I've never received an invitation, but I've seen pictures. There's no view like it in all of Vancouver.

With a membership, you can go in and see clear views of the harbor, see the seaplanes take off. On a cold night like this, you could be in short sleeves, sipping hot toddies by one of the fireplaces inside, looking out over your kingdom.

Without a membership you're out on the pavement with me, watching a man smile at women who are so far out of his league they might as well be in a different stratosphere.

Soon, whatever event has been held here empties out and there is no longer any need to watch the door. A man in a tuxedo says a few words to Nolan and hands him an envelope. He pockets it without checking what's inside and heads for the seawall behind the strip of buildings. It's cold and late, and I'm not sure what he's doing or why, until I see him stand at the railing overlooking a line of docked boats. I understand the fascination, even though I don't share it.

This is where the wealthy go to park their toys.

Nolan puts on a hat, pulls a cigar out of his pocket, lights it, and leisurely smokes it. He's looking at something intently, something I can't see.

My hands go numb in the time it takes for him to finish. I'm standing in the shadows, off the bike path. I think I'm being quiet and am relying on the fact that most people usually look right past me without registering anything about my presence.

But not Nolan.

Without turning he says, "You gonna tell me what this is about?"

I know he's talking to me. And I realize my mistake. Just because Nolan has an eye for the gorgeous socialites of Vancouver doesn't mean that he hasn't also noticed me. I go to the railing and follow his gaze to one of the boats in the marina. The dock lights are giving off enough illumination to see shapes moving on one of the boats. Two shapes, moving rhythmically. If I listen carefully, I can hear moaning. Or that could just be the sounds of the night, amplified by my hyperawareness of the man standing next to me, still smoking.

"You ever seen rabbits fuck?" Joe Nolan asks.

I wonder what kind of pornography he's into, but I don't say that. Don't even respond.

"Yeah, me neither, but I have a feeling it would look something like what those two are up to in that boat over there. The guy who owns the boat comes to the club for some of the events I work. After, he brings back one of the waitresses. Spends an hour tops in there and then sends her on her way walking like she's holding a beach ball between her legs. Works those girls over real good."

There's no emotion in his voice. No thrill of sexual interest, even. Which is unexpected, given what he's just said. If he thinks he'll shock me, he's talking to the wrong woman. Casual misogyny isn't shocking. I don't like it, but it doesn't surprise me.

The cigar is down to the end. He flicks it, still lit, onto the closest boat. "You wanna be one of those girls on the boat? Want me to hook you up with a job?"

"No."

"Didn't think so. You're too old for him, anyway. So how about you get to the point." He looks at me now.

My first instinct is to lie, even though it sits uncomfortably with me. But I sense, somehow, that it wouldn't be the right move. And I've already underestimated this man once. "Back in the day you ran with Jimmy Fang. Fang got busted, disappeared, trial fell apart, you resumed your life like nothing happened."

"Second time today someone's brought that old shit up. I'll tell you what I told your friend, the one with the gimpy leg. That all happened years ago. I don't remember a goddamn thing about it."

He's lying, of course, but that's not the point. The point is my friend with the gimpy leg has already spooked him.

I keep my expression neutral. "You were talking to the cops about your friend Jimmy, weren't you?"

"Get the fuck out of here."

"Look, I don't care about your involvement. I need to know about Fang. Who he might have here in Vancouver still."

He looks around suddenly. Takes in the marina. "Where's the other guy, Sir Limps A Lot?"

"I don't know. I came alone."

"Why do you want to know about this shit, anyway?"

Again, I have a choice. It's hard, but I go with my first instinct. The truth. "Someone's after me. You don't know him, but you used to know the people he's connected to. I want to find him, and to do that—"

"You gotta find them."

"Yeah."

"I ain't a snitch." But he is. I can hear it in his voice, in the way he says it with real anger, real passion. It's not directed at me. His emotion is internal. He's ashamed of himself.

"I ain't a cop." It's partially why I'm here without Brazuca. I looked at the photos of this man, and some part of me knew that Brazuca would turn him cold. That his cop face can't be scrubbed away so easily.

But maybe I have a chance.

"Who are you?" he asks.

"Someone stupid enough to be on their radar."

"Hell." He pulls down his hat. Fiddles with the edge of it. His fingers are red from the cold, and stiff with it, too. He's coming to a decision, and I can sense the struggle taking place inside him. He's wondering if he can trust me.

Maybe I have to trust him a little, too. "My daughter's scared. She's the only family I have, and they know who she is. I have to protect her."

"I don't know anything about them anymore, okay?"

"Yes," I say softly. "Yes, you do." I heard it in his voice, that little hitch, and I know I'm on to something.

He's about to say something, then stops.

A woman wearing a long coat unbuttoned over a short dress approaches from the docks. She looks to be in her twenties. Her hair is a tangle about her shoulders, and she appears to be weeping. We watch her disappear. About a minute later a man at least three decades older than her follows. He's in a tuxedo, strolling off like he doesn't have a care in the world.

I sense the hatred rolling off Nolan because I feel it now, too. Whoever he is, I feel a certain level of disgust for this man who lets a weeping woman he has taken to bed walk alone in this state of distress. That he is somehow the cause of her distress and that the power he emanates, one that seems somehow inherent, is part of why she went to this boat with him in the first place.

"After your friend came to see me, I called my guy at the club and asked if there was a shift for me tonight. They'd wanted me to work, but I didn't really want to come here no more. But your friend got me thinking, so I asked for the shift. I need the money, anyway."

I wonder where this is all going, but I don't have it in me to interrupt. I don't have to wait long. "There's a man who's always at these parties," he continues. "I recognized him the first day I started working events at the club," Nolan says. "He didn't recognize me."

"How do you know him?"

"Drove Jimmy to some restaurant in Richmond once, one of those ritzy spots by the casino, then went inside to use the men's. Saw him with that guy. Got a good look at him, too. But when I went over to talk to Jimmy, he pretended I didn't exist. After Jimmy left, I went into a different line of work altogether. Worked construction for years; then I get some gigs working the doors." He shrugs. "It's okay money. Easier than breaking my back all day every day. A friend recommends me for the Van Club, and first night on the door, I see him. The guy from the restaurant."

"Who is he?"

He doesn't answer. I feel him wavering, regretting perhaps that he's said this much. Or maybe he's remembering what it's like to be a snitch. It's already familiar territory, so I give him a little push. "I have a kid sister, too. Along with my daughter. I know what it's like to have to protect the family."

He considers this, looks in the direction we saw both the woman and the man disappear. He could be feeling melancholy at the memory of the weeping woman, or perhaps his years doing backbreaking labor have sloughed off some of his hard shell.

"His name is Peter Vidal," says Nolan. "He's a lawyer. Married into some money a while back. Then, lucky for him, the broad died. That's his boat we've been watching." He pauses. "You wanna know something, lady? I don't give a damn who you are. You could roll up on Vidal tonight, for all I care. Question him all you want about Fang. I bet he knows something. Guys like Fang were always protected by their lawyers who knew enough about their operations to make sure they never got any time for what they did."

He jerks his head in the direction of the club. Then grips the railing tight.

"You know what bugs me the most about Vidal? His shoes. I can always see my face in that shine. Yeah, I'd bet he's never worked rough a day in his life. Every time he comes to those events, he's got different shoes on, and they all scream money. Guys like that, they don't know what it's like to freeze your balls off watching doors, killing yourself doing hard labor. They're criminals, too, just a different class of them. Those assholes deserve the swift hand of justice, and I hope to God you're it."

For a second, he looks at me like I'm some kind of warrior saint. But he's got the wrong sister.

I hand him one of Leo's cards I lifted from the office to keep from having to speak. In case he remembers anything else. He barely looks at me when he takes it. It's too cold to be standing here by the ocean, but he doesn't seem likely to move anytime soon. This is why I'm the one to leave first. Wondering if I'm the instrument of his vengeance or if he's the instrument of mine.

When I reach the gangway leading to the marina, I look around.

Peter Vidal is long gone.

# TWO

# 15

WHEN I CLOSE my eyes the pulse of Detroit comes back to me. A man's hands on a guitar, his mouth in front of an old-fashioned condenser mic. He takes a deep breath, fills his diaphragm with air, and then his lips pucker as if he's expecting a kiss.

Instead, a hymn escapes.

He warms up to "Amazing Grace," and so do I. We're singing together now and I'm in my head voice, a tone I haven't heard out of my mouth since I was a kid in youth choir. Buck-toothed and scrappy but with a voice like a lounge singer just months away from a lung cancer diagnosis.

Those days are long gone. I've since found the blues to fill the space in my soul, but I remember what it was like to sing up high like that. Reaching for the cracked paint in the ceiling, then past it, too. A gospel, a prayer. Never a celebration.

But it's a nursery rhyme that was stuck in my head while that abandoned building in Detroit burned down, while a man who'd been stalking my mother for decades included me in his death wish. He'd become obsessed with her, blamed her for ruining his life.

Are all women destined to become their mothers? Even

the ones who didn't know their mothers past childhood? For Bonnie's sake, I hope not. My mother lived on the outskirts of a Palestinian refugee camp in Lebanon before she fled to Canada. My father was displaced in a whole other way. An indigenous child scooped up in the sixties, taken from his community and his culture just as sure as my mother left hers.

I have never had a home or good memory of family, other than a sister who doesn't speak to me.

Poor Bonnie. She can do better, even if I can't.


I'm sitting in the dark, feeling persecuted. If I hear Chopin again, I'll smash something against a wall. I put on some Leon Bridges instead. He's singing now about coming home. About wanting to be around. Hell, I want that, too. It's not only the people who have sweethearts waiting for them at the door, holding an aperitif and wearing nothing but a silk robe, who deserve a peaceful homecoming of some sort. People like me, the ones with terrible luck, who don't own a scrap of silk and make poor life decisions—we deserve some semblance of home, too. We may have nothing but horny dogs who wait for us to do their bidding, but our lives must mean something.

Maybe this is what I'm fighting to stay alive for.

In my imagination the city has turned against me, so I close Leo's curtains and sit with my back against the wall. The neon lights still shine through. Whisper understands my mood. She comes over to me and forces her ears into my hands. I massage behind them until she falls asleep on my lap, her deep snores lulling me into a state of tranquility.

When I get to the office the next morning, I'm careful to linger outside for some time, to make sure no one is watching, then use the back entrance. Whisper goes ahead of me into the office Brazuca shares with Stevie Warsame.

Stevie isn't there, but Brazuca is at his desk, staring into his computer screen.

Whisper gives him a look that neither of us seems to be able to decipher. Is it tolerance? Is it . . . affection? I think it's acknowledgment, personally, but before I can dwell on the subject, she turns away from us both and spreads herself across the floor.

"Any more tails yesterday?" I ask.

"No. And I was paying attention."

We mull that over. Brazuca seems well-rested. His eyes are no longer bloodshot, and when I go into the kitchen for some coffee, there's at least half a pot left. He's pacing himself today. I think he can handle a surprise or two, so I tell him about my conversation last night with Nolan. Before I get to Vidal, he interrupts.

"Damn it, Nora," he says. He buries his face in his hands. "We were supposed to talk to him together."

"Where did you go yesterday? After you dropped me off."

He looks away, and I see now that it's back. The ability I used to have, the one that let me figure out when people are lying, has returned in full force. Brazuca was the one man I could never read, but he has changed. He has become transparent to me. Whatever pedestal I'd put him on when he'd been my sponsor has crumbled to dust, and now here he is. Limping along with his secrets.

"You went to Nolan's house, didn't you?" I say.

"Yes, okay? I did. I started to doubt the tail, so I drove around for a while to clear my head, and then I found myself back on the highway."

"And at his house."

"He wouldn't talk to me, though."

It's because he still looks like a cop, even though he isn't anymore. He just has that face. I don't say this, though. There's something unbearably fragile about him right now. "You ever hear of Peter Vidal?" I say.

"I worked a security detail for him once at WIN Security. Some economic forum. Why?"

"That's the name Nolan gave up. Said he saw Vidal with Fang, getting cozy at a restaurant."

This gives him a pause. "Peter Vidal is rarefied company for the likes of those two."

"Now he is. But maybe he wasn't so high and mighty back then." And maybe he's still not all that high and mighty. Maybe he's just gotten better at faking it. "According to No-lan, he married well. Though that doesn't mean his past is clean. He was a lawyer, after all." I decide not to tell him about the woman on the boat. He doesn't look like he could handle it.

He puts up a hand, which tells me I might be right. "Okay, we're doing this wrong. Vidal may have something on Fang, but the Jimmy-Fang-and-Three-Phoenix line is only one part of getting to Dao. The second has to be Dao himself."

"All we know is he's connected, worked for Ray Zhang. I didn't mention this before because I didn't think it was relevant, but he was having an affair with Jia Zhang."

"Are you sure about that?"

"I saw them together on Vancouver Island. The night I went to get Bonnie. They were definitely intimate."

He meets my eyes briefly, then clears his throat and shuffles some papers on the desk. "Okay."

"Rumor has it he was a mercenary of some sort, but who is he? Where was he born? What was his life before Zhang?"

"Exactly. And if he went into hiding, we need to know where he would feel most comfortable."

"All we've ever known about him is a single name," I say, because this has bothered me for a long time.

"We need to look at this like someone hired us to do it. Except you're the client and, Nora, you're too close to Dao. I think you should take Three Phoenix and Vidal. I'll see what I can come up with on my end."

"Okay," I say.

He blinks. "Okay?"

"Yeah, sure. It's a good idea."

He frowns. "I know."

He's unsure about this drastic turn of events, that I'm agreeing with him, but since it's what he wants he lets it go.

The only lead to Dao is Three Phoenix and, now, Peter Vidal. But to pursue it, I need Brazuca and his shaky nerves out of the way.

He may never know it, but it's better this way. For him.

# 16

IT'S TIMES LIKE this that I wish I had a place of my own. I would settle for a room. The cost of rentals in this city are downright Dickensian, and there are two cities here. The people who make up the first cohort are spending their winters somewhere warmer and aren't around to hear the complaints. The second batch of folks are those who are actually getting screwed. Such as Leo and myself. By his living conditions, I can tell the business isn't doing too well. His heart isn't in private investigations right now. In his medicine cabinet, I find three empty bottles of sleeping pills. Tacked on the fridge are invoices from his therapist.

I am drowning in sad men.

The saddest men I see yet are those at the gym in the middle of the day, which is where I am now. The girl at the front desk makes me wait ten minutes to see a sales rep, and I spend another ten minutes explaining to him that I only want to take advantage of the free day passes advertised on their website. Who commits to a year without trying it out first?

"People who are serious about their goals," the sales rep tells me. His muscles are fighting to burst out of his shirt, to confront me about my goals in person. I try, but I can't respect a man who can't at least steal a better-fitting T-shirt. Like I have. Leo's workout wardrobe is top-notch, and it's not like he's going to miss a T-shirt and a pair of sweats.

The sales rep gives me a tour of the gym, which is full of serious people. They lift efficiently, with just the correct range of motion. Their knees never go over their toes on squats. Their grunts of exertion fill the rooms the sales rep leads me through. His sad mouth explains to me the gym rules along with the benefits of regular exercise while his bulging muscles try to intimidate me into submission. I nod every so often and pay close attention to the personal trainers working with other, more serious women. I'm not interested in the women. I'm looking only at the men.

The sales rep notices. "Do you want a consult with a trainer?"

"Not right now."

The sad mouth turns even sadder. "Don't wait too long. Beach season is right around the corner. If you want that bikini bod, you have to start now."

If I ever want that bikini bod, I'll throw myself off a cliff and maybe take a personal trainer or two with me. I store my jacket and wallet in the locker room and then get on a rowing machine with a good view of the main room.

It's midafternoon, just when the yummy mummies and the trophy wives have an hour or two to themselves before they have to take the kids to violin classes or stop in for a quick Botox injection before dinner. It's their playtime, and their playmates are the hard-bodied men who show them how to work their muscles efficiently. How to lift, squat, push, and pull. All with a helpful hand on the shoulder or the small of the back to assist.

I watch the sexual politics at play from the rowing machine while I hope for a rare sighting.

Peter Vidal keeps a low profile, but he was once tagged in a social media post in this gym, and I'm hoping to catch sight of the reclusive millionaire. Waiting around for Nolan to get in touch isn't an option. There must be another way to get to Vidal.

In the end, I row, but I go nowhere.

All this effort turns out to be for nothing. Vidal doesn't show up.

Leo is at the apartment when I get back, opening a can of beer. I see now what has replaced the sleeping pills. Watching him take that first sip is almost physically painful. I've been sober now, yet again, for over a year. I don't begrudge him this liquid courage, but there's only so much I can take.

"Leo," I say softly. "Let's go for a walk."

His eyes are red-rimmed and puffy. He shakes his head.

I leave him and go to an AA meeting. My first in a long time. There are some old faces and quite a few new ones. Nobody minds me. I choose not to share today, and everyone here understands. Whisper lounges at my feet until the meeting is over. I feel unsettled, but I don't understand why until after. I had hoped to see Simone, but she hasn't made an appearance.

When I call, I get her voicemail. Again. "Mmm, I'm busy, boo-boo," she purrs. "But I'll call you back. Maybe. If you've been good. So be good. And leave a message."

I haven't been good since childhood—and probably not even then—but I leave a message for her anyway.

Whisper and I go back to the office, where I find Stevie Warsame uploading photos from his high-tech camera to his computer.

We've worked well together in the past, Stevie and me. He doesn't get personal, which is my favorite quality in a colleague. Once, Leo had asked him about his childhood in Somalia, and Warsame said he didn't remember much before the refugee camp in Kenya. Which shut Leo up real quick.

Warsame looks me over. "So you're still alive?"

"I'm shocked, too."

He nods. We leave it at that.

I put on some coffee and hear the phone ring in the other room. A moment later Warsame sticks his head into the kitchen. "It's for you," he says.

"Who is it?"

He shrugs. "Didn't ask. Says he wants to speak to the lady that works here. You want me to tell him to go fuck himself?"

"Let's see what he wants first." When I pick up the phone, Nolan's voice comes through, low and urgent. There's some excitement to it, too, which throws me more than the fact that he's calling me. Belatedly, I remember slipping him a business card. But I never expected him to use it.

"Lady . . . what was your name again?"

I hadn't given it the first time. "Nora," I say.

"Yeah, so listen, Nora. I got called to work an event at the club tomorrow night. One of the other door guys cancelled. It's no guarantee, but it's put on by the Devi Group—that's the family Vidal married into. If you want, I can get you inside. You can meet him face-to-face." He laughs, and I'm again thrown.

"Okay," I say, after a moment. "What time should I be there?"

"Eight p.m."

I agree to meet him at the doors tomorrow. When I hang up, I spend a good five minutes slumped in Leo's empty waiting room. Since last night, Nolan had a change of heart. He must have gotten home, considered his options, and thought: "You know what I need? A little adventure in my life. Some light detective work would be nice."

This is something I'm somewhat familiar with. The amateur detective. I have unintentionally woken the Hardy Boy inside him and now he wants to help. Christ.

But isn't this what I wanted? Vidal might lead me to Three Phoenix and Dao. So why, then, do I feel so uneasy about this?

It must be Nolan. The way he sounded on the phone. The excitement, yes, but there was also something beneath it. A kind of smugness, maybe. It could be that I don't like that he's my only lead to Vidal. It's hard to trust people in the best circumstances, and it would be a stretch of the imagination to consider this a good circumstance.

But what choice do I have? My background check on Vidal turned up nothing.

It takes me a few minutes to notice the Chopin seeping out of Leo's office. I didn't even know Leo was here. The lights are off in the office, and the door is closed. And yet, spilling forth is our death song. It's a bad omen, this, though I try not to think about it as I walk out into the icy night, a night that is as unlike Vancouver as I've ever experienced. It's so cold out that it's almost surreal.

# 17

WHISPER AND I linger on Vidal's street in Point Grey. Seb's town house is several blocks away in Kits and is all but cleaned up, ready to be sold again for an exorbitant price. I'm sitting in a park that takes up an entire block, and Whisper is off-leash exploring. There are almost no passersby, and no children on the playground in front of me. Nobody is walking their dogs. Empty houses line the street, but there are lights on in Vidal's mansion. The mansion itself is protected by a large stone fence, and there are cameras mounted over the gate.

When I used to live in the basement of the Hastings Street office, at least there were people on the street. They were high, but they were around. There was evidence of lives being lived. Here, the lives—if there are any—are barricaded away. Including Vidal's.

If he's even here.

Before I leave, I call Leo to see if he's at the town house. He slurs his greeting. "It's late," I say, not wanting to speak to him like this.

"No, no, I can—talk."

"Really, it's fine. I'll call back tomorrow." I hang up. It's not even dinnertime, and Leo is drunk. I call Simone for advice on an intervention. She doesn't answer. The sultry message comes on again. I try Brazuca, because at one point he was my sponsor. He was never great on the advice front, but I don't know what else to do.

"I was just going to call you," he says. "Can we meet?"

I give him the address to Leo's apartment.

"I'll be there in an hour. Any more tails?"

"Not since that day we went to find Nolan."

When he hangs up, I feel an unexpected sense of relief.

After I feed Whisper, I heat up some Chinese food from the fridge. Brazuca arrives just in time to eat half of it, go figure.

"What did you want to meet about?" I ask, not yet ready to talk about Leo. We're sitting at the kitchen table, drinking a kind of herbal tea that I found in Leo's cupboard. I don't for a moment let this scene of cozy domesticity get to me. I'm watching for signs of a meltdown, but Brazuca's hands are steady. He's wielding his chopsticks, if not with precision, with a certain amount of capability.

His expression, however, is guarded.

"I may know someone else who might be able to help us find Dao. He has more resources and, frankly, more time on his hands. I went to see him today and he seemed open to helping, but I don't trust him."

He is hiding something.

"Who is it?"

"A former client. I can't give you a name right now." This, at least, is the truth. He's letting me know up front that he's hiding something. I can respect that, so I give him the update on Nolan and share my suspicions that he might want to join the team.

"Shit," he says. "The last thing we need is some guy who doesn't know what he's doing muddying the water. You think he's going to be a problem?"

"I don't know. That's why I have to get to Vidal first at that event, before he has a chance to scare him off."

"When are you going?"

"Nine p.m."

He nods. "Okay, I'll see you there." He's got something else to say, but he can't quite get through it. Whisper allows him to pat her head, perhaps also sensing that he's stalling. I hope he's not interested in a good-bye hug. I can't help but think about the night we'd spent together and immediately try to focus on something else.

The air between us becomes thick with the memories of things better left unsaid.

He clears his throat.

I open the door.

We are careful to step around each other.

"See you tomorrow," he says.

He leaves behind him a sense of restlessness I'm becoming used to.

When Whisper and I reach Seb's town house, the night is quiet. The street is empty. I make sure to linger outside for a while to see if anyone is keeping watch. The air is cold but still. There is no snow, no rain.

After I've made sure that no one's looking, I go in through the back.

Inside the town house all the furniture is gone. There's a single light on in Seb's study, and that's where I find Leo wrapped in a blanket. The desk is gone, and so are the books on the shelves. All that's left of Sebastian Crow in this space is the worn sofa he used to curl up on when he was too tired to go to his room but needed a nap. As the cancer took a firmer hold of him, became terminal, ate him up from the inside, this is where I'd find him.

It's now where I find the lover he'd abandoned.

Leo is asleep with a bottle of bourbon at his side. There's a shot or two left. I'm careful to pour it down the sink before Leo wakes up. Or before I forget that booze was once the greatest joy of my life and that it is a cruel mistress who only takes, never gives. It's a shame, though, because this is the good stuff.

When I return to the study, Whisper is on her belly by the sofa, and one of Leo's hands has fallen over her. She doesn't seem to mind. I leave them there and pull all the shades in the house closed. I'm tired, but I know I won't get much sleep tonight. I drive to Vidal's house. The lights are off, but there's a streetlight right in front of the house. I can see the glow of a laptop screen in one of the darkened rooms upstairs, visible through a gap in the curtains. A few minutes later, a face appears in the window.

Even though I'm in the car, I flinch and draw back into my seat. I don't know if I've been seen or not.

Suddenly I don't want to be on empty streets anymore. It would have been nice to have Whisper here with me, but I think about how calm she seemed on the floor beside Leo, and I remember that he's a part of her life now, too. I don't feel guilty about going to the Hastings office without her.

I sit in Leo's office and read through the latest financials. Krushnik and Co. is still getting work, but increasingly money seems to be paid out to Stevie Warsame more than anyone else. Brazuca hasn't worked for the firm in a month. Leo barely answers his emails. There have been several inquiries for services that he's left unread. As I suspected, things aren't looking good. I shut down Leo's computer.

I can't help but think about why I lied to Brazuca tonight. I was right. His nerves are shot because he's scared. I could see it in the car when he thought we had a tail. I could see it tonight when I let him into Leo's apartment. Brazuca is terrified, but his concern is not for himself. I told him the wrong time for my meeting with Nolan because I can't afford to have his fear clouding what I know I have to do. I can't have it laid bare tomorrow night in front of Peter Vidal, our only real lead.

It's for the best, really, but I still feel terrible about it.

# 18

LEO SHOWS UP to the office dressed in a blue suit and orange-patterned tie. His shirt is tight around the middle, but he wears it with such confidence that both me and Stevie Warsame take a moment to appreciate the transformation that has taken place. Two hours ago, he dropped off Whisper at the office looking like he'd spent the night drinking away his sorrows, which he had. Now look at the wonders a shower and beautiful suit can perform.

He beams at us. "Thanks for leaving Whisper with me last night, Nora. She woke me up this morning and we went for a walk by the sea. It was . . . it was exactly what I needed. I'm feeling so much better now."

"You're welcome," I say, holding myself back from telling him exactly what's on my mind. Which is how insulting it is that he's lying to me, of all people. Stevie's not fooled, either. He's giving him a side eye he reserves for the people who try to bargain down his rates.

"Were you able to close up the town house okay?" I ask.

"Yes. It's done. Finally. How's the search going?"

I shrug. "A couple leads. Nothing solid yet."

"I just have to clear some things from my desk and I'll be

right there with you." He looks vulnerable, all of a sudden. "I'm glad you're back, Nora. And even though you're a pain in the butt—Seb always said so—you mean a lot to me."

Is it getting hot in here? I pull at my collar, scratch an itch below my ear, look at a point over his shoulder.

"Okay," I say. Then I leave. I sit in the waiting room and think about why I wasn't able to say to Leo that he means something to me, too. How much it hurt to keep Seb's illness from him.

Stevie comes out of the office. "Drink?" he asks.

I shake my head. "Over a year sober."

He winces. "That makes a lot of sense, actually." For a moment it looks like he's about to expand on that thought, but thankfully he decides to move on. "Doing some interviews for a background check. Want to come along?"

"Can't today."

He looks relieved.

We chat for a bit. It feels normal, like it used to feel when I worked here. We discuss the news about an alleged serial killer who was caught after eluding the police for decades. He famously went on a killing spree, terrorizing the Bay Area. It was said he was driven to murder because a woman had rejected him.

He continued murdering because he simply enjoyed it.

Stevie thinks it's just morbid office banter, but I'm happy we're speaking like this. About this topic in particular. I don't want to ever forget what people are capable of. Especially given who I have to go see tonight.

# 19

TO LIVE IN Vancouver is to be obsessed with the ocean. There's nothing else of value here. You can find nice trees elsewhere in Canada. You can hike in other places. Mountains abound in this country. There are no shortages of lakes. To choose Vancouver specifically is to choose the Pacific, to sacrifice the entirety of your paycheck to be near it. That is, if you're a hobo like myself. If you're a man like Peter Vidal, and you can afford to park your yacht here in perpetuity, then it's no sacrifice at all.

But the ocean is still the draw.

I can't help but take a few minutes to appreciate the view from the marina at Coal Harbour, circle around to where the seaplanes take off, and then head back to the Van Club.

As I approach it, I peer through gilded doors and into the lobby lit with a cascading chandelier, the light spilling out into the street in little droplets. Even though I'm half an hour early, there's no reason for another bouncer to be at the door. Yet there he is, this guy, unapologetically being a man other than Joe Nolan. I clock his girth first, taking up most of the doorway, and then his guarded expression.

There's no way this man is going to let me through the front without an invitation.

I'm about to try my luck at the service entrance around back when I see a young woman approaching the club, rolling a cello case behind her. Her sleek updo is half-unraveled, but she's in so much of a hurry that she doesn't stop to fix it. It takes me a split second to make a decision while the bouncer is momentarily distracted by a couple in evening wear.

I reach the bottom of the stairs at the same time she does and grab the bottom end of the case.

"I got it," she says stiffly.

"You're late, so let's get this over with." I go up the stairs with my end of the case, and she has no choice but to follow.

"I'm sorry, who are you?"

"I'm helping with this evening's entertainment. I was told to wait for you."

"Really, I can handle this."

We bicker like this all the way up the steps and past the bouncer. I give him a breezy "We're with the band" on my way past. He's about to say something, about to reach out with his hand to stop us, but the cellist is closer to him and she's wearing a silky evening gown under her open jacket. He doesn't want to chance ruining it. It's in this moment of hesitation that he gives up. I'm inside so fast that the cellist has trouble keeping up with me in her low heels. Once we reach the corridor I stop and pass over the case.

"Is this the right way?" she asks.

I shrug. "Sure."

I walk away before she can protest. Like the bouncer, she

misses her chance. I wish I had thought to bring a clipboard with me, because there's nothing as invisible in a crowded room as a woman with a clipboard who is taking notes, but I had stupidly relied on Nolan to get me through this somehow.

No matter. If anyone asks, I'm prepared to tell them that I'm with the band.

No one asks, because as soon as the cellist comes striding through the door at the other end of the room, shedding her coat on an empty chair, the room goes hushed. She takes her place with the band, a rather stripped-down affair, actually. There's the pianist, the cellist, and a female singer. From their dress and the theatrical nature of the singer's makeup, I can tell we're about to be treated to some opera. Looking around the room, which is filled with the most elegant people I've ever seen in my life, this seems fitting.

Vidal isn't in here, and I wonder if Nolan was wrong about this. Maybe that's why he didn't show his face this evening. Amateur detectives are a pain in the ass for a lot of reasons, but their basic lack of reliability is at the top of the list.

I slip out, just as the pianist stretches his long fingers. I've left my jacket at the corner of the room, and underneath I'm wearing a white collared shirt and a pair of black slacks. Both of which I borrowed from Leo's closet, along with his shiniest dress shoes. With luck, I'll be mistaken for waitstaff. Without luck, I'll be tossed out because even Leo's best dress shoes aren't good enough for this postal code.

I've come too far to give up, though.

A staircase leading to the second floor is barred, but the lobby is empty anyway, so it's nothing to throw a leg over the rope. In seconds, I'm up on the second floor. Down the hall from me, beyond a set of glass doors, there are two men smoking on a balcony. This floor isn't lit as well as the first, and I am able to stand in the shadows, watching them smoke. Eventually they shake hands.

The door to the balcony opens, and Peter Vidal comes into the hall. The other man stays outside. I can't see his face, but it doesn't matter anymore because Vidal is walking toward me. What strikes me the most about him is his unfettered confidence. I can see him steering yachts all over the world, as comfortable on deck as he is in a boardroom. I step out of the doorway I'm standing in and am about to say something when the balcony doors open once again and the man Vidal was with calls out, "Nora Watts?"

Both Vidal and I turn to see playboy billionaire Bernard Lam striding toward us, a huge grin on his face. Lam grasps my hands in his large, soft grip. Before I know it, we're embracing like old friends.

When I pull away from him and look behind me, Vidal is gone. No sign of him on the staircase, either.

Shit.

"You know," Lam says, "I was just talking about you the other day. With our pal Brazuca."

Brazuca may be his pal, but he and I are . . . I don't get to think too much about it, because Lam is off again, walking toward the stairs, heading down to the lobby, to coat check, talking the entire time about what a gift to humanity Brazuca is for accepting money to do work for Lam. He shakes my hand at the doors while the bouncer who is still not Nolan looks on.

When he wishes me a cheerful good-bye, I want to murder him.

I'm not sure what just happened, but it's possible that Vidal is still in the building, so I go into the dining room to take a look. As soon as I open the doors, a wave of sound comes thundering over me. It's the piano, the cello, but most of all it's the woman standing at the front of the room, singing.

I have never been able to afford a ticket to the opera. The closest I came was watching a young man, a busker like myself, blast "Time to Say Goodbye" from a boom box on the steps of the Vancouver Art Gallery. His voice soared over the music like nothing I'd heard before. I gave him half of the money I'd earned that day and walked away feeling a lightness inside to match the lightness in my pocket.

So when I hear the band start this song, I recognize it immediately. It's not opera, per se, but for my money it's better. It's something I can understand. Something I can feel. I'm more of a blues gal, myself. The rawness of the blues, the stories of it, they've burrowed inside of me and made a home that I've never been able to root out. But you can't be tethered to your blues every second. There are epic, grand things in life to experience, and what is happening here is just a little taste of it.

Standing just inside the room, I forget, for a moment, what I came here for. This time it's a woman singing, and she is so good that nobody wants to say good-bye to her when it's over. I feel tears in my eyes, and I don't know why. Her voice has wrapped itself around me, but it doesn't feel light, like it did with the busker. It feels like I'm choking on it.

In her voice I hear nothing but melancholy and longing.

Grabbing my coat, I leave to the sound of ecstatic applause. The ecstasy is lost on me, but the melancholy remains. The lobby is stifling. Everything is gold and red. If I sink into one of the overstuffed armchairs, I might never rise again.

The doorman, having seen me shake hands with Bernard Lam, doesn't bat an eyelash at me. Besides, what trouble could I be on my way out?

"Have a nice night, ma'am," he says to me.

I guess shaking hands with Bernard Lam is enough to earn me a *ma'am* and some well wishes for the evening. The song I'd just heard stays with me, dissipates my anger toward Lam.

I was this close.

Vidal was right in front of me, and I could have found some way to confront him about Three Phoenix, about where Jimmy Fang went. Where Dao could be right now. There are so many *could haves* in this, but I don't have it in me to be angry about the loss of opportunity.

At the marina, I look over at the boats. Vidal's is docked in the same place it had been the last time. But there's no one in it. I wait for an hour in the cold. Nothing. No sounds of bodies slapping together, no knock-kneed women limping up the path in tears. No men who exude power and disdain.

No Vidal.

Not even Lam, whom I'd met once and has decided, very inconveniently, to remember me.

I'm out here alone, just me and the night, lit up by a crescent moon shining over the calm sea. Thinking of Lam and his timing, which I'd initially thought was very poor. But it only was terrible for me.

For him, though, maybe it was great. And maybe that wasn't an accident.

Bernard Lam is a man full of surprises.

# 20

BRAZUCA IS WAITING for me in the office the next morning, and he's furious.

"You lied to me," he says. "When I showed up at the club, you weren't there and Joe Nolan wasn't on the door."

I don't deny it. "I was worried Nolan wouldn't talk to you. Turns out it was for nothing because he didn't even show up."

"Is that your idea of an apology?"

We both know it's not. I'm not in the habit of apologizing, especially to Brazuca. There is too much between us to be sorry for. We could be here for days. I heat up some stale coffee and hand him a mug instead. "This client of yours who may know something more . . . is it Bernard Lam?"

He sits up straighter in his chair. I've got his full attention now. There's a shift in his expression, like admitting Lam is his client is his dirty little secret. "What happened?"

"Lam was there last night, with Vidal. All nice and cozy. What does he know?"

"He knows," says Lam, from behind us, "that before the Devi Group, Peter Vidal worked for the law firm Jimmy Fang used for his legal defense when he got busted. And he also knows that you and I, Nora, seem to have a mutual interest in Three Phoenix."

No potential client has ventured through those doors since I've been here, and everyone in the office seems quite accustomed to the emptiness. So much so that we have conversations out in the open where anyone could walk in on us. Like at this moment, for example. Lam stands in the doorway, holding a wool overcoat. He's wearing a three-piece suit, with his tie arranged just so. All that's missing is a sidekick and bowler hat, and then he could really be a Sherlock Holmes cosplayer.

"Good morning, Jon." He nods to Brazuca and then looks at me. "Hello again, Nora. You turn up at the strangest places, you know? I'm in the middle of setting up a meeting with Peter Vidal to support his new development, and then you show up panting after him like a puppy."

I've been accused of worse things than showing up in strange places, but never in my life have I ever panted after anyone. I'm not about to let that one go. "I show up to talk to a businessman with connections to the criminal world and I find you, offering to give him money. What should I make of that?"

He grins. "I've always liked you."

Brazuca looks as surprised by this statement as I am. Why be loose with your affection when you can hoard it inside you until it shrivels and dies? I can see Lam is telling the truth, that he does like me, but it doesn't explain why he feels the need to be here to tell me that. There's only one reason for his sudden visit that makes any kind of sense to me, but he's prepared to make me wait.

That's okay. I'm prepared to dig in. From the looks of it, so is Brazuca.

Eventually Lam gets bored of the stalemate and begins to speak.

"A woman I knew died of an overdose. She took some coke that was contaminated with a synthetic opiate. Jon was looking into the supply chain for me and had come across a Three Phoenix connection. Apparently, the drugs came from underground manufacturing facilities in China. Three Phoenix, though they are dismantled, have a shadow network here they use from time to time for things like drug distribution."

"What's that got to do with Dao?"

"Nothing. Not directly. I've employed people to help me track down the network in China, but it's almost impossible. They exist on encrypted messaging apps and use cryptocurrencies for their transactions. We're not making progress. I need to speak to someone who knows something of this shadow network. I want to do something to get these labs shut down. Or at least get the drugs out of my city. Names to give to the police, prosecutors. The works. I think we should work together. I have the resources you need to find Dao, and you have some kind of personal connection to him."

"Why do you want him so much?"

"I don't. At least not Dao specifically. I want names, and he's my main lead."

Great. Another amateur detective in the mix. "Okay, but why do you want them? What is this about for you?"

He pauses here and looks at Brazuca, as though searching for advice on how to proceed. Brazuca remains impassive.

This is an interesting development.

The last time I'd seen these two together they had seemed like friends. But something has changed between them.

Lam turns back to me. "The woman who died . . . I loved her very much. Making sure these people don't hurt anyone else is . . . of interest."

There's a photograph I've seen once, of Lam at the opening of some art gallery or the other. He is dressed in a tuxedo and has a glass of champagne in his hand. Even though he's surrounded by people, there is a shield around him. Men this powerful don't allow other people into their personal space. They demand fealty, but they don't necessarily give it. It's lonely to be at the top. He'd brought someone into his circle, and her death was a kind of betrayal. Even if he didn't love her as much as he claims he did, he may never have had something taken from him before.

Or maybe he's got too much time on his hands and spending Daddy's billions isn't as spiritually fulfilling as it once was.

As I consider Bernard Lam's offer, I can feel Brazuca's disapproval directed at Lam, and at me by extension. He shifts his weight, blocking my view of Lam slightly. He's doing that thing that men sometimes do, but I'm not his to protect.

"Okay," I say to Lam now. "Let's find Dao."

Lam breaks into a smile. "Good. I have a meeting with Peter Vidal to set up in the next day or so. We're going to discuss my support of his development project. Maybe he'll be inspired to tell me all about Jimmy Fang."

When Lam leaves, taking his old-money smell and mysterious fashion sense with him, Brazuca deflates. "This is a mistake."

"You were playing both sides again. You knew we were both looking for Dao and Three Phoenix but kept it from me. And him."

"I never lied to you."

"You weren't honest, either."

"Because he was a client. The reason Three Phoenix was on my radar at all is because of Lam."

"I don't like secrets."

"Nora, this, whatever it is, is a suicide mission. You see that, right? You need to go to the police. I know you've had a bad history with the authorities. I know you don't trust them, but goddamn it. Can't you see this is bigger than that? Lam may say he has no one else, but he has money and power. He can get away with things you can't. Don't do this. Don't work with him. I don't trust him. Not with this."

"I'm trying to find information to take to the police. They won't believe me without evidence."

He closes the door and stands in front of me.

"I have a friend in Homicide," he says. "Let's go to him. Dao put a hit on you in Detroit. Nate Marlowe was hurt, and that case got a lot of press. That Detroit detective, Sanchez, can vouch for you, that you're in danger. Let's try it that way. For once."

"No." I can't explain my aversion to cops in terms he'll understand. I won't ever trust them. They don't care about people like me, the ones who are not upstanding, the women who believe that someone is after them. What can the police do about Dao when they can't even save women who know where to find their stalkers? "Lam has money and power. You said it yourself. He has what I don't have. And he can get to Vidal."

"Don't get into bed with men like that."

"I think we're safe there," I say, since I'm not planning to get in bed with any man in particular at the moment. I'm a little busy. "But I'll work with him."

He slumps against the doorframe. His desire to be a part of whatever is happening here with me is warring with his instincts, which are clearly telling him to run as far away from this as he can. I'm not surprised by what he says next. "Nora, I have a bad feeling about this whole thing."

And there it is. His nerves. He's at the end of his rope and is smart enough to know it.

"No one is forcing you to look into this with me. I think you should take a step back."

"Is that what you want?"

"Yes," I say, without hesitation.

Every person has within her a certain amount of self-preservation to guide her. But when the self in question has taken the sheer number of knocks that I have, the preservation instinct is ground down. Mine is a fine dust, little particulates that have all but disappeared. I'm not sure what self there is left to preserve. I guess I'm upset because he's finally leaving me alone. There is some small part of me, a wishful, stupid part, that doesn't want him to go.

"Take care of yourself, Nora," he says.

"You, too." And I mean it. I really hope he does.

My phone buzzes an hour later. Brazuca has sent an article. Clicking on it will dig into the data allotment on the burner I've purchased. Since I'm already living dangerously, I do it anyway.

The headline reads: MAN, 49, FOUND DEAD ON SECOND BEACH.

Joe Nolan, who never showed up for his shift at the Van Club, is now dead. His body was found lodged in between two large rocks. A follow-up article says Nolan's car keys were still in his pocket, along with his wallet and a rolled-up joint. His phone was missing, though.

They think he stepped off the path to smoke a blunt, tripped, and hit his head when he fell. He bled out on the rocks just steps away from the path.

Just your average middle-aged stoner who went into the darkness to light up in one of the most cannabis-friendly cities in the world, where marijuana is now legal. He did this on one of the coldest nights of the year. A tragic accident. Nothing suspicious at all.

# 21

DETECTIVE CHRISTOPHER LEE isn't in a good mood. He's not pleased to find Brazuca waiting for him in his driveway when he arrives at his North Vancouver house, across the city over the Lions Gate Bridge.

"What are you, a stalker?" he asks, getting out of his car.

"I thought you enjoyed my company."

"That was in the past. Before . . ." Lee searches for a time he enjoyed Brazuca's company. Comes up empty. "Fuck it. I can't even remember."

Lee unlocks his front door and waits until he disarms the alarm system before turning to Brazuca. "It's been a long day, bro. What do you need this time?"

"Can't I just visit my old partner?"

"Not really. How can I be of service to you today?" Lee's tone is light, but Brazuca worked with him long enough to know his old partner's patience is at an end.

"The man found on Second Beach. Nothing suspicious there?"

"That story in the papers? It didn't land on my desk, so I don't know the specifics. But from what I heard, we're not treating it as a homicide at this point. Unless you know something?"

"He used to be associated with a gangbanger twenty years ago."

"Is this all that old triad shit you've been looking into?"

"Not sure yet. A white guy named Joe Nolan isn't going to be triad, but he went to school with one and they kept in touch."

"But you're talking about twenty years ago, right?"

"Yeah." Brazuca sighs. "That's the problem. We know nothing about these people anymore. They may not even be a gang."

"Any recent involvement in criminal activity on this guy Nolan's part?"

"Not that I know of. Just got a bad feeling."

Lee shrugs. He gets a beer from the fridge. "Want one?"

"No. I'll head out now. I'm off that case anyway. I was just satisfying my curiosity, so to speak."

Lee grins at him. "Once a cop, always a cop."

"That's bullshit."

His ex-partner watches him go. "You know that bad feeling of yours could be indigestion. When was the last time you ate something, bro?"

"Fuck," says Brazuca. He's already at the door. "I can't even remember."

Brazuca backs out of the driveway, thinking about what Lee has said. Once a cop, always a cop. He hopes it isn't true. Nora said she didn't want him on this anymore. Hell, she hadn't hesitated for a second. But can he really leave it alone?

# 22

PEOPLE DON'T DO at-home social calls anymore. That's the sad truth of the society we live in. Nobody wants a relative, friend, acquaintance, or friend of an acquaintance to show up suddenly on their doorstep. A phone call is equally as undesirable because who wants to hear your voice when they don't want to see your face? A text message is also suspect if read-receipts are activated. Emails are preferable, and social media messages the best of them all. With the latter two you can pretend you've never heard of the person or are too busy living your fabulous life.

Krista Dennings can be found through all the communication platforms that exist, living her fabulous life out there in the open, which is why she's so perplexed that I've rung her doorbell. She recognizes me immediately. "You're Sebastian Crow's friend," she says, a frown on her face. Her Afro is a thing of beauty, a feature that makes her stand out in any crowd of reporters. It makes people remember her. Seb would often complain that she got the best tips because she was so striking, but he would say it with a smile. They were friends. At least, until he got sick and forgot he had any but me.

"Yes," I say. "My name is Nora Watts. Can I come in?"

I can tell she wants to correct the *can* with a *may*—but only because I knew Seb long enough to pinpoint these types. Not only is she a journalist, she was also a copy editor for some time. Language is her trade, and the only way to get her attention is to use it very well or poorly.

Poorly wins out. She waves me inside. "Sure, yes. I could use a break, anyway."

There's another woman at the dining room table, with papers spread about her. "This is my wife, Celine," Krista says. "Celine, this is Nora Watts. She's a friend of Sebastian Crow's."

"The journalist whose funeral you attended? I remember. Nice to meet you, Nora," says Celine, in a Parisian French accent. She's an extremely tall woman, even sitting down. When we shake hands, hers almost engulfs mine.

"I didn't see you at Sebastian's funeral," Krista says.

"I was out of town when he passed. I couldn't get back in time."

"What's wrong with your voice?"

"Okay, that's my cue," says Celine, unfolding her long limbs. "Krista is in her grilling mood again. *A bientôt,* Nora." She leaves the room. We hear her on the stairs and a door upstairs shut.

"About your voice?" Krista asks again.

"The effects of poor life choices."

"I can see that. You always had a reckless quality about you."

"What do you mean?"

"I don't know. Just an impression. There's always been something unpredictable about you, I suppose."

This gives me a pause. I'm a woman over twenty-five. I'm so used to people ignoring my existence that it's startling when someone admits they've been paying attention. Then again, Krista Dennings is also a woman over twenty-five. Maybe we've each been paying attention while the other isn't looking.

"I need some information," I say to her. I don't tell her the full sad story because she's heard hundreds of these before. I get to the point, which is something she appreciates.

She listens until I'm done, tapping a pencil against her chin every now and then. "Okay, so what you're saying is you're digging up info on Jimmy Fang? I did that for the better part of a decade. And I got a call about it a few weeks ago from a PI. Celine and I were on our honeymoon then, and I haven't had a chance to call him back yet. A Bazucci or something? You know him?"

"Yes. Jon Brazuca. We work together sometimes. Most of the in-depth articles I've read about Jimmy Fang, the deep dives, had your byline." It was something I noticed in Brazuca's research. Krista's name shining bright at the top of almost every article.

She nods. "Jimmy and I had a bit of a rapport. Some of these gangsters like to talk to women they know they're never going to fuck. You go in, make them feel like a big man, and they get chatty. Jimmy gave me tips, indulged his own sense of ego. I think he liked seeing his name in print. He grew up poor, but he was ambitious. Smart. People liked him."

"Do you know where he went? After he jumped bail?"

"He went to Hong Kong, Macau, the Philippines, and finally, according to a rumor, Indonesia. I think he got a whole new identity in the Philippines and disappeared from there."

"But how could that happen?"

"His people had the resources to get him out. There's a hell of a lot of money floating around British Columbia, in commercial and luxury real estate, gambling, resource development, the works. Three Phoenix was a piddling little street gang that Jimmy Fang elevated through his own personal ambition. Word is he wormed his way into the 14K ranks. Their criminal network is vast and highly adaptable. Technology has made it easier to have reduced numbers but still have their grubby hands in pies all over the world. This province has always had a strong Pacific connection that our good old politicians have exploited for their own personal gain, so we're particularly ripe."

She says this with the bitterness of journalists the world over. A disgust, but an acceptance, too. I've developed a fondness for journalists. They always, always know more than they're saying.

"But any of his associates still around? Anybody who could have helped him leave?" Or who knew where he might have gone, I hope.

"Just his right hand. A guy named Van Nguyen, Fang's cousin-in-law or some such. He was never charged for any-thing but was known to police. Nguyen fell off my radar for a while and turned up last year as a private lender of sorts during one of my investigations into money laundering and organized crime. But he's often out of the country."

I know the name from the research Brazuca had pulled up on the gang. "Any idea what Nguyen looks like now? Any way I can find him?"

"He has a three-million-dollar house in West Vancouver that sits empty, according to the neighbors. He's never there. But." She scribbles something on a notepad. Tears out the sheet and hands it to me. "I hear he has a new girlfriend. She man-ages a casino restaurant in Richmond. Her name is Maggie Miller, a former Miss Vancouver. As for how he looks, much of the same, but older. He keeps a very low profile, and I missed my chance to get a photo."

I think about this for a moment. On the paper she gave me is the name of the restaurant. "Aren't you working a casino angle at the moment?" A few of her recent articles touched on some kind of money-laundering scheme.

She gets a gleam in her eye that I'm well familiar with from working with Seb. A kind of passion that's hard to fake. "Heard of whale gamblers?" she asks, then continues before I have the chance to respond. "It's the high rollers from Asia who want to gamble but don't want to deal with the red tape of bringing money. So they have arrangements with private lenders over there who they pay and then they show up in Vancouver, pick up the cash in restaurant parking lots here—parking lots, for Christsakes—and they're good to go. Casinos themselves are in on it. They don't even make them go to the high-value windows. It's a mess."

"I'm not sure what to do with all that. I just need to find out how Fang disappeared and where he might have gone."

"That's what I'm trying to tell you," she says, as though I'm a particularly bad intern she's been assigned. One with potential but who can't focus on the real issue. "Australian intelligence is calling this the 'Vancouver Model' of money laundering. You don't need soldiers on the street when money moves like this. I'm saying that these guys are so well-connected and rich that they can go anywhere they want. They're into all of the respectable institutions in this city, but they're also into the shady ones, too. Not just money laundering. Human trafficking, human smuggling? Drugs? Et cetera."

"Human smuggling?"

It sounds like a wild conspiracy.

She can see how doubtful I am. "Yeah, but that's not how Fang left. He got on a plane, even though he was on bail. It was a failure of the justice system. Remember, this was twenty years ago. But if you're interested in human smuggling, it's as simple as forged papers, falsifying immigration documents— that sort of thing. Basically, if you want to get something or someone into or out of the country, there's an underground

infrastructure for that. Just like there's an underground banking infrastructure."

"Through those private lenders."

"Exactly. I could send you some information, if you want. I
was never able to find Fang, but I wish you luck. Honestly, you
look like you could use some."

Celine comes back down the stairs. "Always with this Asian
connection," she says to Krista. "You know, I study psychology
at the University of British Columbia, and this comes up in the
paper—an article saying that Canadians are happier in areas
where there are few foreign-born residents. And you know
they don't mean people like me. There is a question you must
ask yourself: Are you promoting this bias with your work?"

"By reporting on criminal activity? That's what I do!" Krista
says. "The reason I do this is so that the government can get
their shit together and regulate things properly."

Celine shrugs. "But they're bribed to not. Paid to look the
other way. Politicians are just as corrupt here, too. I'm saying
the coverage can be taken the wrong way by idiots, and the
idiots become uncomfortable with immigrants."

I get the sense this is an argument they have often, especially when Krista grumbles, "Well, it's their fault for being
idiots. What are you, some kind of social justice warrior? Who
let you into the country?"

"I don't know, but you're the one keeping me here."

They kiss in a way that makes me think that perhaps the
honeymoon isn't over yet, and then Celine asks if I want some

tea. She puts her hands on the top of the doorframe and falls into a stretch, in a way I've only seen athletes do. Krista is equally riveted by this motion.

I say no to tea but make sure to give Krista my number in case she remembers anything else. "Congratulations on the wedding," I say to them both.

Celine beams, argument forgotten. "Thank you!"

Krista just smiles at me. At the door, she gives me a long, searching look. "Sebastian mailed me a copy of his memoirs before he passed. He mentions you in there. You've read it, right?"

"I haven't read the final version."

"You should. You know when I said you were unpredictable? What I meant was I would never have thought you'd be the person to drop everything and take care of a dying man for a year. Who takes care of you, lady?"

On that bright note she closes the door on me.

The phone rings while I'm pulling out of her driveway, but I answer it anyway, hoping it's Simone. It's not. Bernard Lam is on the line. He wants to meet tomorrow.

He's got a surprise for me.

# 23

THE LITTLE MAID feels fragile underneath him. There are stretch marks on her soft belly. Dao likes the little grooves but finds them distracting. Nothing in her employment file told him she's a mother. When he asks about the child, she shakes her head and shifts her body, tilting her hips up and into him. Maybe she's feeling reckless because it's night and they're alone.

Somehow he doubts it, but it's a nice thought.

They've never been alone at night before, and it wasn't his intention to manufacture this particular situation when he knocked on the door of the staff house. There are supposed to be two dayworkers and two live-in servants in the compound. The other live-in, Anto, hasn't been here since yesterday.

"What's your name?" he asks.

She smiles and pretends she doesn't speak English. It was the same when he asked where Anto was.

Doesn't matter.

He didn't hire the staff of the villa—compound, really—but he knows who they are. Like Riya, here, who he is pressing into the mattress. Her employment file gave her age as twenty-four. She looks a lot younger until you meet her eyes and see the old soul that lurks behind them. Which he's doing now, maybe for the first time.

He knows she speaks English, because it is a requirement of their employer that all staff need to understand when they're shouted at in a common language.

Looking down at her, Dao feels no desire. The flare of initial heat is gone, replaced with nothing. In this void of sexual excitement, he wonders about her reason for bringing him to her bed. When he started asking about Anto, she had taken off her dress.

Why doesn't she want him asking about the resident landscaper-slash-handyman?

It's clear the sex is supposed to be a distraction, but all things considered, it isn't very distracting.

Dao rolls off her and puts on his clothes. "Where's Anto?" he asks again.

It's too late for this shit. He'd come back to slick floors and a burst pipe under the kitchen sink. He could fix it himself, but it isn't his job. And he's got too much on his mind to be doing other people's work. Like this lazy bastard Anto.

What, is he taking a nap or something?

Dao goes to the door and looks down the narrow hall. There's another bedroom on this floor and two more upstairs. Nice digs. Maybe a little too nice, and maybe Anto got a little too comfortable.

Well, that's about to change.

He goes to search the next room, but the little maid grabs

his hand and tries to pull him back into bed. There's a sudden stitch in his side, a flash of pain, and he finds himself collapsing next to her. She takes the opportunity to straddle his hips and press her naked body against him.

"Wait," he says, trying to catch his breath. The pain in his belly is unbelievable, and he's fresh out of the pills that take the sharp sting of it away.

She sees him gasping, struggling. She gets off him for the moment it takes to pour him a drink from a bottle of expensive brandy. He wonders if she stole it from the main house. He drinks it in one straight go and holds the glass out for another. She pours even more this time. Looking around the room, he thinks that maybe it isn't hers after all. The room is furnished, but there are no woman things around. No clothes, jewelry, or toiletries. Not even an attempt at making it personal.

A skint room with a bottle of brandy on the bedside table?

Yeah, a man definitely lives here. He'd bet any money this is where that fool Anto sleeps. Or used to, anyway, before he fucked off to wherever he went.

He turns to Riya to give her hell about Anto, but there's that look in her eye again.

And look at that, he's drunk enough for another try.

Afterward, he rolls off her. She seems glad to get rid of his weight. He's exhausted. Feels like he could sleep for a week straight, maybe even longer. He turns over and closes his eyes. He really shouldn't stay, but what's she going to do, kick him out? Soon enough he's off to dreamland. Thankfully, without the actual dreams.

He wakes up to discover that he's still in the same shitty backwater that he went to sleep in. A shitty backwater, yes, but at least he's got a roof over his head and seems to be in a nice bed. There's supposed to be somebody beside him, but he can't remember who because his head is shaking. Or is it the bed? Wait, no. The walls are moving, rumbling. Actually, it's the whole fucking room.

Realizing where he is, and the specifics of living in this particular cursed place, Dao remembers his earthquake training. He throws an arm out to grab the little maid but finds her long gone. So he rolls off the mattress and underneath the bed.

A moment later the room tilts and a part of the wall comes crashing down around him. There's another rattle, a tremor, the feeling of the ground under him being ripped apart.

It feels like he's in hell, but it's really the Ring of Fire. This goddamn, blighted backwater nowhere cursed with frequent volcanic eruptions and earthquakes.

He'd be safe if he was in his own room, not the staff lodging. The main house is reinforced and would have fared better, but of course nobody really gives a damn about the servants. This building was never properly addressed. This house of death, where the expendables live.

He remembers the staff house is backed onto the hills of the region, and what he's hearing is the hill behind him collapsing as the earth slides down around them, and on top of them, too. The bottle of brandy he'd drunk from earlier crashes to the ground, not far away from his face. He curls his body tightly into himself, tries to protect his head and his face.

Somewhere above his head a woman screams. Dao thinks it's the little maid, Riya. He can't see much, but it doesn't seem like she's in here with him. So she's upstairs, then. Or what passes for upstairs now that the whole structure has crumbled.

The bed breaks, and Dao is pinned there underneath, gasping for breath.

It feels like the end of times. The end of him.

It feels like—

# 24

I CAN'T BELIEVE what I'm feeling. I think it's attraction, but that can't be right. I'm trying not to like Peter Vidal, but it's hard because, up close, there's something undeniably magnetic about him.

We're sitting at Café Villaggio, just steps from the harbor, and he's stirring honey into his tea. He gives it a sip, braces, and then drinks again. Lam is late, and Vidal is unsure of why I'm here. He's too polite to ask me to leave outright, but I can tell he wants me to. He's dressed in a pair of dark trousers and a black turtleneck sweater that looks so soft I wonder what it would feel like on my skin. Maybe it's all the talk of getting into bed with people that has me thinking like this, or maybe I just want to be warm and cozy, too.

"How long will he be?" Vidal asks, in dulcet tones. Which I also find pleasing. I'm having a hard time reconciling the man in front of me with the man Joe Nolan had pointed out on the yacht. Though it must be him, and our meeting in this café in Coal Harbour is a nod to his tastes, because of its proximity to his pretty boat.

"Who knows?" I say. "You know how unpredictable billionaires can be."

This isn't the conversation starter I'd hoped it to be. Vidal frowns into his sweet tea. He takes a delicate sip.

The door opens, and Lam comes striding in, in a different three-piece suit today. After shaking hands with Vidal, he throws his overcoat over a chair and tells me he'd like an Americano. I stare at him until he goes to get it himself. When he returns, I can see Vidal hiding a smile. I may be growing on him. At least that's what I think until Vidal says to Lam, "Your associate here refused to tell me who she is. She says you'll explain everything."

Lam blinks, then covers up his momentary discomfort with a smile. "This is my assistant, Nora. I can't keep track of my life without her, really."

Everyone at the table ignores the fact that he's asked me to get him coffee and I flat-out refused.

"Even so," says Vidal, "perhaps we can continue alone."

I don't move. Lam clears his throat. "No, we're fine here."

Now I see it. The power that Vidal embodies is just about equal to the entitlement that Lam projects into the room, at once sweeping over me and bringing me into the circle. I'm here because he wants me to be. It's as simple as that.

Vidal isn't happy about it, but he's willing to let my presence at the round table slide. "Let's get to business, then. I'd be very grateful for your assistance. I'm sorry that the development proposal for the Chinatown complex was turned down. Community pushback, you know. It's my hope that we can . . . make Vancouver more business-friendly. If we can spread the message to the community that more business means more prosperity, then I don't see things like that happening as much moving forward."

It seems like a flaming pile of lies to me, but he says it so nicely, with that gentle voice. I might be willing to give him the permission for his development myself, if I could. This must be what those waitresses see in him before they get onto his boat. Before he sends them home in tears.

"We think," Vidal continues, "that a dedicated space for the arts would go over well, especially if it's backed by your family, given your significant investment in arts and culture. As I was saying to you at the club, the Devi Group was happy to participate in your gallery launch in Seattle."

"That was a fun one," says Lam. "Some of my contacts within the Chinatown business community here might be interested in revisiting your proposal if there was more commitment to the arts. Chinatown has such a vibrant history. It would help if people understood that you're as interested in preserving and celebrating that history as you are in prosperity." He neglects to mention that his contacts really belong to his father, whose reputation in Vancouver's business and cultural circles is iron-clad.

Vidal seems to be buying Lam as a mouthpiece for his father. "And you'd share them for what price?"

And just like that, it's like I'm not even there. There's no place for me to exist between these two and their egos.

They've said meaningless words about community, arts and culture, and now are finally getting to the point.

"Trying to get to the bottom of a private matter, actually. It concerns my family." Lam spears him with a calculating look, from one shark to another. Designed to make him wonder whose teeth are sharper.

Vidal smiles. "My lips are sealed. Go on."

"You were once connected to a Three Phoenix boss named Jimmy Fang. You worked for his law firm, in fact. That is, before he fled the city. We need to know if any of his associates are still here."

Vidal doesn't miss a beat. "That's what it takes to get your family to back the Chinatown development proposal?"

"If I'm happy with the information, yes."

"As much as I'd love to make you happy, I don't know anything about Three Phoenix. Fang, I met. And yes, he was a client at my firm when I was still practicing law. But I have no intimate knowledge of his operation."

Peter Vidal lies so well it's impressive. I'm about to say something to remind them I'm still in the room, but he continues speaking before I can get a word in.

"I do know that before he left the country in a rather scandalous fashion, I saw him a few times with Michael Acosta."

"Acosta's company just bought a two-hundred-million-dollar mine in Indonesia," Lam says to me, suddenly remembering my existence. "But they're into casinos, as well."

Vidal nods. "Acosta has stakes in mines and casinos all over Southeast Asia. On this side of the Pacific he's been more into entertainment, including a major film studio."

This makes me think of something Krista Dennings had said. When she'd been running down Jimmy Fang, she lost him in the Philippines. And had said that he'd disappeared in Indonesia.

The conversation draws to a close shortly after. Vidal and Lam discuss what the Lam family support might entail. They are speaking French to me. I can pick out a few words but don't understand much. Underneath his soft voice, Vidal is more excited than I've ever seen him.

When Vidal leaves, Lam turns to me. "Dao used to work for Ray Zhang, as you know."

I nod. When I met Lam for the first time, this was the piece of information he gave me. At that time, I was looking for Ray Zhang because of his connection to Bonnie's disappearance.

"The official story is that Ray Zhang died in Hong Kong last year from a stroke. His son, Kai, is dead. So is his daughter-in-law, Jia, as well as their son. Zhang-Wei was a family company. After Ray's death, Zhang-Wei Industries was in trouble, and Mike Acosta's Nebula Corporation took over whatever Zhang-Wei international assets they could get their hands on. Zhang-Wei was into mining and real estate all over the world."

"You think Dao tipped him off? That they knew each other?"

"Zhang and Acosta were friendly rivals, but they ran in the same circles here in Vancouver. Head offices for both of their companies were based here."

"Head offices for most of the world's mining companies are in Vancouver." It's something I remembered from the time I'd been looking into the Zhang family and their business dealings.

"Yes, yes. You're not going to give me a lecture, are you?"

"You won't get a lecture from me," I say. I'm not my sister. "When Ray Zhang was out of the picture, maybe Dao transferred his allegiance to Acosta."

"That's exactly what I'm thinking," Lam says. "Maybe Dao was friendly with Acosta—or Acosta's security. Dao had a reputation as someone who worked his way up to the head of Ray Zhang's private security detail. Acosta has done business all over Asia, especially in Indonesia. Dao likely knew Acosta, very well."

"Dao worked for the Zhang family for years. He knew how those kinds of high rollers operated. Knew how to handle their security and the various unsavory aspects of their lives. He was trusted and respected. He would be an asset to any team."

"He always struck me as a company man," Lam says. "A soldier for the Zhangs."

"When we'd first met you told me that he was triad, but how did you know that? Who is he, really?" He shrugs it off, but something jolts my memory. "You said he seemed like a soldier. To me, he had a military bearing. What are the chances that he has some military experience, somewhere in his past?"

"It would make sense. Especially if he worked for someone as high-profile as Ray Zhang."

"And now Michael Acosta. Now what would a guy like Michael Acosta need a ruthless, loyal soldier for?"

It occurs to me, much later, that I should have brought up Joe Nolan's death just to gauge the temperature in the room. I don't see Vidal pushing him onto the rocks, but I would have liked to see his reaction. It's an opportunity missed because I'll probably never be in the same room as Vidal again. But I have Michael Acosta, who might be Dao's new employer. If I—*we*—can figure out what role he plays in Acosta's vast empire, there's a chance we can find him.

*Then what?* asks a voice in my head.

I tell it to fuck off.

# 25

THE DAYLIGHT IS seeping away when Krista Dennings calls. "I'm on deadline so I don't have a lot of time, Nora," she says, as soon as I pick up.

"What's up?"

"One of my sources for the article on the private money lenders called. I couldn't give you her name before, but when she contacted me, I asked if it was okay. Stephanie Kwan's ex-husband owed money to Nguyen's people and Nguyen used the debt in an attempt to get her to sign over the property. But she knew nothing about the loan. She says she's received threatening phone calls from Nguyen's secretary and one from someone claiming to be Nguyen himself but nothing for the past week. On the phone he'd said the next time he spoke with her he'd bring his friends with him. It was an explicit threat. Today her landscaper called while she was at work—she's a chemist—and said some guys had driven by the house a few times and slowed down specifically to get a look at her property."

"You think it's Nguyen?"

"Maybe you should talk to her. She's called the police, and they said they sent a car over but saw nothing."

"She's alright with speaking to me about him?"

"Yes," says Krista, after a moment.

"I'm not sure I understand why you'd be giving me one of your sources."

"Usually these guys prey on newcomers and exploit their fears to extort them out of money and their homes. But Stephanie is a force to be reckoned with. She doesn't take lightly to anyone threatening her, so she was pissed. That previous time, and today, too, when she called to give me the update. I explained to her that you're looking for some information about a threat to your own safety. Maybe she remembers something she hadn't before in her conversation with me, I don't know. I would run this down myself, but—"

"You're on deadline."

"That's right."

"How did you know there's a threat to my safety?"

She laughs, but it's a knowing laugh, one without the least bit of humor. "Nora, I pay attention. It's my job. You don't have any obvious tells, but I could see some part of you was worried. Scared, even." Then she grows serious. "And besides, why else would you be looking into an old gangster like Jimmy Fang? Or trying to use an equally old gangster like Nguyen to get to him? You must be desperate."

After I take down the address, we end the call. Whisper and I get into the Corolla. There's no denying that Krista Dennings is right. I am desperate.

I arrive just moments before Stephanie Kwan does. I'm barely out of the car with Whisper when a sensible Subaru Forester rolls up. A middle-aged woman with blondish streaks in her dark hair gets out of the car, hoisting the largest handbag I have ever seen out of the back seat.

She gives me a frank once-over and turns to Whisper. "Hey there, buddy! Do you want a treat?"

While she rummages in the bag, she says to me, "I'm assuming you're Krista's friend? The one looking for information on that fucking asshole who's been calling me?"

"That's me," I say, watching her hand my dog the treat. Whisper gives it an exploratory sniff and then takes it delicately into her mouth.

"What a lady!" Stephanie says, beaming at Whisper. I like her immediately, this woman. She's still smiling when she turns back to me, but the smile disappears as something just beyond my shoulder gets her attention.

A Bentley pulls up, blocking the driveway entrance. Two men get out of the car, and I try to control my shock. One of them is much larger than the other, younger, too, though the second man wears nicer clothes. I focus on him, Mr. GQ.

Van Nguyen hasn't changed much in twenty-odd years, but for graying hair and a small, sharp goatee that doesn't particularly suit him.

The larger man halts at the sight of Whisper, who's off-leash.

"Miss Kwan, we'd like to speak with you inside. Alone," says Nguyen. "I think you know what this is about." While he's ignoring me, I pull my hood up to cover as much of my appearance as possible.

Stephanie Kwan isn't impressed. "Get out of here, you ass-hole! I've already called the cops!"

Nguyen yawns. "We should settle our business privately."

She reaches into her purse and pulls out a canister of bear spray. The larger man tenses. I see him reach for something inside his jacket. Whisper growls.

I want information on Nguyen, but this is getting out of hand. I move to block Stephanie and wrap my fist around Whisper's collar. "Neighborhood watch," I say to Nguyen and his goon. "Who did you say you were?"

"Oh, I don't think I did," says Nguyen. His voice sounds shockingly young for a man his age. He frowns at me, as if he's trying to place me. He's about to say something else, but Whisper tugs on her leash, moving forward. His attention is on her now.

I step past him, bringing Whisper with me. "Is that a Bent-ley? You wouldn't mind if I take the license plate down, just to put it in our records? North Vancouver is getting dangerous, so we like to keep track of who our friends are."

"Maybe this isn't such a good time, since you have com-pany," Nguyen says to Stephanie Kwan. "We'll be back."

We watch him and the larger man leave. Stephanie doesn't put away the bear spray until they turn the corner.

"Was that everything you dreamed and more?" she asks.

"What?"

"You were looking for information on the guy who says I owe him money for my house. Happy now?"

"Not really."

"Neither am I. I'm calling the police. Again." She fishes in her bag for her keys, then invites me inside, where she gives me a run-down of the phone calls and threats Nguyen's people had made.

"Here are the numbers they used to call me," she says, scrolling through her call list. I log them into my burner. "What's this about? Do they also think you owe them money? Because they didn't seem to recognize you."

Which is strange, if Nguyen is Dao's guy here in Vancouver. If he's responsible for farming out the surveillance, he should know what I look like at least. Or maybe with most of my face and hair covered by the hood, he just didn't put it together in time. "I'm looking for information on someone they used to know."

"Well, you didn't do a very good job of asking them!"

"I know."

She puts out a bowl of water for Whisper. "Maybe I should get a guard dog."

I nod. "That's a great idea."

"Look, don't feel bad. Those guys weren't going to tell you anything anyway."

"I know that, too." I missed my chance to follow them, collect information on where they went, who they talked to. Figure out, somehow, what they know about Jimmy Fang and Dao.

"Thank you for staying with me," she says. "It was good to have someone here when they showed up."

"You really should get a dog."

I stay until a police squad car shows up, then say goodbye to her. I'd wanted to go since Nguyen and his friend had taken off, but I couldn't leave her alone with nothing but bear spray for protection. It's fully dark by the time Whisper and I get back into the car. From our vantage point, Vancouver is laid out in front of us across the water, the city lights shining bright.

# 26

DAO IS SUFFOCATING. There's dust in his mouth. In his eyes. He takes a swipe at them to clear his vision, and the first thing he sees is that he's trapped. The bed collapsed on top of him, and he's breathing into a pocket of air.

He tests his fingers, toes, limbs. Everything is intact but hurts like hell. There's a bump on his head, and that seems fitting. This is what he gets for going to look for a wayward employee and stumbling on the seemingly free gift of sex. But nothing is free, especially not sex, and his life is the price he might have to pay for it if he doesn't get his ass into gear.

He flips onto his stomach and crawls toward the air pocket.

He has no idea how long he's been out, but from his extreme thirst and the weakness he feels, he's been here for quite some time.

It makes sense. He's the only resident, and the compound is minimally staffed. That lazy bastard Anto must be gone, so it's just Dao and Riya, the maid . . .

Who'd been screaming somewhere above his head. It's the last thing he remembered before being crushed.

There's a loose beam blocking his way. He grabs it and pushes it with all his might. The pain is unbelievable, but he manages to budge it. Another push. Some more give. He works like this for some time, taking frequent breaks. He's got no leverage here, only his strength.

Finally, he's moved it enough to wedge his body through.

He can see a speck of the morning sky. He keeps going, crawling through toward that blue, pushing against the debris in his way. He's so damn tired. It feels like he's got nothing left, but then there's a sound. A cry so loud, so unearthly, it almost shatters his eardrums.

Instinctively, he moves toward it. He can't stop now. If he stops, it's over. Part of him wants it to be over. A damn hill fell on top of him, after all, shook loose by an earthquake. And the one before that, and the one before that, too.

The Ring of Fire.

In the Pacific. This archipelago, full of little islands. Rife with volcanos and along fault lines. The meeting point of several tectonic plates and both the Indian and Pacific Oceans.

He's been in Indonesia for over a year, and it feels like it's been trying to push him away ever since he got here. Not that he's wanted to stay. Hell is still hell, no matter how nice the weather is.

There's that cry again. A woman shouting about a baby. Who brought a baby to a natural disaster?

He breaks free and hoists himself onto the ground. Lays there on his back, stunned. The rising sun warms his face, makes him sweat, even though his hands are cold. He sees someone digging frantically through the rubble close by. It's the little maid. Riya. She's shouting at him to help. In English. Which she pretended not to be able to speak.

Women.

She goes over to him and, with a strength he didn't know she possessed, pulls him to his knees, then to his feet. "My baby," she says, her eyes wide and pleading. She's filthy. Her dress is torn in several places, and her hands are bleeding. There's a nasty cut along her cheek that she touches gingerly with her fingertips. Blood on blood. He feels like retching. She reaches to grab him, but he pulls away from her.

"Please!" she shouts, when he stands still for several seconds, just looking at her.

He snaps out of his daze. "Where?"

She pulls him toward the rubble. "I think here. Please."

"Call someone," he tells her. "Get help from the village."

"Can't find my phone," she tells him. "Main line down in the house."

"Then go get someone."

"No time! I can't leave my baby!" She kneels a few feet away. Pulls at the debris with her bare, bloody hands. So he starts to pull, too. Soon, he hears people behind him. Villagers, three men and two women, coming to help on their own. One of them tells him the village is in a bad state and rescue workers haven't even made it there yet. Other areas were hit harder by the earthquake. Together, they clear the rubble from the landslide, which smashed into the staff house, causing it to collapse on itself.

He fights it, but a wave of heat builds inside him.

It gets so bad that he remembers Ahmići. Another cursed place. He'd been so young himself, barely twenty, when the army had sent him overseas. And that village. Both mosques had been mined, but he didn't know that at the time. He only saw the one. Then the bodies in the houses, burned. The people burned. Their corpses.

He is pulled back to Bosnia, a place he has tried so hard to erase from his memory. Now he remembers the children most of all. It was why he left the military, those images of massacred children burned into his brain.

Something broken inside him.

Riya speaks to the others in her language. One of the men offers to take over where Dao is working, but he sends the man away with a single look. There's a baby down here, she'd said. It's now hitting him.

A child is buried under here.

Dao doesn't stop. Now his hands are bloody, too. They work in silence, moving chunks of the building away.

Dao is the one who sees it first. The beam, fallen across a crib. Peeking out from under it is a chubby little arm covered in dust.

Riya goes to the child and pulls its little body out. She's crying, keeling over. Rocking back and forth on her haunches. This is what she was hiding. Why she didn't want him to go asking after Anto the Invisible. She brought her kid here to this place, even though it was against her work contract to do it. There was a no-child policy in the staff house. Boss's orders.

She brought her kid here to die.

The child cries. It's alive. But the knowledge comes too late. Something inside Dao snaps.

He strikes the little maid across the mouth, opening the cut on her face even further.

She stumbles but, in a flash, is up again. One hand holding her child, she hits him back. It takes every single one of the villagers in the compound to pull them off each other, and only then because he's weak with exhaustion. Riya is screaming, she's so furious.

Oh, so now when he's weak she can speak perfect English? Hit him back like this?

In his mind her face blurs . . . she starts to look like Nora Watts.

# 27

ALL THE NUMBERS Van Nguyen's people called Stephanie Kwan from are disconnected. So that's a dead end.

When I need ideas, there's only one person I go to. Problem is, she seems to have disappeared, which is annoying. That's *my* role in the relationship. She has never put me in the position of having to hunt her down before, and I wonder if my warm and cuddly personality has driven her away for good. It occurs to me that though we have known each other for years, I have no idea where she lives.

I ask around our old AA meeting group, but no one has seen Simone lately. That's not like her, but I try not to worry. Maybe she needs some distance.

This depressing thought takes me to the bar down the street. I linger outside for a moment. There's nothing I want more than to drown my sorrows in the cheapest liquor I can get my hands on.

I don't want to go in, but I cross the threshold anyway.

It's not a nice bar. The people here seem sad and mostly alone. There are a few couples at tables, but they seem sad and alone, too. There's a slim, ethnically ambiguous man sitting at the bar, staring into a shot glass. He looks at the glass for a long time, and then he raises it to his lips and knocks it back.

When I slide into the seat next to him, he doesn't blink an eye or look over.

"How did the meeting go?" asks Simone, who is not in drag. Who I'm seeing for the first time as her alter ego, Simon.

Simon is drunk and pretending not to be.

Neither of us knows what to do. I'm having some pronoun difficulty because I don't want to get it wrong. Simone once said that the only people who get worked up over pronouns are those who lack imagination. She'd said it in such a judgmental tone that I didn't want to admit I possibly lack imagination. Especially today. I don't want to upset this friend of mine, who is going through something I understand all too well. A relapse.

Simon stops pretending, presses his head into his hands.

"It was exciting," I say. "Best experience of my life. You should have come."

"Oh, fuck off."

I would happily do that, but I can't leave him here alone in this sad place with these sad people. After I pay the bill, I realize that I couldn't be an alcoholic anymore even if I wanted to. Not at these prices. Not with my bank account balance.

"So," I begin. I'm coming around to thinking of Simone as Simon now, but I don't know if that's what I should be doing. I do know that I'm not meant to see this part of my friend. Simone in her right mind would never want me to because Simone in her right mind has never allowed me a glimpse into Simon.

"I can get home," Simon says. "Don't touch me." He's slurring so much that I don't even bother listening. The cab ride home to his condo in Yaletown doesn't take long, but he falls asleep anyway. When we get inside his apartment, he straightens and goes directly to the bathroom. I stand by the door, listening to him wretch his guts out. While I'm there I take in the condo, which I've never been to before. It is decorated in black and white, with elegant green accents. It doesn't feel particularly masculine or feminine, which is a strange window into this person I know but don't really.

The toilet flushes, and Simon stumbles out. "Get out," he says to me, but there are tears in his eyes, so I have an inkling of what it's costing him to say those words.

I do get out, but I keep the keys when I leave and return in the morning with Whisper in tow, just as dawn begins to rise. Simon is sitting on a stool by the kitchen, sipping strong black coffee. He's not in drag, but he has showered and taken the time to apply thick black eyeliner to his lids. Whisper gives our friend a good long sniff and receives a few pats on the head in return.

Simon pours me some coffee but can't seem to meet my eyes. He disappears into the bedroom and returns as Simone, in subtle makeup and wearing a muted pink wig. I'm not sure if it's for my comfort or for her.

"How long have you been drinking again?" I ask when we're on our second cups.

"Since Benedict Cumberbatch died." She looks at me. "You didn't know."

That her feisty little terrier was dead? Suddenly I'm ashamed. "No, I'm sorry. I should have—"

"Yes. But, as always, you were caught up in your own drama. You could put a drag queen to shame."

Do I feel guilty because I'm angry, or am I angry that I feel so guilty? "Seb was sick. My father . . . I ran into trouble in Detroit. You know that. I was almost killed."

"And when you weren't, you didn't think to call me? Send a text to let me know you're okay? I've been trying to reach you. I've been worried about you."

It's true that when I dumped my phone, I didn't reach out on the burner. Bonnie was on my mind, not Simone.

"I didn't think—"

"You didn't think I'd care enough."

In her expression there's a glimpse of something so infinitely sad that I can't bear it. "Do you think so little of yourself, Nora, that it never occurred to you that you deserve love and compassion? You spent a year looking after a sick man, hoarding all his secrets, taking care of his every need and not letting anybody else in on your burden."

I don't know what I'm expected to say to this. This conversation isn't supposed to be about me.

"Whoever said you weren't good enough to care about?" she asks.

I've never seen the point of tears. There's something inside me that grows cold at the thought of shedding them, at the sight of someone else letting them fall. I don't give in to tears, not even now, because I'll never take the chance that someone will see it as weakness, as I do. But I wonder what it would be like if I did. I feel like we're on the brink of something in our friendship.

"You run away," she continues. "Because you don't want to stay and ask for love. You keep people at an arm's length and blame them for not wanting to come closer when you're the one that pushed them to the corners of your universe. You think I don't know what it's like to feel like I don't have anyone? Like I'm not worthy of love?"

"You're wonderful."

"Of course I am," she snaps. "I don't need anyone to tell me that."

"Are you done?"

"No, actually I'm just getting started. You want to slay Bonnie's dragons and chase all her demons away, but you put yourself in danger because you don't see yourself in her life, being there for her and having a functional relationship. So let me ask you this, Nora: Who slays your dragons?"

Krista Dennings had asked the same thing, in her own way. "I slay them myself."

She nods. "I was afraid you'd say that. One of these days, you'll look around and find that you are truly alone and that you always have been because you're too afraid to let anyone see you. And I know what you're thinking. You're thinking you don't need anyone else because you have Whisper, and I don't even want to start on how fucked up that is. Whisper has people. Whisper has made friends and has a better community than you do. Think about that. Dogs are pack animals. She has others, and at the end of the day, if something happens to her, you have nobody else. You continue this way and you won't even have me."

"*You* continue this way"—I nod to the empty boxes of cheap wine lined up by the sink—"and I won't even have you. So what are we going to do about it?"

"Rehab," she says. "What else? I can't do this alone. I've already made arrangements to go today."

The relief I feel is almost overwhelming. You can't make someone go to rehab. You can't make them value their lives. So at least she knows she's ready.

Business is booming with her cyber security company so she can afford one of the good ones, the one on a Gulf Island where you can't escape confronting your poor choices and destructive habits because it's an island. I drive her to the ferry and fill her in on what's been happening.

When the ferry arrives, she tells me I can keep the spare keys to her apartment but doesn't say why. Only "just in case." After the ferry leaves, I take Whisper for a walk down by the water and think about Joe Nolan, bleeding out on the rocks. Maybe his death was quick. I hope it was. But he doesn't seem like the kind of guy who'd catch a break like that.

One thing is certain. I know, without a doubt, that this path I started him down led to his death. That I am, again, responsible. There's another name to add to the list.

# 28

"WHAT DO YOU mean he wants more?" It has been a day and Dao is in no mood for this shit. "I pay you to pay him to go away."

Jono, his Humas, his local fixer, is adamant. He names a figure, a new demand from the workers. "This is not possible with the budget you gave me last. Sammy says he will not go without more. After the earthquake everybody has more bills to pay. Oh, and he says there are a couple reporters on their way."

They're looking at a protest racket blocking the access road. Picket signs, the works. Catnip for the media. Bad for the mine. A smirking youth with bills to pay watches them from the sidelines.

"Okay," says Dao, eyeing the kid. He can't be more than nineteen. Any more years on him and that smug expression would slide right off his face at the way Dao's looking at him now. "Tell him I'll meet him in twenty minutes round back, by the offices."

"And I will tell his cousin this is not how to do things. For now, I will give the money to Sammy if you just—"

"No, I'll do it."

"But—"

"But nothing. I'll do it. This isn't ever going to happen again, you hear me? You're the fixer, right? Fix it better next time."

Jono looks as though he's about to say something else but thinks better of it. He leaves to pass along the message while Dao's men clear the crowd for his car to get through.

Twenty minutes later, Dao finds Sammy waiting at the back door to the office building, smoking a cigarette.

Sammy sees his hands are empty. "Where's the money?" The smirk is replaced with a frown.

Moving quickly, Dao grabs the boy by his shoulders and slams him back against the wall. He picks up Sammy's fallen cigarette and presses the lit end into the side of his neck. The boy screams.

"You got your money this month," Dao tells him. "And you're not getting any more."

Sammy slides to the ground, gasping, clutching at his neck. "You know who my cousin is? You'll pay for this!"

"Tell your cousin the *community leader* that this company will donate what we agreed on to his *community projects* and not a cent more. And don't you ever pull shit like this again."

Dao watches Sammy scramble away. His cousin isn't a community leader so much as he's a local gangster. But Dao isn't afraid of him. And you let any of them get used to upping their price on you at will, and it'll never stop.

Better let them learn the hard way. That is, after all, what he's paid for. To give them the hard way, but only when they're begging for it.

He feels a lot better now. His phone rings. "Yeah?" he says.

"Nora Watts is back in Vancouver. I saw her myself," says Van Nguyen, his guy.

Dao goes back inside to hear the update. The boy, his cousin the corrupt community leader, and the protest graft are completely forgotten.

By the fence, the DSLR camera keeps clicking away until the big man disappears back inside. The reporter holding it couldn't hear any of the exchange, but what he witnessed was an act of brutality toward this country's protest movement, no doubt about it.

He waits a few more minutes to make sure nobody is coming back out, then he rises, stretches his legs, and heads off to find Sammy Saleh, one of the shining stars of the local conservation effort. Maybe he can get a few pictures of Sammy's wounds, make a nice little package for the news.

The guy who'd slammed Sammy against the wall and burned him wasn't familiar to him. He wasn't one of the local employees or part of the private security team that protected access to the mine. No, he was the guy above it all. Who drove in, his car windows tinted too dark for anyone to catch more than a glimpse.

He was the guy who managed security, the one everyone was so afraid of. Who worked everyone to death and who no one dared to cross.

Someday, somebody was going to catch that fucking violent asshole and teach him a lesson.

# 29

AS I PULL into the alley behind the Hastings office, I notice a man wearing all black lingering outside the back door, pretending to seek the shelter of the awning. He's in excellent shape, extremely broad in the chest. Too healthy for this neighborhood by far and trying to hide it with an affected slouch. But I have lived in the downtown eastside for years, walked these streets at all hours of the day and night. I know who belongs in these alleys, and he doesn't.

I drive past with my hood pulled low. As I do, he steps away from the awning, his focus on the car. In the rearview mirror I see his phone is out and he's speaking into it. Shit. I gun it out of the alley and go the wrong direction up the one-way street it lets out into. There are several honks, but I keep going until I get to the next cross street and make an abrupt turn. It takes me ten minutes of driving to make sure no one's behind me.

Eventually, I get to Leo's place.

Standing outside on the busy street, I look up. A shadow crosses the window inside the apartment. I call Leo's phone. He picks up after the third ring.

"Are you at the apartment?" I ask.

"Nora?"

"Are you there?"

"No."

"There's someone inside."

"Who?"

"I can't make it out, but it looks like a woman." There was a sweep of long hair falling forward when the figure crossed the window. "Who else has access to the place?"

"Nobody. It's a crappy little apartment, though, and security is almost nonexistent, as you know. People leave the rear door propped open all the time to move stuff into their cars out back."

And the lock on that door itself is a joke. I could pick it in under a minute. "Someone's watching the office, too."

"You sure about that?"

I think about the broad-chested man in black. "One hundred percent."

"I'll tell Warsame and Brazuca. Nora, I'm calling the cops to report a break-in. Just so you know."

There's a laundromat about four doors down with a few parking spaces out back. I pull into one of them and use the mirrors on my old Corolla to watch the rear door of Leo's building. There are apartment units up there, and Leo's right, nobody living there is particularly concerned about leaving the door open every now and then. Even though they should be. Because now there is someone who isn't supposed to be up there, rooting around.

It feels like hours but must only be several minutes before a police car pulls up in front of Leo's back door and two officers get out. They try the door. It's open. What a surprise. I wait for them to go in, wait another set of indeterminable minutes to see if they've scared anyone out, and then finally when I see only one of the officers strolling leisurely back to the car from the opposite end of the alley, having just made a block, I realize that all of us were too late. Whoever was up there is long gone. Must have gone out the front, swept away with the tide of nine-to-fivers just getting off work.

They know about Leo's apartment but weren't able to find me there. No matter, the man with the phone already saw me at the office.

"The back door was open, but the lock on my apartment door was forced," Leo says to me, when I call him to give an update.

"Was anything taken?"

"No. The cops think it might have been a crime of opportunity. Some degenerate found the back door open and, as you know, my apartment is the first unit at the top of the stairs."

"Did you tell them about the man watching the office?"

"Yes, but it's an alley off Hastings Street. All sorts of shady characters hang out in that area. They implied that maybe PI work is getting to me, that I'm jumping at shadows. I never understood why you hated cops so much, Nora, but after dealing with this mess, I'm rethinking my position."

"It can't be a coincidence. Someone at the office and the apartment like that."

"I agree. I'm assuming this is about you? They're ramping up their surveillance?"

"It's not safe to go back to the apartment, Leo. For me or you. Is there someone you can stay with?"

"Yes. What about you?"

"Don't worry about me," I say.

I get a text from Stephanie Kwan saying she remembers something and to meet her at the house as soon as possible. What she has to say can't be shared over the phone. The message is paranoid, but then again, so am I. I'm stuck in North Van traffic for far too long, and when I finally get there, I drive right past the house and park a few houses down.

Bright lights are flashing in my rearview mirror as an ambulance speeds away.

I get out of the car and run to the house.

There's a police officer blocking my way. "Please stay back, ma'am."

"What happened?" I ask.

The officer ignores me and goes to the porch while I remain out on the street. A neighbor in a flannel onesie wanders over. "Do you live in this neighborhood?" she asks.

"No, but I know Stephanie. What happened?"

"Well, neighborhood watch heard what they thought was a scream coming from Steph's house and went and knocked on the door. There was no answer, but Brenda next door had a key so they asked her to open it to check if Steph was okay.

Found her with her arm broken. Looks like she interrupted a burglary or something."

"Is she okay?"

"Yeah. She got that arm twisted bad but managed to fight back. Got her hands on her bear spray and just went off on that bastard. Got him real good. And when she screamed, well, that's when the watch went and knocked. Steph said the guy took off then, through the back. Who the hell beats up on a woman, though? It makes me sick!"

I feel the same. I get back in the car.

This is what I think happened. When Van Nguyen saw my face, he couldn't immediately place it, but he knew he should have. Because he was the one who arranged the surveillance. When he realized he saw me here with Stephanie Kwan, he or his goon decided to come back and confront her. He was the one who sent the text.

As I drive away, I take out the phone I have, the burner, and toss it out the window.

# 30

LATER, AFTER I'VE gotten a new phone and updated my contacts, I let myself into Simone's apartment. It's been a long day and I'm tired. Whisper seems to be as exhausted as I am. She barely eats the gourmet dog food I picked up for her, which was expensive. I don't even bother explaining that while she's got the best the pet store has to offer, I'm eating from the discounted deli section of the grocery. I've got bigger problems than the luxury lifestyle she's become accustomed to, courtesy of Leo, who must have a more generous credit card limit than me.

After a long shower, as hot as I can stand it, I turn up the thermostat and try to process the events of the day from the couch. It feels as though I've lived a week in the past twenty-four hours.

Dao's search for me is ramping up. He's sent his attack dogs to use my connections to lure me out.

It's also clear that he's not here to greet me in person. If he had been, he wouldn't have sent others to do his dirty work for him. He would have been in the Hastings alley himself. Waiting for me down the street from Stephanie Kwan's place. Or at Leo's apartment. I can see him now, perched on an armchair in the dark, biding his time until I walk in the door.

He hates me so much he'd send hit men after me in Detroit. That he'd reach out to his shady contacts to find me here in Vancouver.

If I'm so important to him, why isn't he here to come after me himself?

He must have other obligations. Something so important it's keeping him away.

I message Simone to ask her for her Wi-Fi login and password. She responds immediately with the login. The password comes a minute later. It's a nonsensical phrase with numbers and capital letters interspersed. She tells me she changes it often, so don't get too used to it.

Fair enough.

I log on to the internet and, about two hours later, find what I'm looking for. It's the search I've been meaning to do since yesterday's meeting with Lam and Vidal. The reason I went looking for Simone in the first place is she's the only one I trust to help me with this particular search. Because of her relapse, I have to do it myself.

Michael Acosta is the poster child for prosperity. He used to be a fundraiser for the Conservative party of Canada but has left politics to pursue his one true love in life: resource extraction.

Bernard Lam picks up the phone on the first ring. We don't bother with pleasantries. I explain to him what I have on Acosta and his company, Nebula Corp, which isn't much.

"Don't worry about it. I have someone looking into Acosta for me," Lam says.

"Good," I say. "Have them look into the gold mine in Indonesia that Nebula Corp took over recently. It's on the island of Lombok."

"Why that mine in particular?"

I forward him a report.

"Apart from being located in a region that's prone to earthquakes, landslides, floods, and volcanic eruptions, there's evidence of terrorist cells creating problems all over Indonesia. And there's been a certain element of unrest on Lombok for a long time. Violent mobs and organized crime," I say, after he's read it and is back on the phone. "Nebula isn't messing with local police. They've got their own security looking after the miners and protecting their property."

"Unrest sounds bad for business," says Lam, with the understatement of the day. "You think Dao is there."

There's a reason he's not here hunting me down himself. I've killed his lover and his previous employer. He should have no obstacles to exacting his revenge in person because what else is he doing?

He's doing what soldiers do. He's working.

"Yes, I think he's in Indonesia, managing the situation for Acosta."

"Just like he managed difficult situations for Ray Zhang."

"Do you have someone who can look into it? To see if he's

there?" I ask, knowing that if anyone has the resources to find Dao in Indonesia, it's Bernard Lam.

"I have something even better," Lam says. "I have a private plane that can take us there to take a look ourselves."

"What do we do if we find him?" I ask. I don't want to give him the impression that I need a man to make plans for me, because I never have. This is about his intentions.

"Let's cross that bridge when we get there. What do you say, Nora? You up for a trip?"

"I could use some sun."

Lam laughs. "I'll make the arrangements." He hangs up.

It's easy to picture him in his Point Grey mansion, cackling to himself over a cigar, loosening his tie, calling his assistant's assistant to get the plane ready, stat, because he's in the mood to catch some sun while he takes down a crime syndicate.

I wonder if he loved that woman as much as he thinks he did or if this is merely a grand ol' adventure for him. Dao is my endgame, but he's not Lam's, which some small part of me is concerned by. A very small part that I choose to shove away.

Nolan's body may be in a coffin in the earth right now, I don't know. I have pushed him so far from my mind that I hadn't even thought to check. But thoughts of him come back to me now. Who is the instrument of whose revenge here? Lam is using me as surely as I'm using him. But at this moment, sapped of all energy but still unable to fall asleep, I can't bring myself to care.

At least there are no neon lights flashing at me through the window. Here there is only a comfortable couch and my dog on the floor beside me and the blessed night. James Carr is wailing from my laptop speakers—well, Leo's laptop speakers. He's singing about two strangers at the dark end of the street, where they always meet. Not in the light because the light isn't for them. They live in darkness, just like me. No, not just like me anymore. Because I'm heading for the sunshine on a private plane, like the socialite I never wanted to be.

# 31

IT'S THE MIDDLE of the night, and they're in bed. Bonnie can't remember if Alix had turned in to her or if she'd been the one to turn in to Alix. Now the two of them are kissing and she can't remember the last time she felt this good.

This safe.

At first they'd laughed at how crazy it was that two girls from hip-hop dance class ended up spending so much time together, even though they lived at opposite ends of the city. Bonnie out east in the hipster Leslieville stretch and Alix west of the Latin strip off Ossington. It made sleepovers a lot easier to explain to their parents, a benefit that Bonnie is only just beginning to realize.

When Alix put her hand up Bonnie's shirt, she let her, but they had to stop when her fake nose ring got caught in Alix's springy curls.

Bonnie hasn't slept with anyone since she broke up with her ex Tommy last year. She hadn't been ready. But she might be ready now, she thinks. Besides, this is different than it is with a guy. Playful. She wants to tell Alix everything, even the stupid, embarrassing things. Like this feeling she has all the time now, that people are looking at her.

She takes her nose ring out completely, so she doesn't pull any of Alix's hair, and she later goes into the bathroom to put it back in. As she returns to the room, she runs into Alix's mom in the hall. The older woman yawns and reaches up to adjust the silk scarf she's wrapped her hair in.

"Everything okay? Alix hogging the duvet on you? Here." Alix's mom, whose name Bonnie never asked, gives the scarf one final pat, reaches into the linen closet, and pulls out a spare comforter.

"Everything is great," Bonnie says. She takes the comforter anyway, though she doesn't need it. She and Alix may have found a whole new way to stay warm.

The next morning she gets off the streetcar early with a group of people, thinking she could bring some coffee back for her mom. Lynn often doesn't have time to make coffee for herself in the morning, so Bonnie's usually the one to do it. After getting the coffee, she's still got that stupid grin on her face, the same one she had since she woke up this morning. She turns onto her street. She never told Alix about that stuff from her past and about her new concerns that someone is always looking at her.

Like now. It's only a fleeting instinct that something isn't right, that there are arms reaching for her, but it's enough of a warning for her to throw both cups of coffee into the man's face and run, screaming.

A few seconds later, an SUV with tinted windows peels away, tires squealing.

Bonnie stands on her front porch, shaking, her wrists and hands burned from the hot coffee, her heart beating so loudly she can practically hear it.

The front door opens. Her mom comes out. "Oh, hey. Everything go okay at Alix's last night?" Then Lynn sees the frightened look on Bonnie's face. "What happened? Bonnie! Say something!"

"I burned myself with coffee. I bought some for you."

Lynn takes Bonnie's sore wrists in her hands. "Let's get you inside. What happened?"

"Nothing," says Bonnie, breathless. "It's nothing."

She knows someone tried to grab her and that she should say something . . . but she can't bring herself to do it. When she'd been kidnapped by her birth father almost two years ago, she felt as though it was her fault. She got into the car with him. Believed his lies. They kept her drugged, but sometimes she acted like she was drugged even when the effects of whatever they'd given her wore off. She spent so much time silent and confused it was embarrassing. She was ashamed of herself, like she is now. It doesn't make any sense, this feeling. She did nothing but come home.

"Mom, I think . . ." She stops.

Lynn puts Bonnie's hands under the kitchen tap and runs the cold water. "What?"

"Nothing," says Bonnie. It all seems so stupid now. Maybe the guy hadn't been reaching for her at all. Maybe it was just in her imagination.

Lynn leads Bonnie to the kitchen table and sits her down. She pulls two ice packs from the freezer, placing one on each of Bonnie's outstretched wrists. "Now," says Lynn. "Tell me what happened."

"Someone tried to grab me. Then there was this car . . . Mom? What are you doing?"

But Lynn's phone is already out and she's calling 9-1-1.

# 32

I DROP WHISPER off to spend some time with "Uncle Leo," as he's taken to calling himself. Uncle Leo is sober, but it's only the morning. So this isn't a huge accomplishment. There's a moment of self-recrimination when Whisper looks back at me as I stand in the doorway of Leo's friend's place. Then she gets over it and remembers that it's best to keep one's options open in life.

I wait down the street in front of the Sylvia Hotel until a sleek dark car pulls up and a driver in a black suit takes me to the south terminal of the Vancouver International Airport. The terminal reserved for private flights. Check-in is a breeze. They look at my passport with none of the scrutiny exhibited by the border agents when I left Detroit. I'm told Lam already arranged for the return voyage, so those details were taken care of.

I have never been treated better in my life.

"The purpose of my trip is pleasure," I lie, addressing the attendant at check-in. I'm so off-balance I offer this information without being asked.

"You look ready for some sunshine!" the attendant lies back.

What a pleasant life a playboy billionaire can live. To be politely lied to on the way to your private jet, en route to a sunny destination.

"We're not going to the US," says Lam. "Customs will greet us at the plane when we arrive in Lombok. You didn't have to offer up the purpose of your trip."

"I knew that."

He grins. "Sure you did." I can tell he's taking a certain pleasure at introducing me to the wonders of private air travel.

I have with me one of Leo's designer duffel bags, packed with a few changes of the lightest-weight clothing I own. Lam says we're to stay just a week. I'm not sure how long it will take to look into this mine situation, but a week seems like not enough time.

In the restroom I avoid looking in the mirror, because I generally do, and also because I don't want reality to hit just yet. It all feels a bit surreal, to be honest. The driver, the check-in, the private plane I'm to board. When I'd gone to Detroit, there were lineups after lineups. I thought it had put me off air travel for life. Now I see firsthand how the other side lives, and I've got to admit, I like it a bit too much. I could get used to this. I make a note to buy a lottery ticket as soon as I get back.

My luck can't stay this bad forever.


The plane is a Global Jet Express with leather and wood paneling on the interior. Waiting for me on board are Bernard Lam and a man in a bad suit who immediately puts me on edge. Lam welcomes me with a smile, acting as though he hadn't seen me just minutes earlier.

"Who's he?" I ask. I've never seen the man before. He has a crew cut and is as tall as Lam but muscular where Lam is doughy. He has a twitchy energy I don't like, eyes constantly roving.

"This is Ivan. I know I'm supposed to call him by his surname, but he's got one of those ungodly Eastern European ones. Too long." Lam says this with a bit of casual prejudice that's almost shocking. "Ivan is my close protection officer, or my bodyguard, if you prefer, for when I'm forced by my father to do some foreign travel. He's here to keep the commoners away."

Though this is meant as a joke, it isn't really. There's nothing funny about the truth.

"I've never seen you with a security detail before. Only at functions."

"I refuse to have them with me in Vancouver in my daily life."

"Bet your father doesn't approve of that."

"Oh, he keeps tabs on me, but I leave it alone as long as I don't see his people. With these guys around I can't say boo without my father knowing. But at least one of them has to come with me when I travel." He shrugs as if to say, *What are you going to do? This is how I roll.*

"Don't you have a report to file or something?" I ask Ivan. A muscle jumps at the corner of his mouth. He excuses himself to use the restroom before the plane takes off. One final line of coke to get him through the flight. Lucky bastard.

I watch him go, knowing that Lam didn't inform him of his travel plans far enough in advance for him to medicate appropriately. I didn't spend enough time in the military to serve overseas—had left too early for that to even be a possibility—but I do know something about what military types who go into private work go through in order to function in the real world. What they go through is a good portion of their incomes on uppers and downers so they can sleep when they need to and wake up when they get the call.

Like Ivan must have when Lam informed him of our spontaneous trip.

Lam laughs as he, too, casts a glance at the closed restroom door. "Will you marry me?"

"Aren't you already married?"

"Oh yeah," says Lam, a little too easily. "I forgot about that."

"Must be easy to forget when you don't wear a wedding ring. Did you also forget about Clementine?" I ask, having learned the name of his dead pregnant girlfriend from Brazuca.

There is a brief, tense moment of silence. Lam's entire demeanor changes, hardens. "Don't ever say her name again," he says quietly. "You got that?"

"I got it." And it's a relief. This is what I've been waiting for. I wouldn't trust Lam the playboy for a fraction of a second. But Lam the grief-stricken lover is more my style.

"Good," Lam says. "We're waiting for one more person."

"Who?"

"You'll have to wait and see."

Ivan returns from the restroom and takes up his position by the door. I choose a window seat at the back of the plane and ignore the flight attendant who comes around to offer us drinks. I'm riveted by the view outside the window. A man is walking up to the plane with a duffel bag slung over his shoulder. The man has a slight limp and moves with all the energy of a sea slug out of water.

Of course it's Brazuca.

# THREE

# 33

*I'M NOT IN a jungle,* I tell myself.

The humidity isn't pressing in on me. I'm not surrounded by banana trees and assailed by the sound of monkeys screeching. The late-afternoon sun isn't trying to attack my exposed skin, and I'm not calm in the face of these extenuating circumstances, trying to hold on to all my hydration in this extreme heat.

But I *am* calm, and I am in a jungle. Rather, in a bar near one.

Too near for my comfort.

Like many women who've been tempted to leave their homes behind in search of something elusive, some sense of recklessness overpowering them, taking hold of their lives, I, too, have been led astray by a man.

So I am here now in this Lombok bar that has appeared out of nowhere, surrounded by lush trees. The last stretch of wilderness before it opens up to an ugly mining village, which leads to the main road heading into an ugly mine. In the heart of this godforsaken island, one of many in Indonesia.

Right now, I'm watching a group of mercenaries who have bonded over shit beer and are now drinking buddies. Do they know the man who has painted the target on my back? I think it's likely.

I keep my head down and watch them under the brim of my hat. I'm dressed as any other tourist, but that doesn't stop the locals from throwing disgusted glances in the direction of my sundress. I am as disgusted as they are, so I understand. Baby blue isn't my color, and the garment simultaneously provides too much coverage and somehow not enough in this sweltering heat.

I'm trying to fit in, but this dress is absurd.

"You stay here, miss?" the young server asks. She's wearing jeans in this heat. *Jeans.* Her cotton top is long-sleeved, and a pretty pink headscarf covers her hair. This may be why I look so out of place. Lombok isn't Bali in a lot of ways. Indonesia is a Muslim-majority country made up of thousands of islands, little nooks where tourists can get buck wild, separatists can plot, outlaws can hide in plain sight, and locals get on with their lives.

The heat must be getting to me because I completely forget the server is still there, expecting an answer.

"Just waiting for someone," I say. "Is it always this busy in here?"

She shakes her head and clears a nearby table. Shoots concerned looks over at the group of men who are making no attempts to be quiet or blend in.

A sunburned man walks in the front door and heads

straight for me. He sits down beside me at my table and takes my hand, raising it to brush his lips over my knuckles.

The heat and the screeching monkeys haven't improved my mood. I pull my hand out of Brazuca's grip and slap his face good and hard. The resulting thwack is loud. Obnoxious in exactly the way I intended.

There's dead silence from the men at the bar.

I raise my hand to hit him again, letting it hover in the air a moment. Brazuca doesn't flinch. My hand falls. "You smell like pussy," I hiss instead. Also quite loud.

Securing my wide-brimmed sun hat on my head, I walk out of the bar, leaving Brazuca staring after me with a look of absolute amazement on his face and a big red mark stamped across his cheek.

# 34

SEVERAL MINUTES HAVE passed, and Brazuca still feels the sting. Unconsciously, his hand goes to his cheek, reddened beneath a day's worth of stubble by her slap and the onset of a mild sunburn. He finishes the mango juice Nora left behind and picks up the newspaper on the table.

Then there's a hand on his shoulder and one of the beefed-up guys from the bar puts a beer down in front of him. "Alright, mate?" the guy asks.

"Fuck," says Brazuca.

The guy laughs. "Tough luck."

"Guess everyone saw that."

"Heard it, too. Good arm on that woman."

Brazuca nods. "She has violent tendencies." An understatement. They have no idea what Nora's capable of if she's properly threatened. He's never met a more aggressive woman in his life.

"I'm Max," says the guy. "Come join us."

Brazuca follows him to the bar, where a ragtag group of ex-military types are grinning at him over the tops of their beers. They stand out. They're all white, and Brazuca has already noted their accents range from British to Australian to South

African. He thinks there is a Canadian among them, skulking near the back.

Max, clearly a Brit, looks at the others. "He smell like pussy to you?"

"Ain't nothing wrong with that," says one. The Canadian, maybe.

"Sit down, mate," the man behind the bar says, in a thick Australian accent. "These guys are just giving you a rough time."

"I'm in the shit now," says Brazuca, reaching into his shirt pocket for a cigarette and discovering his shirt has been buttoned up wrong. And he's out of cigarettes. He curses soundly.

This gets him a fresh round of ribbing. Max finishes his beer in one gulp and calls for another. "Boyo, you were in the shit the minute you walked in here. Your lady was just waiting for an opportunity to lay into you."

"You could tell she sat here just working up to it," says one of Brazuca's new friends. "Got madder by the minute. I thought it was that damn monkey noise, but it turned out to be a whole different kind of monkey business that got her riled up."

"What happened?" asks the barman. "I'm Connor, by the way. This is my place."

They shake hands. "We were on the Gili Islands for a bit, Gili T, and she decided to come into Lombok a little early. I was supposed to meet her last night. May have gotten a little bit carried away."

The barman and Max exchange a look that says they know exactly how he must have gotten carried away. Gili Trawangan is the largest of the Gilis and is known to be something of a party island. There are a lot of different kinds of trouble a person can get into there, if he's so inclined.

"Since you done fucked up, might as well enjoy yourself," says Max. He calls for another round. Then looks at Brazuca's beer, which he hasn't touched since he joined them. "You gonna drink that?"

Brazuca shakes his head. He's been traveling for days now and probably looks as rough as he feels. "Better not, man. Coming down off something." He gives them a sheepish look and lets them draw their own conclusions.

"Did she say he smells like pussy or he is a pussy?" Max asks.

*This is going to be a long afternoon,* Brazuca thinks. He's not going to find allies in his sobriety here.

He orders a strong cup of coffee and enough food for the table. Then he's back in everyone's good graces.

# 35

"WELL?" I ASK, the moment Brazuca walks into the hotel room.

It's been several hours since I hit him at the bar. I got rid of the sundress the moment I returned to the king suite we're sharing and am in a pair of cutoff shorts and a T-shirt. Even with the AC on, it's still too hot.

"Hang on," he says, and disappears into the bathroom. Ten minutes later he emerges, freshly showered and in a change of clothes. Still unshaven, though. He passes a comb through his damp hair and looks out the window. Spread out in front of him is a view Lam has paid good money for. The ocean, peppered with colorful fishing boats, sparkles as the sun sets. Couples lay tangled underneath resort awnings, some in bathing suits and others in evening wear. It's a far cry from the little mining town I'd scootered into this afternoon, the one with the bar.

The reason we're sharing is because Lam found it amusing that Brazuca decided to join us last minute on the flight. He hadn't bothered to call ahead and make arrangements for another room. On the plane, Brazuca and I fell into the routine of two people who'd rather not be on a trip together. Lam laughingly said it seemed natural for us to continue the ruse.

For all intents and purposes, we're a couple giving it our last shot but failing. There's enough history between us to sell this.

"That slap was a good move," Brazuca tells me, without turning from the window.

"I was inspired."

"Hell of an inspiration. But it was the right instinct. They would never have talked to me with you there, and it made them sympathetic to me. They're actually not bad once you get to know them a little."

"And what did they have to say?"

"You were right, they're part of the security detail at the mine."

Ex-military types in a flock like that . . . it seemed obvious that they were blowing off steam after work. Especially given the proximity of the mining village that Nebula supports, now that they've taken over the mine there. "And?"

I can tell he's enjoying stringing me along.

"Let's go find Lam," he says, grinning. "He should hear this, too."

Lam is in the private bungalow with its separate suite of rooms on the hotel property. Right off the beach. How he managed to swing this on such short notice is beyond me, but it's possible a minor sheikh or two have been kicked out to make room for him.

His bodyguard is there, out by the pool with Lam and a woman I haven't seen before. She's tall, fat, and more beautiful than any person has the right to be. She has the hair of a model in a shampoo commercial, long and glossy, even with all this salty sea air. Her and Lam match in a way I can't explain. When he sees us coming, he sends her away with a kiss on the cheek.

"A bit young, don't you think?" I say.

Lam shrugs. "Legal."

"You didn't want to introduce us?"

"She didn't want to be introduced. Her oil baron daddy is looking for her, and she wants to keep a low profile." This makes sense. The woman looked to be in her early twenties. Also looked like money in that indefinable way that some people do. The way that Lam does. It also makes sense that within a day of being here, he would already be mingling with the heiresses of the island.

He checks to make sure Ivan's out of earshot and lowers his voice. "So what did your little trip into town tell you?"

I wonder what Ivan would think of all this if he knew what we were saying. Brazuca and Lam got into a bitter fight about keeping him in the dark when we arrived at the hotel. I don't care either way, but Brazuca has a point. If we're stuck with him, might as well use him. But Lam doesn't want him reporting the particulars of our trip to his father. It's why he brought only one bodyguard with him and not a horde of them, like he should have.

I understand his thinking. Nobody has ever particularly cared where I go or what I do, but I'd imagine it would get irritating if all of a sudden someone did.

Brazuca takes a seat on the lounger beside Lam while I

remain standing. It's cool enough now that I can bear being outdoors without a frozen drink in my hand.

"Nora found a bar where some of the private security team for the mine hang out. They had some interesting things to say. There's been some petty local gang activity. There was also an earthquake and some pretty bad landslides a few days before we got here. People are on edge."

"Okay," says Lam, somewhat impatiently. "And Dao?"

Brazuca smiles, but there's no warmth to it. Lam doesn't notice or doesn't particularly care. "They talked about the head of security at the mine. A big Chinese bloke, ex–British military. He's been on their asses for about a year. Everyone hates him. The security teams because he won't fraternize with them and some of them think he's a gangster. The workers because he's tough on them. The villagers because he's Chinese, but from Vietnam. Some just don't like his face."

"Did you see him?"

"No. Apparently he's been laying low because of some dustup with a protester."

I stare at Brazuca. "Chinese from Vietnam?"

"There's a sizable ethnic Chinese population spread across Southeast Asia, Vietnam included," Lam explains. "During the Vietnam War, many Vietnamese fled and ended up in refugee camps. Some of them made it to Hong Kong."

"Then, for Dao, the UK," I say. "And then wherever the Zhangs needed him to be. Which may be why Dao seems like a ghost. He's moved around."

Brazuca looks at me. "We need Simone."

"She's in rehab. But I think it's one of those facilities where patients can bring their computers. She took her laptop with her when I dropped her off at the ferry."

He thinks about it for a moment. "If it's the Gulf Island facility she stayed at a few years ago, then yes. They allow phones and laptops."

"Who's Simone?" asks Lam.

"Cyber expert," Brazuca says.

Lam frowns. "An addict, though? I can find you someone else. I've got a guy."

"I'm sure you do. But I like my guy so I'm going with her," I say.

He doesn't like my tone. Maybe it's disrespectful, but I couldn't care less. "You know what your problem is?" Lam says. "You hate the rich."

"I eat the rich."

"Come take a bite." He opens his arms. I'm perversely tempted. He's lost weight, but there are still quite a few prime cuts left on him.

"Alright, kids. Let's stay focused." Brazuca gives me a quelling look, as though I'm the problem. Or maybe he thinks it's sexual tension, and the idea of me and Lam makes him as uncomfortable as it does me.

I turn away. When I chew Lam up, he won't even feel it. Problem is—and this is the real issue—I'm not sure if I have more to gain by keeping him whole.

"Do whatever you want," I say, reaching for my phone. "Ex–British military via Hong Kong? Ethnic Chinese from Vietnam? This is all information that we haven't had before. I'm going to talk to Simone."

"Let us know what she finds," says Brazuca.

I walk down to the ocean to make the call. Simone answers on the first ring and listens to the updates. "What took you so long to bring me in?" she asks.

# 36

LAM INSISTS ON paying for Simone's services because "it keeps people honest."

"I'm not above taking a rich guy's money," she says, when I broach the assignment with her. "Is he cute?"

"He's Bernard Lam." Before we left for Lombok I had told her I was working with someone to find Dao, but I didn't tell her who it was until now.

She recognizes the name immediately. "Well, in that case, I wouldn't mind taking a lot of his money. He's got a billion or so to spare."

"His daddy does, anyway."

"Oh, it's all the same to these people. As much as I love to do free work for you, Nora, I enjoy being paid even more." Ouch. She says this without bite, though, so I know it's not personal. "If it's going to help you find Dao and figure out why the hell he's got such a hard-on for you, then I'm all for it. What you've given here is enough for me to get a start, anyway. I've got some contacts in the security world I can tap now that we know he's working for Michael Acosta. I'll get back to you soon."

While we wait, Brazuca makes one trip back to the Australian's bar to see what else he can find out. I drive my rented scooter toward the mine but turn around just inside the village on the outskirts of the mine property. Things begin to look too industrial, and a tourist on a scooter stands out here. There are more than a few hostile glances thrown my way, at my baseball cap and aviator shades. A few curious ones at the smutty novel I pull out while ostensibly searching for my island map, both courtesy of the hotel lobby. The map is still crisp, but the novel is water stained and dog-eared. As far as disguises go, a sex-obsessed tourist with a poor sense of direction is about as effective as one can get overseas, but I'm still uneasy here in Lombok.

But it's not like I can leave. Dao is so close I can feel him. If this island is where we put our past to rest, so be it.

On my way back to the hotel, I stop at a roadside restaurant that looks more like a hut. Order a plate of steamed vegetables and tofu covered in a fragrant peanut sauce. Wash it down with a glass of papaya juice. The meal is a hundred times better than the hotel version I had last night. This is the healthiest food I've eaten maybe in my entire life. I can feel my body healing. Feel it getting stronger. I could get used to living like this. Bringing my dog on my private plane for a bit of fun in the sun. My skin has turned a dark brown from all this sun exposure, but at least I'm doing better than Brazuca, who has taken on the appearance of a man being boiled slowly but can't seem to crawl out of the pot.

"You like the gado gado?" the chef asks, as he clears my dishes. He's the chef, the waiter, the busboy, and the host.

"It was delicious."

"Thank you. You go back to your hotel before it gets dark?"

"On my way back now."

"Good. That is good. Be safe."

"It's not safe after dark?"

He hesitates a moment, his round face holding something back. "Nowhere is safe after dark."

Truth.

The reports from Simone and Lam's cyber guy come in. We meet up that evening to go over them, Brazuca and Lam reeking of zinc oxide from their sunscreen. Ivan isn't in sight, but we know he must be around.

Dusk hangs in the air. The sun on its way out reluctantly, leaving tendrils of pink and orange behind. Our faces are lit by paper lanterns strung over the back patio. Lam's sobriety matches mine and Brazuca's, for once, but his face is flush with some emotion. Excitement, maybe. Our motives are unclear to one another, maybe even to ourselves, but we've come too far to go our separate ways. In all honesty, I might be in this for Lam's private plane, but I've never made Lam any promises. Who knows what's going on with Brazuca, except that he is most undoubtedly being paid—and paid well—to be here.

The best I can figure out is that I want Dao because he's

hunting me. Lam wants Three Phoenix, which he thinks he can get through Dao. Brazuca is collecting a paycheck but wants this to be over so he can go back to healthy eating. Whatever our reasons, we are together now, outdoors on a warm night. In a shaky paradise.

So we get into it, the legend of Dao.

# 37

DAVID TAO WAS born in Vietnam. At the age of two, his widowed mother fled to a refugee camp in Hong Kong. She and her son were resettled not long after in East London. When he was eighteen, he signed up for military service and served with the British army's peacekeeping force in Bosnia. Whatever he saw there must have put him off keeping peace for life because he left the military right after that. He found some work in private security and was assigned a detail for a high-profile diplomatic event. At that event there'd been a security threat to one of the VIPs. Dao was the man who identified it and managed to avert a crisis.

Ray Zhang of Zhang-Wei Industries was the VIP.

"That's where they met," I say.

"He caught Ray Zhang's eye," Lam replies. "Poor school performance but he had a gift with languages. Military training, and he spoke English, Vietnamese, and Cantonese fluently."

"A good close protection officer is hard to find," says Brazuca. "He had the skills."

"It's about loyalty, too. Ray Zhang and Dao were loyal to each other. Dao stayed with the Zhang family for years. He became head of their personal security detail and their fixer."

"What's with his name, though?" I ask. "How did it become Dao?"

Lam shrugs. "Maybe someone got it wrong once and it stuck. Maybe it's a nickname. One of the meanings of Dao is a sword."

"Nice bit of orientalism there," I say. "So he went into the military, not a gang."

Brazuca nods. "But it doesn't mean he didn't have dealings with organized crime. Ray Zhang was rumored to have some shady links. He gambled recreationally, too. It's possible that Dao's connections to Three Phoenix came through him."

Lam can't contain his excitement. "I was unsure if his connection to Three Phoenix went deeper, but if his ties were to Zhang only, then we have a way in. He has no real loyalty to these people."

"What's the way?" I ask, even though I already know the answer.

"Money, of course. Do you think he wants to work for Acosta for the rest of his life? Jon here worked Clem's case for me, even though he had reservations. Why did he do it, then? Because I offered him more money than he'd dreamed of."

Brazuca says nothing to this. He's too busy contemplating the stars above us. You could almost believe it, that he's this absorbed by the night sky. You could, if you didn't see him pass a hand over his knee, the one on his bad leg, the gesture a familiar one to me. Back when we used to go to meetings together and there was that moment where we were asked who wanted to share, Brazuca would do this.

It means he's holding back.

After a moment he turns to us. "I've been back to that Aussie bar. Most of the mine security, the foreigners, live in the village. But not Dao. Acosta has a villa he keeps on Lombok, and that's where he stays."

"Is Acosta here now?"

"No, he's in Europe. Dao watches the compound."

"Shut up by himself for months at a time," I say.

Brazuca nods. "The guys that work in the security business, they're part of a world we have no idea about, not really. They've seen things we can't ever imagine. They live off moments of pure adrenaline. When they come down, they come down hard."

"You're talking about drugs?" Lam asks.

"Sometimes."

"Well, that only makes it better. I hope he's a junkie." Lam is unable to disguise his disgust. Or unwilling, maybe. You'd think a man who lost a loved one to an overdose would be more sympathetic. Maybe junkies he's not in love with don't count. "Brazuca, can you make contact?"

"Yes."

"Good. Tell him you're representing a party who wants to contract his services. If his loyalty is for sale, I'll be the one to buy it."

"What about me?" I ask. "It's personal between us. He won't let this go."

"That's why we have this," Lam says. He pulls up a news

report on his tablet. It's been translated into English and covers an incident at Acosta's Lombok mine, where an unidentified employee was caught using physical force against a protester. There are photos of a man slamming said protester against a wall and pressing a lit cigarette into his neck.

You can only see the attacker from behind and a brief side profile but the man in the photos, from what I remember, is Dao's approximate height and build.

"Where did you get this?" I ask.

"Just came up on a local media source. Not big enough to make international news, but I have some news contacts I can use to stir this up."

"I'm not sure that blackmail is going to work on Dao," Brazuca says.

"That's just leverage. I'll offer money first," says Lam. "Do you know how easy it is to buy people? A man like Dao has been around extreme wealth for years, but he's never had it himself. I'm giving him the opportunity to have some of mine for a price. The price is information that will lead to shutting down those drug labs for good. And you, Nora. You're part of my price. I take care of my people. Jon can tell you."

Brazuca excuses himself and leaves the patio, exiting through the back gate. He says something to Ivan on his way out, but I don't hear what.

"What's his problem?" Lam says.

"Probably the heat. Are you worried?"

"About Jon? Never. He'll do his part. When we set up the

meeting, Nora, you will of course be there but out of sight, please."

"It's your show," I say. "But Brazuca will have to be in the room. And we'll have to figure out a way for me to listen in."

"Of course," Lam says. "We both have a stake in this."

I leave before Lam has the urge to shake on it or play a few rounds of golf to seal the deal—whatever it is that high rollers like him do. The ones with enough money to buy people off. To think that no matter what, their vast stores of cash can get them whatever they want. People's loyalty. Their knowledge. Along with their love and their hate.

But you can't buy hate as strong as what Dao has for me.

I'll play along with Lam for now—it seems I have to. What I want is some dirt that will put Dao away for life. I'll have to look into that report, see if there's something to be done with those photos to build a case against him. Somebody's got to care about him bullying local protesters, right?

It doesn't seem like enough, even to me, but maybe it's a place to start. There could be a pattern of this kind of behavior, one that might put him behind bars.

On the way out, I say good-bye to Ivan, who's standing guard by the back gate, near a statue of a mermaid. It looks like he wants to say something to me but stops himself before he forms the words. That's okay. I don't need to hear them. I understand a warning, even an unspoken one. It's what he's warning me about that concerns me. It occurs to me that I should tell him I have no plans to put his boss in danger, but what does it matter what I say? Besides, Lam is putting himself in trouble just fine without my help.

Maybe that's why Ivan looks so upset—or would, if he was capable of showing any emotion at all.

I take the path leading from the suite to the beach. It's not a private beach; it only seems that way. Leo doesn't answer the phone when I call, so I try Stevie Warsame and ask him if there are people still watching the office.

"Not that I've found," he says. It's very early in the morning there, and I wonder what he's doing up. But I don't ask. "Krushnik thinks he's spotted someone. Even called the cops about it, but these guys are good. They don't stay long. I would spend more time on it, but I got two cases I'm dealing with."

"Leo isn't helping out?"

"No, and I gotta talk to him about that. Brazuca up and disappeared, too. What the fuck is going on here? I didn't sign up to run this company."

He sounds so aggravated I don't point out that he is a partner at the firm. I wouldn't want to run a PI outfit, either, but no one has ever made me a partner of anything.

"You coming back anytime soon?" he asks. "I could use the help. Did you ever get your PI license? I knew you were working on it before you left us."

"No," I say. "I'd like to, but you can't count on me right now."

"Don't I know it," he snaps.

I sit on a lounge chair by the beach for a long time afterward. A man who resembles Brazuca walks up from the beach and into the hotel, but at this distance I can't be sure it's him. Maybe it's the sound of the water or the cool, salty breeze coming off it, but I have no desire to leave this lounge chair. I doze on and off while lovers whisper to each other from nearby lounges and Bob Marley seeps from speakers nearby. Even though we're nowhere near Jamaica, there's nothing like a beach and Bob Marley. That's what people think, anyway.

Maybe for some the reggae is enough to ignore the hotel security doing sweeps of the beach and hotel grounds. A little "One Love" and people forget that love sometimes isn't enough to ignore that the locals are struggling, frightened, and that this island is no stranger to unrest and disaster. Could be they're like Lam, who has never learned to be scared. Has been taught he is the largest predator in the world. An idle man with time and money. Who tells me he can buy grudges from a deadly, military-trained operative who sits in his employer's villa obsessing over women from his past.

# 38

THE SUITE LAM booked for us has two separate bedrooms that can be accessed by a shared living room. The bathroom is large but also shared. As I step into the suite, part of me hopes now that we've found Dao, Brazuca will no longer feel the need to keep up the ruse of being mismatched lovers. But such is not my luck.

He's waiting for me in the living room. He has something he wants to say but doesn't know how to broach the topic. So he sulks into his hibiscus tea until it occurs to him that I might want a cup, too. He makes me one without asking. Hands it over, somewhat grudgingly.

Now we're both sulking.

Our addictive personalities have led us here. Together again, wishing we were drinking something stronger.

I want to say something, too. Rather, ask. Why he takes these hits from Lam, the jabs about him being bought and paid for. But I can't seem to get there. "How are you going to make contact with Dao?" I settle for instead. He'd been quick to respond when Lam asked.

"He eats at a restaurant near that villa he stays in. Every day at breakfast and for dinner in the evening."

"You've seen him?"

"Today before we met up for the debrief."

It takes me a moment to absorb this. Suddenly it seems real, the fact that I am finally this close to the man who put a hit on me in Detroit. Who threatened my daughter. There's something else I'm missing, but I can't remember what it is.

I stare into my tea. "How did you get this intel?"

"My buddy at the bar. The owner. I've been playing the rejected lover. They feel sorry for me, so we've been chatting. They really hate him, Dao. He keeps his distance. I asked them about buying property in a gated community, somewhere nice and safe. Didn't take me long to figure out where Acosta's house is. There's a village nearby where he must get supplies. Then I sat around a café with a paper and watched a strip of restaurants. It was easy."

"So you know what he looks like."

"Let me show you." He pulls out his phone and scrolls through a series of videos that show a tall Chinese man with a shaved head entering and exiting a small restaurant.

"I never guessed he was born in Vietnam."

"He's not Chinese enough for the Chinese—even the Zhangs, who he was loyal to until the end, called him by a Vietnamese name that isn't even his—but he's too Chinese for the locals."

"Everyone's a critic," I say.

He laughs quietly to himself and then turns off the AC. He opens a window, letting the fresh sea breeze in. There's something easy about him standing there. Comfortable, even.

"Back at that chalet in the mountain," he begins, bringing up the subject we have avoided for this long.

"Do you really want to go there?"

"I could be up for it, Nora. Do you?"

I feel like one of those people who only cheat on their spouses when they go away on business trips. Maybe it's because I'm out of my comfort zone and in this lovely hotel room. Remembering the last time.

Away from home, no one has to know. "I could be up for it, too." As soon as I say it, I realize it's true. This is a night full of surprises.

He looks at me for a long moment. "Can I tie you up this time?"

I hesitate. "Yes."

"Come on then."

We go into his room where he ties my hands to the bed-posts, but not my legs. Then he disappears for a moment and comes back with a cold bottle of beer from the mini fridge in the living room. I meet his eyes.

This is repayment for what I did to him.

Two years ago, I tied him up, straddled his chest, opened little bottles of liquor, poured them into his mouth to fuck up his sobriety.

Because he'd lied to me and I felt angry and betrayed. But now those lies don't seem to matter.

This is what has been building between us since I slapped him at that jungle bar.

Part of me wants him to pop the top off the bottle. A very big part, one that used to consume every part of my life. He knows this. Smiles and straddles my hips. He puts the cold bottle against my neck, gets lost at the sight of it there. I can feel the condensation pooling on my throat. He takes the bottle away, but the chill stays. I think he's going to open it. Want that badly.

Instead, he touches his lips to mine and whispers, "I would never do that to you."

There's a moment of relief and frustration. Part of me wanted him to, badly. That little demon in my head that's always there, begging for a drink. "You think you're better than me?"

He laughs, settles on top of me, and pulls my legs up. Hooks them around his waist. "I know I am."

Then we stop talking. Thankfully. He brings that easiness about him I was admiring from the window here, too. It's so easy between us, this. Easier than it should be.

"I wanted to walk away so badly," he says much later. "When Lam showed up at the office, I wanted no part of this, whatever it is."

"I know."

"So why can't I?"

He doesn't expect an answer. Doesn't get one, either.

"I almost had a drink today. Before the beer just now," I say, thinking of that godawful heat cut only by the ocean breeze. What could one fruity cocktail hurt? Unless, of course, it becomes two, then four, then a couple of vodka shots after that.

"Me, too."

It takes me a minute to work up to what I say next. "When I heard we were waiting for someone on that plane, right before we left Vancouver, I hoped it was you."

"I don't trust Lam. That's why I came here."

"Neither do I."

There are no blues songs in the aftermath; there is only the sweet silence of the night broken intermittently by the sound of our breathing. One of us is lightly snoring, but I can't figure out who it is before I fall asleep.

# 39

EARLY YESTERDAY MORNING, just as dawn broke, I put on a black one-piece bathing suit I bought at the hotel gift store, charged to Lam's room, went down to the beach, and waded chest deep into the ocean. Then began to swim. I didn't stop for a long, long time. I swam until my limbs got so heavy I almost didn't make it back onto the sand. When I did, I lay flat on my back, taking in big gulps of air. One of the resort waiters offered me a fresh coconut out of sheer pity.

This ocean is different from what I'm used to. It's either the Bali Sea or the Lombok Strait, but I can't remember which. It should be similar to the views I've seen from Vancouver. Sand. Ocean. Mountains. Fishing boats. But there's nothing familiar about this. The water is warm and clear. The boats are painted canoes with brightly colored wooden legs creeping out from the center, like cheerful spiders that sit atop the sea. Even the mountains look different. Lush and inviting in the blinding sunlight.

Like something out of a picture book.

As I sat and looked out at this pretty picture it struck m that there was an emptiness in me that should have been fill with fear. I almost drowned once. I shouldn't have felt so f out on the water. But all my senses were alive. I could feel the sand underneath me. Taste the salt on my lips. Feel the cool coconut water going down my parched throat. Hear the surf gurgling toward me. Watch the sea move in the sunlight, so clear and pure.

About twenty feet away a woman I recognized as a waitress at the resort restaurant waded into the water. She let the waves lick her thighs for a few minutes, splashed water on her arms to the shoulder, then waded out again. She proceeded to scrub sand over her arms and legs in brisk circular motions and returned to the sea to rinse it off. When she emerged again, her skin was pink and clean. I watched her meander away down the beach, around a bend and out of sight. Then, inexplicably, she returned this way almost immediately, her movements quick. As soon as she was within sight of the resort she slowed again. There's something about this stretch of beach we were both on that felt safe. Who knows what lurks beyond the bend?

A kind of peace settled over me as the sun rose, brought on by the simplicity of a woman's early-morning ablutions. There was a certainty building inside, growing out of the emptiness. What has happened since we filled in the blanks with Dao hasn't changed it.

Which is why, as I get out of bed the next day, I feel no guilt, no regret.

I take the small bag I packed earlier and leave Brazuca behind without looking back.

Almost twenty-four hours after my swim in the ocean, the dawn breaks gently over the horizon as I get on my gray Honda scooter and drive away.

Money and blackmail, of course, Lam said. This wasn't his first lie to me, but it was his big one. There's a reason he wants to keep me away from the meeting. My presence here is the little worm you stick on the end of a hook.

To Bernard Lam, I'm nothing but bait.

# 40

ACOSTA'S ESTATE IS on a street full of other estates. It's an enclave of wealth and power on a poor island, so of course it's a gated community. The locals trickle in from the nearby town to work at the villas beyond the security checkpoint, but I'd never pass for one of them. In Vancouver I'm taken to be the help on a regular basis. But that's not going to work here.

I'm on the side of the road, just before the entrance to Acosta's street, where Dao lives. Beyond the gates there seems to be damage to some of the houses, but I can't see a way in to take a closer look. So I turn my scooter around and head into the town.

The town is eerily quiet, and about half of the buildings are flattened. This must be the effect of the recent earthquake. The damage is worse here than I've seen anywhere else.

I take a seat at the café across from the restaurant that Dao was photographed going into. It's possible this is the exact spot Brazuca sat when he took the pictures. I order a Balinese coffee and scroll through the news while I wait. The local journalist who took the photos of Dao and the protester has done profiles of mining issues across Indonesia. There's a lot of information here, but nothing more on Dao. Maybe I can get some better

NO GOING BACK 213

photos than Brazuca did. Hopefully one or two that would identify him as the man who hurt the protester.

Hours pass, but he doesn't show up. I'm starting to get some curious glances from the café workers, so I pay my bill and leave.

Turning my scooter around, I head back to the hotel.

In the hall outside the room I share with Brazuca, I take a deep breath before entering. Steeling myself for something. Preparing my excuses for abandoning him after good, even great, sex. Sex that was uncomplicated in a way it has never been before. At least not for a very, very long time.

When I open the door, the breath I've been holding releases on a tiny exhale of air and sound.

The room is empty. Brazuca's things are gone.

The front desk has no idea where he went. "Miss, the room is paid for. We can do no refunds," says the concierge. He muffles the receiver on the phone, and I can hear people talking in the background but not what they're saying. When he comes back his voice is urgent. "Miss, please stay in your room. Don't open the door for anybody."

He hangs up before I can ask why.

The grounds outside are deserted, but there are a few fishing boats out on the water in the distance. If I squint, I can see the fishermen pointing to an area of the shoreline that's beyond my view, around the bend I'd seen that waitress hurry away from. The one who'd been rubbing sand into her skin and washing it off in the sea.

In the room, there's no good-bye note to be found. That's to be expected, because I hadn't left him one, either.

There's movement that draws my eye down by the beach, near the path leading to Lam's little suite. A head of lustrous hair catching the sunlight.

Four men round the bend and head straight for the beach house, a smaller target than the larger hotel.

Then I'm moving, rushing out of the room, down the stairs, and onto the path leading to the beach house. A hotel porter tries to grab my arm, but I shake him off. As I get close to the house, I hear men whispering to one another, see them move forward. They all seem to be armed. One of them is most definitely the protester Dao had slammed into the wall. The protester leads the pack—they're about to try the door, when there are a series of shots.

Coming from inside.

Then all hell breaks loose.

# 41

SPRINTING TO THE back gate, I see Dao emerge from the house. He's backing up, holding Lam by the scruff of the neck in one large hand, and in the other is a pistol. Ivan emerges from the house after them, bleeding from a wound in his arm—but he's still holding a gun.

"Don't move," Dao says to Ivan.

That voice is a dagger to my spine. Immobilizes me. Weakens my knees. It is the voice that haunts my dreams.

Once, a long time ago, when Ray Zhang's son, Kai, attacked me and they thought I was near death, Dao had told Kai to get rid of my body, not knowing or caring that I was still alive. Though I didn't hear it the second time, I can imagine him on the phone when he sent those hit men after me in Detroit. Telling them that yes, he'll pay the price for my murder. Maybe he even haggled a little.

Ivan's gaze flickers to me. Just a small movement, but it's enough to cause Dao to shift slightly, still keeping Lam in front of him and Ivan in his sights.

Dao looks at me. So does Lam. They are the same size, both very tall men, but Lam doesn't stand a chance.

"I told you," Lam says, his mouth bloody. "I told you she was here!"

"So what do I need you for?" Dao says.

He sounds different. Now that the first shock of his voice is past, I notice something I should have seen as soon as he started to speak. He's so hoarse he's almost wheezing, and his posture is bent. As though there's some kind of injury he's being mindful of. An image of Ivan disappearing into the plane's restroom crosses my mind as I see the same thing in Dao. His heightened energy. His aggression.

I see the moment Lam becomes expendable to him.

The shift of Dao's finger on the trigger.

"David, stop," says Lam, perhaps sensing the change in Dao that I now witness.

Dao replies in a language I don't understand. Whatever he says, it's not hopeful. I see shock cross Lam's face.

Dao pulls the trigger.

Lam falls.

Dao points at Ivan and shoots, but he has overestimated Ivan's loyalty to Lam. I guess money can't buy everything after all, because Ivan's already turning away to run back inside. He falls, too, but just in the door.

As Dao is turning to me, there's a commotion inside and the men led by the protester come charging out. They must have entered through the front.

They see Ivan slumped over. Lam on the ground and Dao

standing over him. They begin to shout in confusion and move toward Dao.

I feel a tug on the back of my shirt.

"Run!" Brazuca hisses into my ear. He reaches for my hand as a hail of gunfire pelts after us.

# 42

I DON'T TRY to turn back, but as I run away from the person I came here to find, I feel a keening sense of relief and loss at war with each other. The battle is internal, but Brazuca must sense it because he tugs harder at my hand even though I'm faster than him and should be pulling him along. But he's doing pretty well, even with his bum leg.

Then we are in the hotel and I'm surrounded by staff, who shove me and Brazuca into the ballroom where a handful of other hotel patrons gather. Apparently, the word of a security threat has spread throughout the hotel. I hear some muttering about a gang.

Brazuca is still holding my hand. Neither of us seems to be able to let go. A woman in a wedding dress is sobbing in the corner, in the arms of her groom. Various people in semi-formal wear are scattered about the room casting concerned looks at the bride and groom. Two men are slightly damp and wearing swim trunks. They look too tired to speak.

"The protester from the photograph, the one Dao beat up . . . he was there," I say quietly to Brazuca. "I think he must have followed Dao to the hotel."

"Someone he knew may have seen Dao go in and called

him. Those security guys from the bar said Dao had been laying low."

"Maybe the protester's not just some innocent activist after all. Not with a group of armed friends like that." The AC is cranked, and a shiver passes through me. "They don't stand a chance against Dao."

"You don't know that. He was heavily outnumbered. Maybe . . ."

I know what he's thinking. That maybe my problem has been taken care of. Maybe Dao is dead. I want so desperately to believe it. Something of that desperation must be showing.

"Nora," Brazuca says. "You can't . . . you couldn't save Lam."

"Lam?"

"Yes, Lam. We both saw him take a bullet." He pulls a chair out for me and sits beside me. "Do you need medical attention? What's going on?"

Brazuca takes my hand. I can't bear the thought of pulling away right now. His touch anchors me, and I need it because there's a shift taking place inside me. A growing awareness.

"Dao," I say. "He was bent over, like he was injured."

"Maybe he got shot. I wasn't inside. Lam asked me to leave at the last moment."

"No," I say, frowning. "It looked like an old injury."

"What are you talking about, Nora?"

"Why was he there? I thought you were supposed to make contact this morning." I see the guilt on his face. But I can't fault him for it. I have kept things from him, too.

"Made contact yesterday. Lam didn't know about it."

"You didn't want me at the meeting."

"Can you blame me? I didn't want you in danger. The second he saw you everyone else faded away." He pauses, not sure how to proceed. Two policemen come in and speak to the concierge, who's consoling the mother of the bride.

Brazuca ignores them all. His attention is completely on me.

"I was a cop for a long time, and I saw some things . . . even when I worked for WIN Security, there were rough spots. You see the worst of humanity in these fields. The very worst. But, Nora, I've never seen so much hate in someone as I saw in Dao today. When he looked at you . . . every little bit of rage inside him is for you. It doesn't make sense to me, but it's the truth."

That I'm the complete focus of Dao's hatred doesn't surprise me. I'm not sure anything can anymore. "What happened at the meeting?"

"I wasn't there. I have no idea what went on in that house."

"Dao was shot," I say slowly.

He shakes his head. "Didn't look that way to me. I'd just come in the back gate behind you when I saw him shoot Lam."

There's a tear in his blue T-shirt, at the shoulder, exposing a swath of skin that's less burned than the skin on his face and arms. There's nothing I want more than to press my fingertips to it, touch it with the tip of my tongue, taste the salt of man and sweat. Last night I hadn't touched him there, not specifically in that place I'm staring at now. Other places, yes, but this river of skin flowing over muscle and bone is still uncharted territory for me. There's still so much I don't know about him.

The first time I fell in love was when I was fourteen years old. It was with a boy named Zack. Of course. All the bad boys were named Zack back then. The second was a man who worked at a gas station during the day and took night classes. He wanted to be an accountant. I marveled at the idea that someone with such broad forearms would want to spend his days at a desk, calculator in hand. He belonged outdoors but didn't want it, and I also enjoyed the way he didn't seem to know himself.

There were a couple more after that. Then I stopped falling. It hurt too much. There was no point. The falling in was almost immediate, but the climbing out was a slow, arduous process of discovering just what I was thinking in the first place.

Oh, right. I wasn't thinking.

I release a breath that I've been holding. In this room, I'm at once cold and wide open. Wondering if this is what falling in love has become. Not a rush of feeling. Soft words late into the night. The intensity of sexual desire. Maybe I'm too old for all that. Maybe it is one man, revealed to me a single inch of skin at a time. I think about the slap in the bar, done for effect more than anything else. Now the thought of that violence sickens me. Which makes no sense, given what I've just witnessed.

"No," I say. "*Before.* Two years ago, Dao got shot on a boat.

The night he and Jia Zhang took me out on the water, they were going to get rid of me. But it didn't work."

"You survived."

"Yes," I say, thinking of the way Dao stood today on that back patio. As if there was an old injury to consider, his posture off. His bearing not straight and tall as I'd remembered. "But he got shot that night."

"This is the first I'm hearing of it."

It plays for me like a reel of an old noir film that has some gaps, a victim of age and the general wear and tear of having been preserved in a memory such as mine. Me, the heroine of the story. The record keeper.

Insanity.

The night Kai and Jia Zhang died, I was on a boat. There was a scuffle. And there was a gun. I remember getting my hands on it and what happened next.

"Brazuca, it was me," I say, with a sudden urgency. "I did it. They had me trapped, and I was fighting for my life. I shot Dao in the gut."

I remember now.

# FOUR

# 43

DAO GOES BACK to the villa for his passports. They're in the room safe where he left them. There are three. One with his own name, one with the name of the man he'd become since getting to Lombok, and the third is a clean identity he hasn't used yet. He stuffs them all into a pack, along with some clothes, his pills, and money. There's blood on his shirt, so he pulls it over his shoulders and puts it in a plastic bag. He'll get rid of it later. When his hands stop shaking, maybe. He hasn't been this out of it since the night Jia died and he could do nothing to protect her. He'd wanted to, but the shock of the bullet tearing through his flesh took his breath away, and when he caught it again, it was too late. Jia was gone.

There's a sound behind him.

He goes into the hall and sees the maid Riya, who he doesn't really think of as little anymore. She's rounding the corner, hurrying in the opposite direction. Shit. She still comes every day to clean, to get paid, but he has no idea where she's been staying. Did she see the blood on his shirt? When the authorities come looking for who killed that lying, blackmailing son of a bitch Bernard Lam, will she conveniently remember seeing him here? What about when Sammy Saleh, his uncle, and his gang show up?

He shouldn't have hit her after the quake. Shouldn't have ever let it get personal. There's only one thing left to do now.

He draws his gun and clicks the safety off. Makes his way silently down the stairs on bare feet. At the foot of the stairs now. A pause, then her voice coming at him softly from the entrance. He finds her there with a laundry basket at her feet, likely the reason she'd come into his room in the first place. She's got her hand on the door, and she's saying something to the child from the landslide, who's now balanced on her hip.

Her hand lingers on the door, as though she can sense him behind her. But she doesn't dare turn. Maybe she knows he's got a gun.

"I didn't see anything," she says.

The child wipes her sleepy eyes and blinks awake.

His hand is on the trigger. But she didn't see anything, she said.

He hesitates a moment too long.

She slips out, closing the door behind her. The sound of it shutting sets him in motion. He strides across to it and flings it open. There she is, hurrying away. She punches in a code at the gate and leaves before he can step outside.

His phone vibrates in his pocket as he stands there, on the brink of going after her. There's only one person who'd be calling him now. "Is it arranged?" he says, when he answers.

Nguyen hesitates. "Yes. I'll send you the details."

"Use the new number. I'm ditching this phone." And the gun, too, when he gets a chance.

"Your employer—"

"I'll deal with that." There's a pause. Nguyen is thinking, which is never a good sign. "What now?"

"Getting you out of Canada the last time was tricky. You sure you want to come back?"

"Don't worry about me. I'll see you when I get there."

He ends the call and stares at the gate, closed again. Shit. There's not enough time to deal with the maid now. He puts the gun away and goes back upstairs to grab his stuff. He hates this place. Always knew this gig was going to end. The only thing now is to keep moving. Look forward. Never mind that the reason for his escape is solidly in his past. That kind of thinking could get you confessing your feelings to a shrink or something.

He passes the full-length mirror in the bedroom that is no longer his.

Would you look at that? His hands are no longer shaking.

Good. He'll need them steady for when he gets to Vancouver.

# 44

MAYBE I *AM* one of those voluptuous heroines in a noir film. I've seen something, remembered something else, and am starting to question my sanity while I put together pieces of a puzzle.

Am I lying to myself? Are these memories true? I am a woman of means with stunning good looks, but who will believe me?

I raise a pale, trembling hand to brush a strand of hair off my face only to look down at the hand and realize it's not pale at all. It was never pale to begin with, and now it's darkened by the hot Indonesian sun, the blunt nails and strong fingers speaking of years of hard work and a poor moisturizing regimen. It doesn't shake, either. It's as steady as the Vancouver rain that falls just outside the window, turning to snow as the temperature drops.

Well, there goes that theory. I'm nobody's heroine. Part indigenous, part Palestinian—two bloodlines where basic human dignity has been historically denied. Who would put me in one of those stories? Who would believe me if I told them my own?

Besides, I've only ever seen one film that could be classified as noir. A Hitchcock, I think. All I remember of it is a woman being attacked in a room by a flock of birds and reading that the actress who played her actually had been attacked at the behest of the maniac director who wanted her terror to be real. He'd switched out the planned mechanical birds for the scene for real birds at the last moment.

The actress was powerless to stop it.

Everywhere you look there is a story of a man terrorizing a woman for reasons of his own. This is perhaps my only connection to those fragile kittens in the movies.

The terror, my companion.

"Come here," Brazuca says, from across the room. We're back in Vancouver. He's bare chested, having long thrown out the shirt with the tear. Seems to have given up on wearing shirts altogether when we're alone.

In bed we push past the secrets, obfuscations, evasions, and outright lies. We are honest, for once.

I've always hated the term *making love*. It has never felt right to me, to suit those words to this action. But I'm reluctant to call whatever this is fucking. *Sex* too banal. *Intercourse* too clinical. I hear kids these days call it *smashing,* but that seems wrong on too many levels to comprehend. It's none of those things and all of them, except for the last. It's an exploration to see what fits. I can't figure it out yet, this thing between us, but I know I won't ask him about it. It's too new. Too much can go wrong. It changed the moment I pressed my mouth to the inch of skin exposed by the rip in his shirt.

Everything tilted.

"You ready to talk about what happened in Detroit?" he asks.

"I was looking for the truth about my father's death. But the whole thing went sideways," I say.

It tilted there, too. Maybe it never straightened. I'm living a sideways kind of life, but it seems okay right now, here in this bed with the curtains drawn, cocooning us in. The only view is of a telescope in the living room. It's strangely comforting, the idea that just past this room if we were to fit an eye to the small circle of glass, we would see the world out there. But we'd have to get up first, cross the threshold, and look through the glass.

Insurmountable obstacles.

This sideways life of mine doesn't feel right, but it's okay because Brazuca seems to be living sideways with me. He is also askew.


In the aftermath they found Lam's body. They blamed it on local gang violence, an attempted robbery gone wrong. Two of the locals who were part of the gang were found beside Ivan at the house entrance to the back patio. By the time the police got in there, Dao was gone.

"He's got as many lives as you do," Brazuca said.

We played up the tourist card, of a couple caught in a trag-edy. Brazuca was a friend of Lam's, and I traveled as Brazuca's girlfriend. The attack on Lam was seen as a crime of opportu-nity for a group of violent youths looking to snatch a wealthy man whose family would pay to get him back or had at least put kidnap insurance on him. Though several people had seen another man of Chinese descent on the property, nobody knew who he was.

There was death all around us and with it an atmosphere of confusion that we used to quietly make plans to leave. When we heard Lam's father was on his way to Lombok to collect Lam's body, Brazuca and I accepted a police escort to the air-port. We flew to Singapore, Seoul, and finally back to Vancou-ver. On these flights I did nothing but sleep.

We collected Whisper from a reluctant Leo and went back to Brazuca's apartment in East Van. A pattern establishes it-self. Walk, eat, and go to bed. Dao hangs there between us, but we're exhausted by the thought of him. We push him aside for now. The Canadian climate is a blow after all the sun we've experienced, leaving behind reddened cheeks and cold fingers. We mostly stay in. It feels better this way.

"Do you believe me?" I ask Brazuca.

"Yes," he says, after a moment. He's telling the truth, but he looks uneasy. It could be from hunger, I think. He eats only half as much as I do. I feel a burning urge to row in place, so after I walk Whisper, I head to the gym. My mind is too busy for anything else. Before I leave, I look back at him from the door. He's half-turned, his smile disappearing, a grimace of pain replacing it.

Two days later, he returns from a doctor's visit with news of an ulcer. The day after that Bonnie calls to tell me she's in the city. She speaks in a mashup of sentences that takes me a moment to pick through.

"You're in Vancouver?" I ask, feeling dread creeping over me.

"Mom and I are staying with my dad for a bit. Can we meet?"

"No, go back to Toronto." I don't mean to say this, for it to come out the way it does. Made harsh by sudden confusion.

Bonnie doesn't take this well. She's quieter when she speaks next. "I can't. There was a van and a man tried to grab me . . ."

"No."

There's a moment of silence. "You don't think it happened?"

This . . . this is exactly what I was afraid of. "I know it did." All I can think of is that she's here, right where she shouldn't be. Close to me.

And the film reel keeps spinning.

# 45

THINGS HAVE CHANGED between Bonnie's adoptive parents, Lynn and Everett. When I first met them two years ago, their marriage was a cautionary tale in getting married. Now divorced, they're at ease with each other in the kitchen of Everett's rented apartment in a way I would not have expected of them. There's even a hint of warmth underlying the concerned looks they shoot each other when they think Bonnie and I aren't looking.

It's the first time I've seen the three of them together like this, Bonnie and her parents. Back when she'd gone missing and they reached out to me to see if I knew anything about her disappearance, everything about their relationship with each other seemed strained.

But now, through the miracle of divorce, they finally seem like a cohesive family unit.

"Whoever tried to take her, the vehicle was stolen and later dumped," Lynn says. "There was some CCTV footage, but they couldn't identify anyone. Only the driver was visible, but his face wasn't clear."

I look at Bonnie. "And you said it was likely two people?"

"One guy tried to grab me, and seconds later the car pulled away. I think there were two of them."

It's difficult to find a trusted accomplice for your sexual predation, if that's what it was. Which makes me think it wasn't about sexual predation at all. That it was targeted. Lynn and Everett think so, too.

It's time to come clean. "There was a man who worked for the Zhang family—"

"Dao?" Bonnie asks.

"Yes. He's alive. He remembers me, and you, too. Two years ago, when I went looking for you on Vancouver Island, in Ucluelet, I shot him. I think . . . I think he's holding a grudge."

"You mean he was trying to kidnap me again?"

"Not him personally. He's been hiding out overseas. But he might have had people watching you. And his grudge isn't with you. It's with me. He knows if you go missing, I'll come looking."

"We're going to the police," Everett says.

Lynn puts a hand on his arm. A friendly gesture. They've come a long way, these two. "We've already been to the police in Toronto. There wasn't much they could do. What are we supposed to say? This whole thing is beyond me, Nora."

How do they think I feel? Turning to Everett, I say, "Does anyone know about this apartment? Can Bonnie stay here?"

"It's leased in my name, but my . . . partner, Adele, her brother has a cabin in Whistler that's vacant. He's never there, so she has full use of the place." At the mention of his partner, he glances at Lynn, then Bonnie. Neither seem perturbed. A certain tension in him, one that's not related to his daughter's safety, releases.

"I can work remotely for a little while," Lynn says. "Ev, is there Wi-Fi at this cabin? And is it okay with Adele if I stay there as well?"

"I'll check with her, but it shouldn't be a problem. It's got four bedrooms, so you'll have privacy. I can come up on the weekends. And there's Wi-Fi, of course. Who can live without it?"

"How soon can you guys pack up and get there?" I ask, trying to keep the urgency out of my voice.

Everett looks at the clock. "We can leave tonight after the traffic slows."

"Okay, I'll come with you."

"That's not necessary," Lynn says, rightly assuming that being in my presence is dangerous.

Bonnie shakes her head. "No, I want her to come up with us, Mom. Please?"

If there's one thing parents of an only child can't resist, it's their one child. They've got no others to put their hopes on if the relationship goes sour. As both Lynn and Everett know, because they agree quickly.

"I'll be back later," I say, rising from the kitchen table. Bonnie brushes her hair off her neck, then immediately pulls it forward again. She's too late. I've already seen the red bruise there. She meets my eyes and gives me a quick darting smile. Neither of her parents notice the hickey or the smile.

She follows me to the door. There's something on her mind.

"What's wrong?" I ask. "Do you remember something?"

"No, it's not that. I'm just . . . I don't know why a person would want to hurt someone else. How could you want to kill?" she asks. "Not like an accident or that you're defending yourself. But really want to cause harm."

"I think you just have to be capable of it. It has to be inside you."

"I don't think it's inside me. I'm not . . . I'm not like that. I could never hurt someone."

She'd be surprised at what she's capable of. And maybe one day she'll have to test that theory. But it's not something I want for her.

I say softly, as gentle as I can, "I don't think so, either."

Then I walk away before she has too good a look at what's inside of me.


In the Corolla, which I've picked up from Simone's building, I run that moment in my mind again and again. Her question about morality. A mutual acknowledgment of a secret.

Bonds have been made on less.


The police station on Cambie is right under a bridge. If, like me, you enter the lobby of the station and are ignored by the cops, criminals, and regular civilians standing around, you may feel the need to bury your pathetic instinct to seek help. Maybe you feel that there's no support here, that no one will help you despite the evidence that someone is trying to kill you and take your daughter. *Again.* Maybe you feel the need to take the walkway up onto the bridge, try to climb over the railing, fail, and instead consider flinging yourself at the cars speeding past.

This pit stop wasn't planned, yet here I am. Standing in the lobby and trying to imagine a situation where a cop would give me the time of day to explain. *Excuse me, sir, but there is a mercenary after me. Sorry,* alleged *mercenary. He blames me for the deaths of certain members of a family he was close to. Do I look like a femme fatale from an old-time film to you? Point is, someone—this alleged mercenary—sent some hit men after me in Detroit and has now tried to take my estranged daughter. Also there was a run-in in Indonesia I should probably tell you about where he murdered an eccentric billionaire bent on revenge.*

Then I would feel guilty because I think of this imaginary policeman as a man and what does that say about my feelings on gender equality?

Whatever instinct brought me here has failed me. I wait just inside the door for someone to notice me, some sign of interest. Two police officers stare at me as they walk past. "This isn't a shelter," says the woman cop. "Go warm up somewhere else."

"Hang on," says her male partner. "Not sure there are shelter beds free tonight. Weather report's calling for more snow."

"Really?" she replies. "Climate change is a bitch. At least it's good for the skiing."

I leave while they move from discussing their weekend plans to the likelihood of more traffic accidents and the possibility of overtime pay.

I'm not even a blip in their memories.

I walk out of the station to discover that snow hasn't started falling behind my back, but something else, something ominous, has appeared. I've looked away, blinked, and there is now a Salvation Army Santa ringing his bell on the corner.

My endangered daughter who's no longer estranged has shown up with a hickey on her neck, just in time for the holiday season.

# 46

AS SOON AS I open the door to Brazuca's apartment with his spare keys, I hear Whisper crying. This momentary distraction takes my attention away from what I should have noticed the moment I walked inside.

There's a man here. No, men. Plural. One who has stepped behind me from the bedroom and one who is in the living room with Brazuca.

The man behind me isn't armed, from what I can see, but this does nothing to reduce how tense he makes me. He's not much taller than me, but he's lean and muscular. And he can move silently, which says something about his training. It says "don't fuck with me." Shouts it, really.

"Ms. Nora Watts?" asks the man sitting in an armchair next to Brazuca, who's on the couch. He's Chinese, fit, and compact. I put him somewhere in his sixties, maybe older.

"Who wants to know?" I'm just buying time while I adjust. It's obvious who he is. My instinct is to delay this conversation as long as possible. Reality, however, won't wait any longer.

"Nora," says Brazuca. "This is Edison Lam, Bernard's father."

Lam's father nods. "You were one of the last people to see my son alive, Ms. Watts. I would like some information from you. Do you have some time for a grieving father?" Though it's posed as a question, the lethal intent of the man behind me, Mr. Lam's private security, tells me it's not.

Whisper is now barking, the noise coming from the closed bathroom door. It puts me on edge. "I'm sure my boyfriend told you everything you needed to know," I say, nodding to Brazuca. I make a split-second decision to continue the ruse we'd used in Indonesia. A couple with some intimacy issues. There's a flicker of understanding from Brazuca to me, but it's gone so quickly I think I'm the only one who sees it. I hope so, anyway.

"We decided to wait for you," says Mr. Lam. I can't imagine calling the quietly dignified man in front of me anything other than *mister*. Everything about him demands respect, takes it from the room, and pulls it inward toward his body. Edison seems a ridiculous name for a man like this, yet here we are. It's possible he has another name, one that reflects his heritage, but I don't know it.

Brazuca's voice takes on a gentle tone. "We told the police everything we knew back in Indonesia. Your son hired me to help him look into someone that was hiding out in Lombok. My girlfriend came along for the ride."

"You've worked for Bernard before."

"Yes, sir," says Brazuca. "We met back when I was with the police and we developed a rapport."

"I see. And this . . . rapport led him to ask you a few months ago to investigate his whore's death?"

Brazuca keeps his expression neutral. "Yes."

"Am I correct in assuming this someone you were searching for is in connection to this?"

"Yes."

"Who is this person?"

"His name is David Tao, but most people know him from a single name he went by: Dao," I say. "He once worked for Ray Zhang's family. Now he works for Michael Acosta. Acosta's company has a mine on Lombok, and Dao was head of security there."

"Why did Bernard want to find him?"

Brazuca interrupts before I can speak. "He thought Dao knew something about the criminal organization involved in Clementine's death. That's the woman who died."

Maybe Edison Lam wants to call her a whore again, but he doesn't. He's excellent at reading the room. His first use of the vulgarity was to shock us, get us to reveal something. To use it again would potentially alienate us. My respect for him grows. I can see why his son hated him so much. What would it be like to grow up with a billionaire father who outshone you in every way?

There are a series of three short barks from Whisper, still locked in the bathroom. If she's unhappy with this situation, she should join the club. Nobody in this room wants to be here, with the exception of Mr. Lam.

"I'd like to let the dog out," I say.

The bodyguard, a tougher version of Ivan, with deep blue

eyes, moves to block the bathroom door. "Not right now." I can't quite figure out his accent, but it intrigues me.

With a slight shake of his head Brazuca tells me to let it go. "Is there anything else you need to know?" Brazuca asks.

It takes a long time for Mr. Lam to respond. "Did Bernard find what he was looking for? Did this David Tao give him the information he wanted so badly?"

"We don't know," Brazuca says.

"Baby, Bernard is dead and his dad is just trying to get some closure. I think you can bend confidentiality this once," I say to Brazuca, who looks shocked at being called a term of endearment. I turn to Mr. Lam. "Dao was at the hotel the day your son died, but they met privately. Jon wasn't allowed to go to the meeting."

"Where were you instead?" he says to Brazuca.

"Nearby. Waiting to be called in, just in case."

Mr. Lam looks at me. "And you?"

"I went for an early-morning ride, before it got too hot."

"Do you have any reason to believe that Dao had a hand in my son's death?" asks Bernard Lam's father.

"He would be a fool to cross someone as powerful as Bernard and, by extension, you."

"Yes, but there are fools all around us." I wonder if he's talking about anyone in this room particularly, but he continues before I can dwell on it further. "I know this man Dao. I have seen him at various events with the Zhang family, but I did not pay him much attention because he was just a bodyguard. I think he deserves some of my attention now, don't you?"

"He might be able to answer your questions about Bernard's last moments better than we can," Brazuca says, careful not to glance my way.

"I think you might be right. Do you know where I can find him?"

"No."

"I suppose I'll have to look."

"If he does turn up, please let us know," says Brazuca. "I have a few questions for him, too. I worked for Bernard, but he was also a friend."

Mr. Lam hides his disbelief well.

When he leaves with his bodyguard, I let Whisper out of the bathroom. She walks through the apartment, sniffing the surfaces the two men touched. She's agitated, but then again, so am I.

"If he finds Dao, he won't tell us," I say.

"Not a chance. But if anyone can locate him, it's that man."

"It would have helped if we could tell him that we saw Dao kill his son."

"Yes, but then we'd have to tell him that we were there when it happened. Which would mean we lied to the police in Indonesia. We'd lose his trust."

"I'm not sure we have his trust, but I think you're right." I think of Bernard Lam and how he'd wanted to use me. I'm not sure I can allow myself to be used that way again. I trust Bernard Lam's father as much as I trusted Lam himself.

"I need some air," says Brazuca.

"Will you take Whisper for a walk?"

"I really need to be alone right now."

He doesn't look well, so I don't push it. It's the first time he's asked for space. Perhaps it's the first time he's recognized he needs it.

# 47

THE CAR IS idling down the block, just like Brazuca knew it would be. Even someone like Edison Lam couldn't find decent parking on this street.

Brazuca casts a glance behind him, but he doesn't see Nora in front of the apartment. Doesn't see her up in the window, either. Her sight line from the window doesn't extend far enough to see where he's going, so if she's not on the street, he's safe.

He knocks on the glass of the black-tinted SUV. The door opens, and the bodyguard steps out. "I have some information," Brazuca says, before the bodyguard has a chance to tell him to get lost.

"Let him in," says Edison.

Moments later, they're seated beside each other in the back seat. The bodyguard and a driver up front.

"Sorry, my girlfriend is still upset. I didn't want to say this in front of her."

"It is a strange thing to hear a mature man such as yourself refer to an equally mature woman as a girl. Friend or no."

"With all due respect, sir, would you like the information or not?"

Edison laughs. "I see why my son liked you now. He enjoyed being flattered, but he didn't respect anyone who did it. You're not one to flatter."

"No, I'm not. Let me get to the point. When I was looking into Clementine's overdose, I came up against some bikers who work with Three Phoenix to bring product into Vancouver. I may have made some enemies, but they know something."

"Hells Angels?"

"No. Another group with a much lower profile, but they are believed to have links to a larger biker syndicate. The main person involved was a longshoreman named Curtis Parnell. He was able to directly confirm a relationship with Three Phoenix."

"A longshoreman means the ports."

"Yes, that's how they got some of their illicit product in, at least. Dao has been in touch with Three Phoenix."

"Thank you for the information."

"I'm not done yet. The second line of inquiry you could take would have to go through WIN Security." Brazuca glances at the bodyguard and driver.

"My friends here are not with that company, but I'm familiar with them. What do they have to do with Dao?"

"Ray Zhang was a client. Dao was head of his private security, but he'd work with WIN if he needed a larger detail."

"You just gave me two lines of inquiry to find the man who might have been with my son when he died. How can I repay you?"

"Just find Dao. This is speculation on my part, but I don't believe he simply witnessed your son's death." Brazuca isn't sure why he doesn't tell them that he saw Dao shoot Bernard Lam. Maybe he's just gotten so used to holding back that it's second nature.

Edison Lam exchanges glances with his bodyguard. "You think he was involved? What would he have against my son?"

"He's mentally unstable and has been recovering from a serious injury. I think your son tried to buy him off, and that didn't sit well."

In a move that seems to shock Bernard Lam's father as much as it shocks Brazuca, Edison reaches over and puts his hand over Brazuca's. "Thank you." In this moment he's not a pillar of industry, a respected, ruthless businessman. Here in this car he's a father grieving for the loss of his only son. "You were a police officer," he says.

Brazuca nods. "A detective."

"So you know what it's like to witness loss." Again, it isn't a question.

He's seen far too much of it. "Yes. Everyone has their own way of dealing with it."

"Human beings are complicated creatures," says Edison. "But they're motivated by primary emotions. Love, lust, greed, hate, jealousy. My son, I never understood what motivated him until that woman died. It was love. I didn't think he was capable of feeling that strongly about a person."

"Justice," Brazuca says. "He wanted justice for her death."

"Justice is a moral construct. Something being right or wrong. My son once said to me that morality is for the lower classes. I think he heard it somewhere. So he only felt morality in relation to one person."

"At least he felt it."

Edison Lam shakes his head.

The bodyguard speaks for the first time since Brazuca got into the car. "The drugs that come here, they're synthetic. The chemists that make them adapt to new formulas, new laws. These aren't large-scale industrial activities. They're small and are easy to dismantle. Producers are on edge, especially now with people being so scared of potent opiates accidentally contaminating more recreational drugs. How did he intend to track down those little labs?"

"I never asked him, but I warned him over and over that it was a futile game he was playing," Brazuca says. He looks at the driver. "Can you take me a few blocks down?" He doesn't want to talk about morality and justice anymore.

The driver nods. Strangely, Edison Lam doesn't remove his hand until Brazuca gets out of the car. Standing on the pavement and watching the SUV drive away, he can still feel the old man's touch. The lingering warmth. He might be imagining things, but it felt like a promise between them.

Brazuca hopes to hell that Bernard Lam's father finds Dao before Nora does. Nora's tough, but by his calculation she's all out of lives. He has no doubt that if she comes up against Dao she won't be left standing at the end of it. He'd seen the kind of rage Dao has inside him for Nora. She can't compete with that.

If Nora faces down Dao, she will die. He is absolutely certain of it.

He returns to the apartment an hour later with two steaming orders of noodles and tofu in a vegetable broth. It's the only kind of food his stomach can take at the moment. Nora's not there, and neither is Whisper. He waits until the noodles have gone cold and then forces himself to eat, though he's not hungry.

His telescope, the beauty he'd bought secondhand, is set up at the living room window, pointed up at the sky. Looking through the eyepiece, he roams, searching for nothing but the feeling this activity brings him. After a while, calm settles over him. There's a text from Nora waiting when he finally pulls himself back into the room. She went to see her daughter.

Right.

He'd forgotten to ask Nora how it turned out, but it must have been alright if she's seeing the girl again. Another thing he hasn't remembered until this moment is taking his antibiotics. There's too much to keep track of. He pushes it all out of his mind for now, showers, and goes to bed.

The sheets don't smell like him, but that can only be a good thing for a bachelor. Crawling into a bed that smells like a woman who's just been in here with you. So that even when she's gone, you're not alone.

During the six years he was married he didn't sleep well beside his wife, especially toward the end. But it was the thing he missed the most about her presence in his life. Having a living, breathing reminder that at least someone would notice if he didn't wake up. Now that he's divorced, even this small reminder is enough. A woman he'd never thought he'd have in his bed has been here and left behind traces of her presence. Her scent, the groove on the other side of the bed. A warmth that still seems to linger. He's shocked that he's thinking of Nora—goddamn Nora, who has in the past done everything she could to push him from her life—in this way. But he is.

# 48

WHISPER IS IN the back seat of the car, fast asleep. I'm following Everett's Audi on the Sea-to-Sky Highway.

Before we set off for the Whistler cabin, he casted a dubious look at the Corolla. "You got snow tires on that thing?"

"Yes."

"Because to travel on that highway after October, you need snow tires."

"I'm aware."

He was about to say something again about the snow tires, which I don't have, when Bonnie came out of Everett's place with her backpack and a rolling suitcase.

"Can we go now?" asked Bonnie, saving me from having to lie once again.

Who has the time to change tires for a different season? In any case, Everett insisted that Bonnie ride with him and Lynn in his Audi. Bastard. I wouldn't drive badly with my dog in the car.

The highway dips and rises, hugging the coastline. In the daylight it's a beautiful drive, one many people make just for the pleasure of going around a bend and coming out of it to see the ocean spread out in front of you. It's so pretty it's dangerous. I'm glad we're doing this at night. The snow has held off, thankfully, so at least there's some small reprieve. And I have the radio to keep me company.

That is, until the Detroit song comes on, and I hear Nate's voice.

I switch it off before I can hear my own. But it's too late. The mood changes. It's no longer a pleasant night drive with only the taillights of the car ahead of me to keep me focused. It's a drive to hide away a girl I've put in danger by simply being alive. I used all the countersurveillance tactics I learned from life and Stevie Warsame before going to meet Bonnie and her family, but Nate reminds me that it's never enough. I can't seem to help myself, though. Now that I know Bonnie's not safe and that someone has tried to take her, I have to know where she is.

This, perhaps, is what danger does. It helps you to stop questioning your instincts.

Less than two hours after starting out, we're at the cabin. From the spill of light on the porch a woman emerges and beckons us inside. Everett goes first, with Lynn and Bonnie trailing after. I let Whisper out to stretch her legs. She sneezes at all this crisp mountain air and urinates by a nearby bush.

We wait.

Five minutes later, Bonnie comes looking for us. We go inside for a family reunion.

"You didn't tell me there was going to be a dog," says Adele, Everett's new lady. Well, maybe not so new. He'd been having an affair with her while still married to Lynn.

Everett glances at me. "I didn't know the dog was coming."

"She's a good girl," Lynn says, having met Whisper exactly once before tonight. "I'm sure she'll be no trouble at all."

"I'll walk her before we go to bed," Bonnie offers.

Adele nods. "Okay." She doesn't like Whisper in the cabin but is prepared to put up with her because it's Everett's family. I get the feeling that mother and daughter have met the new woman in Everett's life before, but this might just be their first time being in such close quarters. And now there's a dog to factor in.

Adele starts making pizza, rolling out the dough on a huge marble counter in the kitchen. It takes so long to make that nobody's hungry by the time it's done. But we still eat it. Everett and Lynn sit at the table and try to pretend this is a completely normal experience, all of us being together like this. Bonnie and Adele don't pretend. They pick at their food and avoid looking at each other. I eat quickly and excuse myself from the table as soon as I can.

Everett looks up from his phone. "Before you go, we should discuss something. I'm thinking of hiring a bodyguard for Bonnie when she goes back to school in Toronto."

Does he have the money for that? "That's a good idea." I turn to Lynn. "How long are you planning to stay here?"

She glances at Everett. "I'm not sure. Maybe through the holidays?"

"That's fine with me," says Adele. She's still not sure why I'm here, and neither is Everett. I think only Lynn understands my presence. Maybe she understands better than I do.

It's so quiet in the bedroom they've given me that I can hear every creak, every scurry, imagine every thought. I can hear Whisper's breathing, and by the rhythm of it, I know she's awake. When there are no more creaks, scurries, and thoughts, we open the door and walk through the house. The thick rugs and runners down on the floors keep her nails from clicking as she follows me. I check the doors and the windows. Everything is locked up tight, just the way things were the last time I looked.

There's a flickering light coming from the kitchen. Someone has left the television on, and there's a rerun of an American morning show playing in the background, on mute.

I find the remote in order to turn it off when, on the screen, I see a man sitting at a stool, a guitar in his hand. Then I'm searching frantically for the button to turn the volume up. The sound comes on, and I lower it until it's just above a hum. Loud enough that I can hear every note the man plays on the Fender Strat he's got in his hands. He doesn't look well, but apart from his gaunt, tired appearance, it doesn't seem to faze Nate Marlowe that he's on live television so soon after getting out of the hospital.

He handles it like a pro, goes about strumming like there's nobody in the world watching. Maybe there isn't for him, in this moment. This is what music does to him. What it does to me.

He starts in on the song, a song I know by heart, that pulls at every fiber of my being so that I'm now standing directly in front of the TV set. His voice isn't the same. It isn't like butter, rich and delicious, as it used to be. It's hoarse. He can't hit his high notes anymore, so he sings it low, raw. He sounds like me. When he gets to my verse, his pitch changes and falls even lower. Watching, I'm like a string on that guitar, wrenched taut. Softly, so very quietly, I sing the chorus with him and go into the next verse. He looks up, directly at the camera, and it's like he's looking right at me through the lens.

The song ends, much too soon, and I become aware of a presence behind me. I turn to see Bonnie, mussed from sleep and a kind of wonder glazing her eyes. "You're her," she says. "You're the woman on the song with that singer. The one he recorded before he got shot. Because you were in Detroit!"

I don't say anything to this. But my silence is confirmation enough.

"Everyone's obsessed with this story," she says, moving closer. "He said he couldn't find you, after. He said he didn't even know your last name."

"You should get some sleep," I say.

"Nora . . . I didn't know you sang."

"I don't. Not anymore." Again, this comes out wrong, as my words so often do with this girl a part of me so badly wants to reach. I soften my voice. "Nobody wants to hear a woman over thirty sing a song. Number one rule of the music business: Be young."

She giggles. Reaches up and pulls her hair into a bun, forgetting about the mark on her neck, which she has been careful to conceal before this.

"New boyfriend?" I ask, nodding to the hickey.

"Girlfriend, actually. Maybe. Her name is Alix."

"What happened to Tommy, your old boyfriend? The one I met."

"Oh, him. We broke up."

"Because of Alix?"

"No, because of us. Our relationship was over. It's tough to do long distance, with me being in Toronto. So we broke up, but it was a mutual kinda thing. You don't have a problem with me dating a girl, do you?" Her gaze is direct, unflinching.

"I don't have a problem with you dating anybody." I think of Krista Dennings and her tall French wife. If that's what's in store for Bonnie, I'm more than happy with it.

She smiles. "The thing is, I'm not even sure that we're officially dating or anything yet. So I'm not ready to tell my parents about Alix . . ."

"No problem. I won't say anything."

"I never thought you would," she says, sweeping a lock of black hair off her face. The hair doesn't seem to want to stay in the bun. Pieces of it slip out to frame her face. She gazes at me with the most piercing look I've ever been on the receiving end of. "You know, when I used to think about who my birth mom was, I never imagined you. Okay, that sounds really bad! Sorry. I mean, I've met you, we text, and I send you those dumb photos, and still. You're, like, a mystery."

"What do you want to know?"

"I don't know. Tell me something."

"Wait. I'll do one better." I hand her the key from around my neck, still on its leather string. "This belonged to my mother. It was from her home, back in Palestine."

"Palestine?"

"Yes."

"How . . . how did she get here?"

"From Palestine, she lived on the outskirts of a refugee camp in Lebanon. Someone sponsored her to come to Canada, and she eventually went to Detroit for a wedding. That's where she met my dad. In Detroit," I say. "This is all I have of her."

"My grandmother . . . what was she like?"

"I don't know." Then I laugh. "I have no answers about her. She left when I was a kid. But I can tell you about your grandfather—my dad. That's why I went to the States. I was looking for clues about his life. He was born in Winnipeg, but he grew up in Detroit. He was . . . his friend told me he was a good man. He was kind."

"That's why you were there? And how you met Nate Marlowe?"

"Yes. Your grandfather was adopted, like you, but he knew nothing about his birth family. He spent his whole life trying to find out."

She puts the key around her neck while I tell her what little I know about my father. Lynn comes into the kitchen at some point and fills a glass of water from the tap. But she doesn't leave after. She lingers with us, listening. It doesn't feel like an intrusion, her being there. It feels like the most natural thing in the world.

It's enough, maybe, to help me forget life outside this cabin in the woods. Just for a little while. Talking to her now, in the hush of this kitchen, I am able to push aside the thought that Brazuca hasn't responded to my message telling him that I would be away tonight.

Also the memory of him limping away from Edison Lam's car like he has no care in the world, while I clenched Whisper's leash in my fist and led her away, deep into an alley behind me, into the shadows, around and back to a place where I could watch him go while still remaining hidden.

Keeping, as always, to the dark end of the street.

# 49

I WAKE UP to a missed call from Leo and a video waiting
from Simone. I open the video first. When I click on the link,
shaky footage of what happened on the back patio in Lombok
starts to play. After a moment, the focus clears. The events
unfold the way I remember, but from a different angle. Then
the memory fades and new information comes my way. Dao
takes cover behind the sculpture of a mermaid and returns
fire. The gang take cover, too, but two of them are shot. One
is the young protester. Dao doesn't stop to ponder this. The
chaos is enough for him to turn, jump the wall, and disappear.

Rewinding the video, I pause just at the moment he turns.
The focus adjusts, zeroes in on his face. I stare at it for a long
time. There are creases on his forehead now, and two brack-
eting his mouth. There's a cut bleeding freely on his chin. It
seems as though he's looking straight at the camera—or at the
person holding it.

"Who took this video?" I ask Simone, when I get her on the
phone a few minutes later.

"Gimme a sec. I'm just getting back from morning medita-
tion and my ass is numb from sitting on the floor so long."
There's a rustling sound, and then she comes back on the

phone. "Okay, so I was doing some searches inspired by the news report with the photos of him manhandling that protester, and I found the video. Some socialite staying at the hotel recorded the murder, 'accidentally' uploaded it on social media from Bali. Claimed she was too distraught to think clearly, but the thing was widely circulated before she pulled it down."

I remember the flash of dark hair down at the beach. It's what caught my attention at the window in the first place. Lam's heiress, the daughter of the oil baron.

"Cristina Guerrero is a twenty-three-year-old Colombian student currently enrolled in Business Studies at Yale," says Simone. "Her father made his money in oil, but personally I feel it might be cocaine."

"That's a bit biased."

"Apologies, you delicate flower, you. Rehab is a fucking trip, as always. Anyway! The dad married a beauty queen who died of an eating disorder ten years ago. Dear Cristina was packed away to boarding school soon after. I found an interview done with her in a fashion magazine where she said her mother starved herself to death so she wouldn't have to. But with her bone structure and money, the whole world is her playground. She hopes to use her business degree to get into fashion for plus-size women. In her spare time, she's a lifestyle guru and posts health and well-being advice from exotic locales around the world."

"Must be so hard for her," I say. We giggle.

"Oh, I agree. Especially now that she's witnessed a murder—a cold-blooded execution, as she called it in her online post. Her followers have gone up by hundreds of thousands. People concerned about her take on health, well-being, and fashion now that she's been so traumatized, no doubt."

The lack of alcohol is making Simone a little testy, but it's okay with me. She can be testy as long as she's sober.

"This is it," I say. "This video shows that Dao murdered Bernard Lam. Have the local police identified him?"

"I'm going through news reports using a keyword search, but no, not as far as I can see."

"Then he's long gone. He didn't plan on killing Lam, and now there's a video out there . . . he's not sticking around. He must have left right after that shootout."

"I mean, if I murdered somebody and had access to Michael Acosta's resources, I would have made moves, too . . . There's no doubt in your mind he's coming after you, right?"

"None."

"Well, if the police won't identify him, there's only one thing left to do. I'm going to release this video through social media and get the comments going. And I'll drop some anonymous hints that the same guy who roughed up the protester is the one who killed our friend Bernie. Everyone and Interpol is going to be looking for David Tao now. Thank God for heiresses with top-of-the-line phone cameras."

When I hang up, I also feel a moment of gratitude for the existence of heiresses, one in particular. It's a feeling I never thought I'd have. Every day there's a new surprise waiting for me, a new betrayal.

The doors and windows of the cabin are still locked. Lynn is sitting in the kitchen with a French press in front of her. Whisper is at her feet.

"I let her out a few minutes ago," Lynn says.

"Thank you," I say, very carefully. I'm not sure how to read her mood. The last time we were alone in a room together, Lynn and I, she told me her marriage was over and she was taking Bonnie to Toronto. She left behind photographs of Bonnie's life. She didn't have to do that, but she did. It was the start of something between us, but neither of us wanted to acknowledge it. But we knew it was there. A kind of under-standing.

A beginning, perhaps.

She pours a cup of coffee for herself and one for me. "How are you holding up?" she asks.

"Couldn't be better," I say. "What about you?"

She sighs. "It's been so long since someone asked me that question, I don't even know how to begin answering it."

I'm not feeling up to conversation, either. We sit in the quiet kitchen and finish the French press. She makes another one. We drink that, too.

"I have to get going," I say.

She nods. "Go get him."

"I will."

Her voice takes on a hard edge. "I mean it, Nora. I don't

pretend to understand what's happening here, with you or with Bonnie. But it has to end. And I'm not stupid. Everett wants to be a big shot; he wants to hire bodyguards and all that. He doesn't see. Whoever tried to take Bonnie, it wasn't about her at all. It was about you. So I'm going to support his decision, and I'll do the best I can to protect our daughter, but you're the one who has to fix this."

"I know."

"Good. Here, take this with you." She breaks off a banana from a bunch and packs some of the leftover pizza from last night, along with two bottles of water. After I feed Whisper and let her stretch her legs once more, Lynn sends me on my way.

She told me to take responsibility for the mess I've created, which hurt, but it is a fair assessment of the situation. I'm to do it for *our* daughter, but before I go, here is some sustenance for my journey.

I drive away from the cabin with the knowledge that I've been reprimanded and nourished simultaneously. It's a new experience for me. Does Bonnie experience this every day? Is this what it's like to have a mother?

I wouldn't know.

# 50

TO SAY THE heavy snowfall caught the city by surprise is a ridiculous understatement. People are in a state of shock, interspersed by moments of panic. No one knows what to do with their hands. Should they try to dig out their vehicles, which they don't know how to drive in these weather conditions, or do they dial their workplaces to say they aren't coming in? Tips on how to drive in the snow fill local news reports while those who had moved here to get out of this kind of vengeful weather curse their misfortune and sneer at the masses who are seemingly struck helpless by flakes of fluffy white precipitation.

I am on the side of the cursing and sneering few. It takes me, as Leo would say, literally forever to get to Mountain View Cemetery.

It's such a letdown, visiting a grave.

Herein lies the rotting body of a person who was once alive. Here's a stone slab with some basic identifying information on it. I'm reading the words on the headstone, but they don't make sense. Well, they do, technically, but they're not what I think about when I think of Sebastian Crow.

Is this all that's left behind of him? A name. A date of birth and a date of death. A profession.

There's nothing sentimental about this piece of stone stuck into the earth, not even a nice quote or bit of poetry to make his existence on the planet seem worthwhile. To show that he had a good life, an interesting one. That he had loved and was loved in return. Maybe loved a little too much, actually, given Leo's mental state after his death.

There's nothing to show what kind of heart Seb had, which is a shame because, love squabbles aside, he had a good one. It was the one he showed to me. There's this feeling I can't shake, that I have let him down somehow by going to Detroit to learn about my father's life there. I left a dying man alone in order to figure out what happened to an already dead one. What kind of sense does that make?

It was supposed to be me figuring out the headstone. Why hadn't I thought of this in advance? About what should be included on this ugly piece of stone? The bit of poetry was my responsibility, because I was the one who was with him in what had to have been the most painful year of his life, watching him lose the battle to cancer. He'd chosen me to be with him at the end, and I let him down. And I don't even know what poetry he liked, if he had even liked poetry at all.

I really shouldn't be in this nice silent graveyard, making a clear target of myself. But where else am I supposed to read Seb's memoirs? The snow has stopped falling and the ground has hardened with the cold, so I put down a blanket, which Whisper immediately settles over, and pour some coffee from Seb's old thermos that I've lifted from Leo's apartment. The temptation to add some whiskey to the thermos is as strong as ever, but thankfully Leo is keeping all his booze to himself these days. I read for a while, nodding at certain passages, my favorites. None of this is new to me because I'd helped Seb craft this book. The stories are his, the life was his, but I had something to do with the organization of it, with the vetting of information.

This book feels like an old friend.

It feels like my friend.

When it gets too cold to sit any longer, I pack everything away and wander farther into the cemetery to a grave I have never visited before, though I have known for some time where it is and who it belongs to.

In my life, I have been close to two investigative journalists, both dead now. Mike Starling and Sebastian Crow weren't the attractive, charismatic sorts you see on television. They weren't rugged, go-get-'em types. People didn't just fall into bed with them with little or no effort on their parts, and nobody with eyes would put them on television for a viewing public for their telegenic appeal alone. It didn't matter that they weren't pretty. What mattered was that they were good. They were the real deal. The ones who would never get famous, never be booked on American talk shows to talk about their work. When their work came out, it was relegated to the much shittier Canadian press, but they didn't mind because it wasn't about personal exposure; it was about the work.

They were obsessed with their stories.

This obsession I can understand. In truth, I'm feeling more than a little obsessed right now. I'm standing in front of Starling's grave, reading the words on his tombstone. Unlike Seb, he got a quote. Someone was looking out for him. There, carved in marble—a nice touch—is part of a Martin Luther King Jr. quote: ". . . unarmed truth and unconditional love will have the final word."

It is a generous bit of dishonesty because everyone who knew Starling was aware that he was a Hunter S. Thompson man who liked to laugh into his rum and drunkenly mutter, verbatim, "It's a damned shame that a field as potentially dynamic and vital as journalism should be overrun with dullards, bums, and hacks, hag-ridden with myopia, apathy, and complacence, and generally stuck in a bog of stagnant mediocrity."

But how he really felt about his profession isn't tombstone material and, to be honest, the lie looks much better in the dim winter light. I'm feeling tenderly toward Starling. I was somewhat prepared for Seb's death, through the writing of his memoirs and taking him to his appointments. Watching his rapid deterioration. But I wasn't ready to see Starling go, because he had been murdered, found floating in a bathtub full of bloody water. Found by me, which was a strange bit of karma because it was his connection to me that killed him in the end.

Dao, the man responsible for this hit on me, was responsible for Starling's death two years ago. He is responsible for the attack on Nate Marlowe and was the engineer behind Bonnie's kidnapping.

Nothing stirs in this graveyard, not even the wind.

I feel a presence behind me. Leo's eyes are bloodshot, and his tie is askew. He looks like he slept in the clothes he's wearing.

"Where did you sleep last night?" I ask.

"What?" he says absently. "Oh, I had a date. That's not what I called you to talk about. Whoever has been watching you has given up on the office, but they're still on my apartment." Whisper goes to him, and they spend a moment engaging in an ecstatic lovefest.

"I left some stuff there. They figure I'll be back at some point to pick it up."

"That's what I thought, too. Warsame was able to follow them to a bar in Surrey. The first time he did it, it was a man he followed and the second time it was a woman. Nora, they went to a biker bar."

"That fits with what Brazuca said. Three Phoenix still has a pipeline into the country, and they're filtering product through a biker gang. Guess the bikers are still surveilling me for them."

"There's one more thing you should know." Leo pauses. "Brazuca ran into some trouble with one of the bikers a while back. A guy named Curtis Parnell. Warsame helped him with the case, so he's got more information than I do. But from what I heard, Parnell has an axe to grind with Brazuca."

"What's the bar?" I ask.

"I don't know," he says, lying.

"Leo," I say. "They tried to take my daughter. Again. Someone was waiting for her at her house in Toronto."

"Fuck," Leo says, sounding stricken. He gives me the name of the bar. Then he says, "She must have been so scared. How is she doing?"

"She's seventeen years old. Who would actually know?"

"Good point." He looks at me. Smiles. "You like her."

"What?"

"Your daughter. You like her."

I think about lying to him, but what's the point? "Yeah, I like her a lot. She's dating a girl right now. Asked me if I had a problem with that."

Leo laughs. "What did you say?"

"What do you think I said? I told her I fly the rainbow flag at Pride every year."

His smile widens. "Oh, God. I'm picturing it right now. You. At Pride." He shakes his head. "She was testing you. I hope she turns out to be a lesbian, for her sake. They have better orgasms than straight women. I read that in a magazine—wait, it's *more* orgasms. I'm not sure if they're better or not."

"You're just a font of information today," I say.

"Don't knock it till you try it. But seriously, what are you planning to do about Dao?"

I update him on what happened in Indonesia, and on the

video. "He's not in Indonesia anymore, that's for sure. He's either on his way, or he's here already. He played his hand by trying to have Bonnie taken. He's not waiting anymore."

I don't know how I know this, but I do.

"You didn't answer my question," Leo says sharply.

"I'm going to lay low and let the police do their jobs. Simone is boosting the video and making the connections between that and when he assaulted the protester."

He nods. "Good. Getting his identity out there and the nature of his crimes. Still at Brazuca's?"

"For the moment."

"Can Whisper stay with Uncle Leo tonight?"

I look at her on her belly, enjoying his rubs. Can't bring myself to deny her more. "Yeah."

"I'm sorry I asked you to meet me here," he says, looking at Seb's plain headstone. "I thought I was ready to see it, but this was a mistake."

"You still miss him."

"I don't even know if that's it. When he asked me to leave, it shook me. I was angry—but I'm not angry with him anymore," Leo says. "I used to be. When he died, I was even angrier. Now I understand his reasons and I've accepted them. He gave me no choice."

"Maybe he thought he was doing what was best for you."

"No, he was doing what was best for him. He wanted to do this without me. He asked me to leave the house, but in truth, he left me. People leave you, and you learn to live without them. When you learn to live without someone, that's the end. You figure out you don't need them, and no matter what happens, it can never be the same. The Seb that I knew and loved, I hold him in my heart and I won't ever let go of that memory of him. But he left me, in more ways than one. He lay down the night he died with Whisper at his side, and he never called, never texted. He wanted to be alone."

I pat Whisper on the head and bid her to stay. She has been through so much but seems to understand her new life very well. Maybe even better than me. I imagine she even likes the variety of it. Me, Brazuca, Uncle Leo. She belongs to all of us and to herself most of all. I leave her there with Leo, who is still lost in contemplation of Seb's grave.

I'm suddenly cold. It must be all that sun I've gotten used to, to feel this way due to a little snow. I pull my hood up to ward off the chill.

# 51

WHAT I LOVE about the violent sycophants of the world is their lack of imagination. For a biker clubhouse, the dive bar decor is unsurprising in every way. There are pool tables and dart boards. The bar is a wooden slab where cheap booze abounds. If you want a nice glass of wine or a good Scotch, you'd have to go elsewhere. Not that there's anything wrong with cheap booze. I was once a connoisseur, so I'm in no position to judge.

It's just like the movies except the bar doesn't go quiet when I enter.

There are no shocked gasps, no furrowed brows or angry mutterings. But I know my presence has been noted carefully. I know there are cell phone cameras pointed my way. There's a man and a woman at the bar, both on their phones. There are available seats all around them. There's an air of menace about these two that makes everyone but me think twice about sitting too close. I have nothing to lose but my life and the few remaining dollars in my pocket.

As I approach the barstools I check my pocket just to make sure. There are no dollars left. Well, that's disappointing.

I sit next to the woman and smile at her in my best attempt at sisterly affection.

Her expression doesn't change.

"Can I get you something?" asks the young waitress wiping down the counter. She's South Asian, but I guess it's not that surprising that she's here, given the large Indian population in Surrey. Though it is a biker bar, so her presence does strike me as odd. Or maybe I don't know bikers as well as I think I do. Maybe they're big into diversity these days, who knows?

"No, thanks. I'm just here for the sparkling conversation."

"Buy something or leave," says the woman I'm still smiling at.

"Why so hostile?" I ask. "You and your friend here have been looking for me, haven't you? I just stopped by to make your jobs a little easier. Why don't you call your little friends who put that watch on me and let them know I'm back in town. In case you forgot where I live, here's the address." I recite the details of Leo's Chinatown apartment. Including the postal code. It feels good to be helpful sometimes.

The man and the woman say nothing, but the young woman behind the bar scuttles away quickly.

Ah, now there's that silence I've been waiting for.

"I've been thinking," I say. "About how fugitives from the law get into the country. There are lots of ways—used to be easier to come through the US, but with all these illegal border crossings from the US into Canada these days, the RCMP is cracking down. Sad, I know. Some of our most enterprising criminal organizations have had to adjust. But there are still ways. Places like, for example, Southeast Asia, where a well-connected person can get a fake passport cheaply. That's if you're flying. But Vancouver offers a variety of options—that's what I love about this city. A few years ago we caught two boatloads of migrants. And that's just the ones that made the papers!"

"You got a point?" asks the man.

"Oh yeah. Sorry, I forgot. I'm getting to it, though."

"Well, hurry up," says the woman.

"There are lots of ways a man—or woman, but let's just say it's a man—can get into the country if he's tapped into one of these human smuggling networks. My point is, since you asked, when he gets to town, let him know I'm waiting for him, won't you?"

"Are you done now?" asks the woman.

"I think so, yeah."

"Good. I've got a point, too, hon."

"I'm all ears," I say, knowing full well that when another woman calls you *hon,* she wants to rip your throat out.

"My point is that I would like you to get up and walk toward the ladies' room nice and easy, where we can finish this chat privately."

"No thanks, sweetie pie, my business isn't with you. It's with Dao."

The name doesn't register with her, but the man recognizes it. I file that away for later. "I like your jacket," I say to the man. "It's a nice color. What would you say it is?"

"Green."

"Wow. You've really got a knack for description. I think I've seen this jacket before, at a Water Is Life march a little while ago. Then again, maybe I'm wrong."

But I'm not. This is the man from the protest, the green jacket I'd been following right before someone tried to grab me.

I slide off the stool. "I just have this feeling—I don't even know where it came from. But it's this powerful instinct that if anything happened to me—if, say, I get hurt in the time it takes me to get from here to my car—you'll have someone a lot more dangerous than me to answer to. That dangerous someone may want the pleasure of chatting with me himself."

While they're still processing that, I leave. They'll figure out soon enough that Dao doesn't care how hurt I am when he finds me, as long as he's the one who gets to do all the murdering.

But I'm not taking any chances, either. I get out of there as quickly as I can and keep an eye on the rearview mirror as I make my way back to the city.

It's late by the time I return to Leo's apartment. He's sleeping elsewhere with Whisper for the time being, so I'm alone. I barely have time to remove my shoes and turn up the thermostat, when there's a knock on the door. It's only been five minutes since I walked through it. I don't answer it.

Lynn's directive rings in my ears. Take care of it, she said.

I'm about to dial 9-1-1.

Then my phone rings. It's Brazuca, calling to see why I'm not answering the door even though he has seen me enter the building.

I let him inside.

"Where've you been?" he asks.

"Where have *you* been?"

He hesitates, wondering if this is a loaded question, which, of course, it is. But before he can speak, I tell him about the video and the apartment being watched by the man and woman I'd followed back to a biker bar.

He looks away. His face is bathed in the neon pink light from the Szechuan place. "So we're just going to sit and wait for Dao to show up?"

"He knows we're here. Well, that I am, anyway."

"Fuck. Why go to that bar and bait him?"

"It's time to finish this."

"I gather Simone is helping to spread this snuff video?" Brazuca asks.

"Like the helpful global citizen she is. She tells me she's even moved to let the Canadian authorities know that this fugitive might be in Vancouver. Out of the goodness of her heart."

He smiles, and the meanness goes out of me.

For a while, we talk about other things. He tells me about

his telescope and gets lost in various constellations. I hear how his mother had taken him once to the Canary Islands and he'd seen the night sky in a way he'd never seen it before. He wants to go to Alberta and see a new purple-colored ribbon of light in the aurora borealis that scientists are calling Steve. Even though it's now known that Steve is actually a twenty-five-kilometer-wide concentration of hot gasses, he still thinks it's worth a trip to Alberta, which is insanity. Nothing is worth going to Alberta.

Contemplating all this helps to pass the time. We're getting to the end of all this talking about every topic except for the thing that's on both our minds.

Brazuca yawns.

He should be tired. It must take a lot of energy to be that deceitful. There's a moment when I have the courage to ask what he said to Bernard Lam's father in that car. But I don't have the courage to hear the answer. I don't think he would sell me out to use as bait the way that Bernard Lam did. I can't bring myself to believe him capable of it, though it has become clear to me that just about anyone is capable of anything.

The moment passes, and we settle in for the night.

Somewhere out there Steve is flashing purple and creating awe in the universe. We're bathing in some pink light of our own, until there's a flicker, the Szechuan place across the road goes dark, and we are alone in the way I've come to associate with him. Ever since he was my sponsor and we'd sit beside each other in the cold of the night and retreat inside ourselves. Alone but together.

I still don't know what to call the sex, but it's good in the way it can be when someone is familiar with your body. I haven't learned someone like this in far too long. Better this than talking. The inch of skin at his shoulder is still my favorite place to visit and stay awhile.

Brazuca doesn't seem to mind.

I'm not sure his lies matter to me right now.

# 52

THE NEXT MORNING I find Brazuca sitting at the kitchen table. Abandoned to the side are two breakfast sandwiches from the shop around the corner. His full attention is reserved for the object on the table in front of him: a pistol in a sleek pancake holster meant to sit on the hip.

"Is that licensed?" I ask. "Did you have it with you last night?"

"Yes and yes. Here." He offers it to me in the holster, but I shake my head.

I know how to fire a gun. Have more than a passing familiarity with them. But I don't have to feel it up, the way some gun nuts do. I have no desire to romanticize it, to take it apart and put it back together. To wax poetic, call it Baby, and go out with it to destroy some innocent beer cans. I never forget that Baby killed my father and is responsible for what happened to Nate Marlowe in Detroit.

"Why did you bring it?"

"Thought it would be useful to have it if you're going to be staying here." Brazuca isn't offended that I won't touch his gun, but he's got something on his mind.

"But."

"But I think it's time we try something different. Your idea of a trap is a good one, but I gotta say there's a better way to do this. I spoke with Detective Christopher Lee, my ex-partner at VPD, while you were sleeping."

"You told a cop about me."

"Not everything, but some. I had to," he adds, somewhat apologetic. "Did you see this?"

He pulls up the video Cristina Guerrero took in Indonesia and pauses it at the moment Dao jumps the wall. His shirt snags as he lifts himself over and his torso is briefly revealed. There's a scar running down his abdomen, but his lower belly is oddly distended.

Brazuca zooms in and indicates toward Dao's bloated stomach, an anomaly on his lean, muscular body. "Experts have pored over this video, and I even asked an ER doctor friend of mine to take a look. Judging from the scarring and the condition of his lower belly, he was in serious pain. She thinks he had a bowel obstruction from a previous gunshot wound to the abdomen. Something about adhesions and scar tissue . . . apparently it can recur with those types of injuries and it's very painful."

"And I shot him. I caused it."

"Yeah, you did." He hesitates. "Look, Nora. It didn't seem like it at the time, but our play on Lombok worked. There's a video of him committing murder, and he's linked to the mines and Acosta through the protester he attacked. That's what gets him arrested and out of your life. Edison Lam will make sure he pays for Bernard's death. You have nothing to lose by getting the authorities involved. Nothing."

My memory backlog of cops being shitty to me, not believing me, not helping when I needed it, looking at me as though I don't belong on this land, comes back. After discovering Brazuca was talking to Lam and being ordered to end this by Lynn, I must have gotten reckless. But Brazuca is right. It's time. "Okay."

He looks relieved. "Okay. My old partner is willing to talk to us. It'll extrapolate from there and more agencies will get involved, but I thought he'd be a good person to start with."

"Alright, let's go."

He pushes a breakfast sandwich toward me but makes no move to unwrap his. "Eat something first."

I shake my head. Suddenly I can't wait to talk to the cops, for the first time in my life. To tell them everything, talk about the video, let them do the work for a change.

I grab my jacket and toss Brazuca his own. "We can eat on the way."

That's why my stomach is empty when the truck comes speeding into us in the alley behind the building, a huge souped-up pickup ramming into the rear end of Brazuca's MINI.

Brazuca was just in the middle of putting on his seat belt, but it wasn't fastened. His head goes slamming into the wheel.

I get whiplash, but I'm belted in so there's nowhere to go.

I'm still stunned by the suddenness of it. My door is yanked open, and a man I vaguely recognize reaches over, unbuckles my seat belt, and hauls me out. He shoves me into the bed of the truck.

Brazuca is left behind, bleeding from the head.

# FIVE

# 53

WHEN BRAZUCA WAKES, he's in the hospital but he can't open his eyes. His lids have anchors on them. "Nora," he rasps.

"Easy there, bud," says a familiar voice. "Let me tell the doc you're awake."

Brazuca hears footsteps, and then Lee, his old partner from Homicide, returns with a doctor. By this time, he can just manage to open his eyes to slits. It's too sudden, the room too bright. He blinks, and when he tries again, his vision clears a little.

"Where's Nora?" he asks the both of them, his voice sounding as though it belongs to someone else, someone who slurs. For a terrifying moment he's transported back to his days as an alcoholic, to the few times he got blackout drunk and couldn't say a clear word when he woke up. But then he thinks of the crash and remembers why he's been asking for Nora in the first place.

"You've got a concussion," says the doctor. "And fractures to your skull. You're pretty banged up, Mr. Brazuca, but you'll live."

"Nora Watts."

The doctor whispers something to a nurse, and they both leave. Lee remains standing.

"Tell me," says Brazuca.

"Your tiny little goddamn car I've told you to upgrade a million times was rear-ended this morning by a stolen pickup truck. We caught the plates on a red-light camera. The pickup was driven by a woman. According to a witness, upon striking your vehicle, a man exited the passenger side of the vehicle, approached the passenger side of your vehicle, and pulled a woman out of your car. The woman was put in the bed of the pickup, which was then locked. The truck took off. It was heading for the highway. Then we lost it."

"How long?"

Lee hesitates.

"How long have I been out, Chris?"

"Four hours."

"Shit."

"It's a stolen vehicle, and we put out an alert for the car as well as Nora. Do you have any idea where they would have taken her?"

Brazuca tells them about the bar she'd just gone strolling into.

"A biker clubhouse? You sure that chick messed with a biker gang?"

Brazuca nods wearily. That's Nora alright.

Lee comes back an hour later. Nora wasn't at the clubhouse. Neither were the man and woman who'd taken her. "We're looking for her," Lee says. "But what's this got to do with this fugitive?"

"Everything," Brazuca says. "We find him, we'll find her, too."

"I think you need to do a better job of explaining what's going on."

"It's going to take a while." He tells Lee this not as a deterrent but more as a general warning.

"You're lucky, bro. I've got all the time in the world. But hang on, let me get someone in here." He goes to the door and brings in a woman.

Everything about her is shiny. Her blond hair, her lipstick. The silver pen she takes out to jot notes. The sheer brightness of her hurts his eyes.

"Detective Ellie Strauss, from the Fugitive Task Force," she says. "I've heard a lot about you, Mr. Brazuca."

Brazuca ignores the attempt at making nice, which is more in her tone than in her statement. He gets right down to it, this mess he's found himself in with Nora. It does take a bloody long time to get through it all. As the minutes tick by, he can think of nothing but Nora's life seeping away as Dao draws closer. He doesn't even think of himself. Maybe that's what a concussion does to you.

After they leave, he remembers when he was in Detroit, searching for Nora.

He's under observation because of the head injury, the doctor had said. He's doing some observing himself, which has turned from concern for Nora to the mess he's created for himself by his inability to stay out of her life.

Sleep is elusive tonight, so he mostly stays up. Waiting. Thinking. He so badly wants Nora to be okay.

# 54

IT'S JUST ME and Baby in the bed of the pickup.

Baby and I?

A woman with dark red hair comes to mind. She's someone's mother, but not mine. She would know if it's *me* or *I*. Whose mother is she? There's something important I'm trying to grasp about mothers and their children. But I can't figure it out.

It could be that I was left in the trunk of a pickup truck for far too many hours. By the growl in my stomach it could be a day. By my thirst, it feels a decade longer.

I think phones are the instrument of the devil, but I would have sold my firstborn child for one as it grows colder.

Then I remember that my firstborn child is what this is all about anyway, and I can't sell what's not mine. But I can still find a way to protect her.

The man waiting for me is prepared for a fight, but he isn't expecting Baby.

I'm ready when he opens the trunk. I hear a sound like a garage door lifting. The first three shots go wild, but they shock the hell out of him. I fall out of the truck. Try to stand. Fall again. Fire another shot wildly. There's a shout and a cry of pain.

The garage door is still open, so I run. Trip on an old tire on the ground, get back up, and run some more. There's shouting behind me, but I'm free, goddamn it. I make it out onto a road dotted with potholes.

I'm somewhere rural, which is terrifying. If you've ever heard the name Robert Pickton, a serial killer who preyed on women in British Columbia for years, you'd understand. He lived on a farm in rural BC. These isolated stretches are no good for women, no good at all. Bad memories come slashing out at me in the dark. I'm weak from hunger and thirst. I drop the gun twice but have the good sense to put the safety back on after the first time. Time moves slowly. The memories won't be pushed aside.

There's a car idling on the road ahead. Turning to look behind me, I see someone dart out of the shadows, but I can't find anything to aim at. My vision blurs.

The car door opens. Van Nguyen and his friend emerge. They recognize me immediately.

"Hey, it's the neighborhood watch!" says Nguyen. He grins at someone behind me.

I turn, raise the gun. It slips from my hand, and as I bend to pick it up, someone kicks me in the back. A spear of pain ices up my spine. When I can open my eyes again, to see past the pain, there's the woman from the bar. She kicks me again, this time in the face.

"You're early," the woman says to Nguyen.

"Be glad I was. I heard a gunshot," he responds.

"This bitch had a gun on her when we picked her up. She came out of the truck shooting."

Nguyen tsks. "Sloppy. Shoulda checked."

"Curt's been slipping recently," says the woman. "But he didn't deserve that. Let me kill this bitch."

"No. She's the package. You know that."

"She has to pay for Curt."

"Is he dead?"

"No, but she shot him! I called a doc we've got. Should be here soon. Let me have her."

"You don't demand from us. We get you your stuff."

"Yeah, well, we bring it in from the ports! This is bullshit, and you know it. She has to pay."

"You were asked to deliver a package and you did. You have our thanks."

Hands lift me, and I am put into another vehicle. This time the trunk. Before it closes on me, I hear Nguyen say: "Don't worry. She's as good as dead."

But good as isn't the same as dead. Cold comfort, but it's all I have.

# 55

THE MANHUNT IS a joint affair. Because of the video showing Bernard Lam's execution, authorities in Indonesia request assistance through Interpol, which means the Department of Justice becomes involved. Local police work with the elite Fugitive Task Force out of Toronto.

Conservative American pundits howl for Canada to do a better job at policing their borders. Liberal Canadians gently remind everyone that America is not a model they want to emulate. Conservative Canadians shout that maybe they do.

Because tensions are high, nobody in the country is apologizing.

Some souls unfamiliar with the country's colonial history wonder what is happening in their nice country.

Aspersions are cast all around.

All law enforcement involved are reminded of that time two bike cops in Montreal were responsible for apprehending one of the FBI's most wanted during a routine stop. If bike cops can do it, why can't they? There are jokes on the radio about hiring some Montreal bike cops to teach Vancouver PD a lesson.

The weather joins forces with the criminal element against

the good men and women in uniform. Also against the bad ones, because weather doesn't discriminate. There's snow-storm after snowstorm. Nobody in the city can get their hands on road salt. Between astronomical gas prices and this lack of ability to get out of their own driveways, Vancouverites give up and stay home.

After the first day, Lee starts to assume Nora Watts is dead. Secretly, so does Brazuca.

The stolen pickup truck is discovered parked on the side of an abandoned logging road in Abbotsford. The truck had been doused with gasoline and lit on fire, so all the police found was a burned-out shell of a vehicle. And human remains that have yet to be identified.

When he's released from the hospital, Brazuca sits in his apartment, by his telescope, and puts his face in his hands. He hasn't been taking his antibiotics, so his ulcer has returned. With friends.

He gets a call from IHIT, the Integrated Homicide Investiga-tion Team. They're investigating the pickup truck death.

Brazuca is asked to come in to go over the Nora story yet again. He does, with the same level of detail that he'd given to Lee and Strauss at the hospital.

"You're telling me," says Detective Hiroshi Ito, "that a man who worked private security for a VIP developed some kind of grudge against a local woman, the passenger in your ve-hicle at the time it was struck, and that he had put a hit on this woman. He used a biker gang to kidnap her."

Ito is famous in police circles for his quiet manner, which is at odds with the steroid-filled life he'd lived as a youth. Though he was born in Vancouver, he had a few sumo wrestlers in the family tree and decided to continue the tradition by becoming a competitive body builder. The running joke was that he couldn't handle the pressures of competition and took the easy way out by becoming a police detective.

"Yes. I've already explained all this to Vancouver PD. The man you're looking for also has connections with organized crime in China through the family he used to work for, or maybe he'd had them before—I don't know. I personally think he's using his organized crime links to evade the authorities. He did that once before."

One moment he feels light-headed. The next he feels weighted down.

It goes on like this for several minutes as he tells Ito how Dao had disappeared after Bonnie was found, the time she'd been kidnapped. "He has a network in place here. It might be a loose network, but the ties are strong for him to have accomplished what he has. Maybe they owe him favors; maybe he's paying them."

"That's a hell of a lot of speculation. I find this hard to believe." Ito isn't as incredulous as he sounds. He's clearly been following all the salacious details of the case.

"Let me give you some examples. Two decades ago an alleged triad boss from Macau set up his family in Vancouver and funneled assets into the country. A rival gang put out a contract on his head to the tune of one million dollars, to be executed in Vancouver. About two years before that, Jimmy Fang, head of Three Phoenix here in Vancouver, was involved in a street gang rivalry, money laundering, drug and arms trafficking. He jumped bail and fled the country. He's suspected to be in hiding in Southeast Asia. A Vancouver man was recently arrested on charges of selling encrypted phones and access to an encrypted network to Mexican cartels. Vancouver has ties to organized crime circles from all over the world and it gets messy. You know that."

This clearly isn't new information to Ito. He doesn't speak for a long time, just looks at Brazuca thoughtfully until Brazuca can't take it anymore. "Want some more examples?"

"Yes, and when you give them, also make sure to tell me where you think they would take the woman. Nora Watts."

"I don't know!" Brazuca shouts. He recoils almost immediately. The outburst came out of nowhere. Ito doesn't look shocked, but then again, he wouldn't. He's used to dealing with irrational people. Brazuca can't ever remember losing his temper quite like this before.

With his dark eyes wiped of expression, Ito reminds him of Nora. Who used to look at him in a similar fashion. Like she could see right through him.

To add to his troubles, just minutes after the interview, Krushnik calls to ask if there's been any news. He can hear the dog barking in the background, so he ends the conversation as quickly as he can. The noise is like a jackhammer pounding into his head.

Back in Detroit, Nora survived a burning warehouse. What a cruel joke if she'd been the one burned in the pickup. A cruel, cosmic joke that only happens to people like her. Who were living on borrowed time, anyway.

She should have died a long time ago, he thinks.

Then he wonders where that thought came from.

# 56

IF SHE'D BEEN wearing steel-toed boots when she kicked me, my back would have been broken and my cheekbone shattered.

I'm in so much pain, even still, that I don't know how much time has passed. Eventually the car stops and I'm pulled out again, this time carefully, with Nguyen holding Brazuca's gun on me while his goon drags me from the inside of a garage into a basement.

Nguyen follows us down.

His man zip-ties me to a chair as Nguyen watches. From the way he's looking at me, I get the impression he isn't one of those sick fucks who takes pleasure in other people's pain. He's just okay with it as long as it serves his purposes.

"So much trouble," he says to me. "For just one woman."

"I'm going to die . . . tell me . . ."

"Yes, you're going to die. You fucked with the wrong person, lady. I feel sorry for you to be on Dao's bad side."

"It was you," I say. "You helped him escape. Back then. You helped him . . . now."

"He paid good money for it. He had a lot put away in China from some of our other businesses, and Ray Zhang left him some dough, too, but he didn't care about that anymore. He just wanted to know where you were, what did you look like, were you happy. I told him, who cares if you were happy? Just get rid of you if you're such a problem. And I thought when he said yes to the hit in Detroit, that was the end of it. Then you come back and he wants more eyes on you, plus on the little bitch pup of yours in Toronto."

"Boss," says the goon. "What do you want me to do with this?" He holds out Brazuca's gun.

"Ditch it."

"How long we gonna keep her here?"

"What is this, four hundred questions? Get upstairs, I'll take care of this." Nguyen is losing patience. He's had a hard day lending people vast sums of money and is clearly over this conversation regarding my fate.

The goon flinches and disappears.

"You shot him," Nguyen continues. "Man doesn't forget a thing like that. You shouldn't have done it. Plus, both the old man and the baby he was trying to save died. What a shit-show. And now look at you."

Sometimes when you're beaten down, the soul accepts that death is an inevitability. I've felt this way once or twice in my life. Once the question of death is out of the way, the soul gets salty.

"I should have done a better job," I say, around the blood in my mouth. "Aimed better."

"Ain't that the truth! Don't you worry, he'll be here soon enough. You can discuss it with him." He turns to leave, then remembers something. "Oh, by the way, scream all you want. You're in the basement, and this is a six-thousand-square-foot property. The houses on either side are unoccupied."

As soon as he gave me the square footage, I knew our location. At his house in West Vancouver, where Krista Dennings said the neighbors hadn't seen him in months . . . years? I can't remember. It strikes me that no one is going to come around with an apple pie or to ask for a cup of sugar. That as soon as he leaves, I'll be alone in the dark.

"Wait!" I said, stalling for time.

"What?"

I say the first thing that comes to mind, something that has not taken as much space there as it perhaps deserved. "There was a bouncer who died a couple weeks back. Joe Nolan."

"Who?" Nguyen continues up the stairs, as casual as could be.

But I'd already heard the lie.

He knew exactly who Joe Nolan was, when I mentioned his name. Nguyen is who Vidal must have called to take care of a messy situation. He just took care of it too well, for poor Joe Nolan's sake. I was feeling sorry for Nolan, because I was feeling equally sorry for myself. I'd been so close to going to the police and telling them everything I knew and some things I didn't. How I wish I had.

After Nguyen leaves, I work on trying to loosen the zip ties. Nguyen's man comes back down with a bottle of water. He pinches my nose until I open my mouth to gasp for breath and then pours as much of it down my throat as he can.

"Bathroom," I sputter.

"Piss yourself. What do we care?"

Charming.

He leaves after doing the bare minimum to keep me alive, switching off the lights and plunging me in darkness.

Now I'm back to the zip ties, rubbing at them until my wrists are bloody and raw. I'm still working away at those when the door opens again and someone comes down the stairs, armed with a small but powerful flashlight. I blink as the light catches me.

"Hello again," says a voice I vaguely recognize but can't quite place. "You really did a number on those wrists, didn't you?"

I shut my eyes tight against the glare and then slit them open again, only a sliver this time. It doesn't help. I still can't see a damn thing. "Who are you?"

And the voice laughs.

# 57

BRAZUCA GOES TO a meeting for the first time in a long, long while. The scratches on his face are mostly healed, but people still flinch at his appearance and his shuttered expression. There's a hard edge to him now that nobody likes. Tough. He doesn't like it, either, but he's not going to change for these losers. Sitting and listening to his fellow alcoholics repeat their sad stories and their limp motivations, he feels nothing but distaste.

Simone slips in toward the end of the meeting. He catches her stealing glances at him throughout the meeting. With her electric blue hair and violently green nails and lipstick, she's easy to spot. Especially when she tries to make a quick exit.

He catches up to her in the parking lot. It's a cold and blustery night, but even so he thought she'd be less annoyed to see him. "What?" she asks when he puts his hand on her arm.

"Nora . . . have you heard anything?"

"No," she says, looking inexplicably angry.

"If you hear from her—"

"Nora's gone! Okay?"

"That seems cold."

"Yeah, well, fuck you very much. What do you think must have happened to her by now, Jon? She's dead! You see that, right?"

He does see it. But he doesn't want to. What he wants is Nora back.

Simone can tell, and she pities him. "Don't you want your life back, Jon? Don't you want to be happy? There are signs, and then there are signs. Don't let her take any more of your life. Don't let her jeopardize your sobriety and your mental health."

She spins on her sky-high platformed heel and walks away.

There's nothing for him to do after that but go home. He thinks about calling Bonnie, but Strauss had warned him that, due to the high-profile nature of the case, they're not revealing details about Nora's disappearance until they figure out whose remains were in the pickup. If she's still alive, Nora is in the hands of the people who want her dead. There's no use reaching out to her daughter without answers.

There must have been a call placed from Ito to Lee after Brazuca left his IHIT interview because Lee stops by with some Korean barbecue on his way home from work. Ito worked homicides for IHIT, and Lee worked homicides for the city of Vancouver. Maybe they're friends, Brazuca thinks, but he doesn't care enough to ask. Lee eats most of the barbecue while filling Brazuca in on the developments of the case. There aren't any, so Lee just talks at him while throwing him perceptive looks over his food.

The way Lee eats everything in sight without question reminds him of Nora. Though she regularly forgot mealtime unless you reminded her, she had a big appetite for a woman her size and always ate everything on her plate. As though she knew something no one else did about a famine just around the corner. He thinks of her body, the surprising wiry strength of her. With a jolt he realizes that, again, he's just put her in the past, though she hasn't been found yet.

Lee thwacks him on the shoulder before leaving, a semblance of a manly embrace that he should return but doesn't.

"I'll keep you up to date, but you know you can call me anytime, bro," Lee says. Then he zips his coat, which he hadn't bothered to remove, and is out the door before Brazuca can respond.

Suddenly he's tired of it all.

His ulcer and its friends are twisting inside of him. They're getting to know one another, becoming drunk off his stomach fluids and making little ulcer babies to plague his nights. He can't take this anymore. What his life has become, he doesn't know. He thinks of Nate Marlowe.

Bernard Lam had given him an obscene amount of money to work on Clementine's case, and Brazuca has some savings of his own. The only purchase he's made since the money cleared was his beautiful telescope. He stands in the middle of his living room, guts churning, and looks at it while he comes to a decision.

When the truck smashed into his MINI, the left side of his

head took the brunt of the impact. He heard a door open and had managed to slit one eye, just in time to see Nora hauled out. He couldn't move, could do nothing to stop it. There was a moment of perfect lucidity that rose past the roaring sound in his ears.

For a split second, he could see clearly.

What he saw was a face he recognized all too well. Curtis Parnell, the biker who'd been affiliated with Three Phoenix. When Brazuca was investigating the supply chain for Bernard Lam, trying to find who was responsible for his mistress's overdose death, Brazuca had made an enemy of Parnell. He shouldn't have been surprised to see the biker there, but he was. Parnell took Nora, and now she's gone. Dao is gone, too. He tried to save her and failed. Now he feels nothing. No outrage, no fear. Weary resignation is all that's left of him.

He puts his phone to charge and lies down. Waits for it to ring with news about Nora.

It doesn't.

# 58

BONNIE REPLAYS THE Indonesia video over and over. She has seen it a hundred times. Her father, Everett, walked into her bedroom at the cabin once, when it was playing. He was angry at her for watching something so violent, but she didn't have the heart to tell him it was the guy from the time she'd been kidnapped.

The video becomes an obsession. Dao looked different from how she remembered him. Thinner. Even more frightening.

She's so scared. But it's not like she can go back to Toronto, where someone tried to grab her off the street. She focuses as much as she can on schoolwork. The private school she's enrolled in is based on modules and not on classroom attendance, so at least she's not falling behind. But it's still hard to concentrate and she keeps waking up in the night. Even though the burns on her wrists were mild and have disappeared, she still feels them stinging.

It snows every day. With its snow-capped mountains and never-ending forests, it's the most beautiful place she's ever been—and she grew up in Vancouver.

Lynn also works from the cabin. Every day they go to

Whistler Village for lunch. Everett and Adele are on a work trip, but they promise to visit this coming weekend.

"I haven't heard you talk about your friend Alix in a while," says Lynn. "What's she up to?"

"We got into a fight," Bonnie says, picking at her salad.

"Why? What happened?"

"She posted a photo of me on social. My account is set to private, but hers isn't." She catches Lynn's worried look. "I told her to take it down as soon as I saw it. But she knows how I feel about posting stuff."

"What was the photo of?"

"Me in front of the ski lift in Whistler Village. We were messaging the other day while I was waiting for you outside and she asked for a pic."

"You mean right here?" Lynn asks, gesturing out the window. "Did she tag your location?"

"Yeah. But the photo was only up for a day. And I told her never to do it again." Alix knows Bonnie's adopted, but she doesn't know any of the details of Bonnie's kidnapping a couple of years ago or why she's so secretive about her whereabouts all the time. Bonnie told her that she left Toronto to spend time with her dad in Vancouver. Alix is her first friend—well, more than a friend, really—that Bonnie has who doesn't know anything about her crazy past.

Lynn puts down her napkin. She looks worried. "Have you heard from Nora?"

"No. Her phone is off. She's not answering any of my calls."

Lynn pays the bill and they leave. She is still preoccupied. Still worried. They had gone through this after the kidnapping. Online safety one-OhMyGodThisIsSoBoring-one. Lynn had consulted a professional skip tracer who'd turned her skills from finding missing people to advising people how to stay hidden if they wanted.

"Listen to this," said the woman who'd come by the house, back when they first moved to Toronto. She was in her fifties, dressed sharply with little cat-eye glasses perched on her nose and startling blue nail polish. She had the urgency of one of those evangelical preachers you'd see sometimes on TV. "You're on a social media platform and you tag your location. Someone can look at that location and come find you. You keep tagging your locations and they know your whereabouts, what you do at certain times of the day. They can work out your schedules, your exercise routines. They know who your close friends are because those are the people in the photos with you, who are liking and commenting on your posts. If they can't find you, then they'll find one of your friends and work out where you are. They can get a snapshot of your school life, your home life. Be very careful."

Lynn explained how Bonnie's birth father had been able to find her using underground chat forums for adoptees. The woman nodded. She knew all about them. She pushed her glasses back up the bridge of her nose and tucked a strand of silver hair behind her ear. "Be careful of what your friends post about you, as well. If there's someone who's known to be your friend and their profile is public, you can also be in trouble. Don't let people tag you in photos. Best not to get photographed at all."

Both Bonnie and Lynn thought that was a bit much at the time, but now it seems maybe the woman was right.

Bonnie feels uneasy. It's just one lame pic of her in Whistler! Doing what thousands of other teens do on the daily. A selfie with duck face. One photo and she's upset with Alix and her mom all at once. Fuck. She thinks of Nora, who she feels would somehow understand.

But Nora's disappeared again, just when Bonnie needs her the most. Just when that video of Dao turns up. Just when Bonnie could use a little extra protection in her life.

# SIX

# 59

SIMONE COMES IN the door with groceries. She likes to shop late at night because of her disdain for queues. According to her, life is too short to wait around for people to rummage through their personal belongings for cash, credit cards, and coupons. She has more important things to do with her spare time. Like fill me in about the goings-on of the world.

"Brazuca was at the meeting tonight," she tells me. I nod and wait for her to continue. Which she does, as I help her pack away the groceries.

"He did not look good. I told him what you asked me to. That you're gone and to forget about you." She catches my look of relief. "I'm not sure it was the right thing to do, Nora. It's supposed to be for his safety, but that man cares about you. He's hurting."

"At least he's alive."

"If he comes to me again, I'm not going to be able to lie. It felt awful to do it this time."

She hands me a candy cane. I give it back. She shrugs, unwraps it, and pops an end into her mouth.

"Did you share? At the meeting?"

"Nope. But I went for coffee with Angela afterward. You don't know her, she's new. Just got through her first month sober."

I nod. It's an accomplishment we both understand.

We make dinner in silence. Simone gets through half the candy cane and tosses the rest into the trash. Her stint at rehab went well, she said. At the facility they had cooking workshops and she's developed a love for tortilla soup. We make some more now, even though we haven't finished the last batch Simone started on, before I showed up at her door. One of us will get tired of this soup eventually, I'm sure, but it won't be today.

"Any luck on your end?" she asks. "With your guy?"

"Not yet. But I have high hopes for tonight."

She sighs. "One day, having high hopes for a guy tonight is going to mean something different for you and I'll be so proud."

A laugh escapes me. "You sound like Leo."

"Your dog sitter seems like a sensible person."

She notices the look that crosses my face at the mention of my dog and puts a hand on my shoulder. "Sorry, I didn't mean to bring Whisper up. I know how much you miss her. You'll see her when this is over. And Bonnie, too. Dao can't hide forever, and I'm shocked that he's made it this far. Everyone is looking for him. I'm still monitoring all the news outlets and social media. The forums are lit with speculation about him.

I'm going to know as soon as the fucker turns up. I've got that Fugitive Task Force number on speed dial."

"Thank you."

"What are friends for?"

Ever since she found me standing at her door with my wrists bandaged from the zip-tie abuse, she has been gentle with me. I explained that I didn't try to kill myself and, after a while, she believed me. Her hair, nails, and lips are as brightly colored as ever, and she seems alright. Not great, but alright. She's getting more vibrant by the day, which means rehab gave her back some of her spark. She has spent hours in her office catching up on her work contracts and monitoring the net. Like me, Simone prefers to be alone, but she leaves her door slightly ajar to let me know she's there for me.

I want to ask about Brazuca, to have her describe him. I can't think about him without picturing what he looked like bleeding in his car. Which reminds me of the car, and what happened.

Sitting there in the darkness with my wrists bloody and raw, it took me a split second to realize the man in the basement with me wasn't Brazuca. It wasn't Dao, either.

"I waited as long as I could," Edison Lam's man said. "Had to make sure no one else was in here. Had to make sure, also, that no one was going to show up anytime soon."

He led me up the stairs and to a sliding door out back. I stumbled to the car and climbed into the rear seat. I put my hand over my heart to slow it down. I was nothing but a heartbeat in a rigid skeleton. If it wasn't for that thump threatening to pound right out of my chest, I would have thought I was dead.

"I don't think you were honest with us, Ms. Watts, when Mr. Lam asked you about his son's death," the bodyguard said, from behind the wheel.

"How did you find me?"

"I followed you to the apartment. Saw them take you. Then followed you from there."

Of course that's how it happened.

"They had me for a long fucking time!"

I caught his nod in the rearview mirror. "Yes, well. I wanted to see how it played out. Thought maybe David Tao would show up, but I realized the house was empty. There are cameras, but they're not hooked up, and though there's a security company sign on the lawn, there was no alarm."

"Yes," I said. "This is a property Nguyen owns, but he doesn't live here." Then I asked him about what's been on my mind since I got taken. "What happened to Brazuca?"

"My colleague stayed behind to make sure he got to the hospital. He did. He'll make it." He glanced at me in the mirror. "There's a bottle of water beside you."

I drank the whole thing. The bodyguard who was now so obviously more than a bodyguard said nothing. We were on what appeared to be a dark country road with houses scattered at intervals. "I guess we're going to see your boss," I said.

Looking back, I'm not sure if a smile crossed his face or if I simply imagined it.

We didn't go see his boss, Edison Lam. We went to the building where Leo was crashing, but he wasn't there. So he took me to Simone's place. In that car ride I told him everything I knew about Dao. He explained that Brazuca tipped him to the biker connection and that since the video of Bernard Lam's murder had surfaced, Mr. Lam had been cooperating with the authorities.

"But they don't know about your private investigation," I said.

He shook his head.

I must have told him what I did because I was too tired to raise my normal defenses. There was no need to keep up with the innocent girlfriend act, which didn't come naturally to me anyway. Plus, it's easier to share your secrets with a stranger. I never asked him what his name was and he didn't bother to tell me.

"Do you know where Dao is?" I asked.

"David Tao is likely in British Columbia, but we don't know where. Van Nguyen is a new angle."

"Is it safe to assume that Mr. Lam is continuing to investigate this privately? He's not going to sit back and let the authorities in on this, is he?"

He didn't answer, which was answer enough. "We'll be in touch," he said, before I got out of the car.

I'm guessing he wasn't using the royal we. He's not the queen. He was letting me know that he and Edison Lam will be wanting answers to their questions, but not that day. Out of deference to the time of night, my obvious state of distress, or for some other mysterious reason of his own.

# 60

I'M LEFT STANDING on the promenade with my hood pulled close, watching the harbor. There are no stars out tonight, no moon.

But there's a light on in Peter Vidal's yacht.

A man in a long navy jacket approaches. His head is bare, even though he's been standing here watching Vidal's boat as long as I have.

"You're not cold?" I ask.

"This is not cold compared to where I grew up."

"And where is that?" Because his accent betrays nothing.

He ignores the question. My savior could say he's from any northern clime and I wouldn't be surprised. Or maybe his origin story is as unimportant as his name.

"It's time for our chat now," Edison Lam's bodyguard says to me.

"Mr. Lam is back in town," I say.

He's not surprised at the conclusion I draw. "Yes."

"It was nice of him to ask you to keep an eye on me."

He nods. Yes, it was nice. "We should get going."

A man of few words. I like that.

I also appreciate the fact that he was honest about surveilling my movements. His teams are very good, and it has been fun to see if I can slip by them. But they're top-notch, Edison Lam's guys. The best that money can buy. I can't shake them, despite my best efforts. It would be a nuisance if I didn't know that no one else can get through their defenses, either. I'm safe, while they're watching. It's a more comforting thought than it should be.

Following behind him I feel a transference of tenderness, the sort I'd begun to feel for Brazuca. Now, I only think of Brazuca—because I've never called him Jon; even our intimacy has never allowed for it—lying in a hospital bed. Every once in a while, his face is replaced with Nate Marlowe's, then Leo's. Sometimes it's Seb Crow, my dead friend. I wasn't responsible for Seb's death, but if I had been around during his final days, maybe I could have eased his passing somehow. Spared him a little pain. These men, the three who are still alive, of blood and fragile bones . . . I can't do anything more for them. Except maybe stay away.

For now.

We go to a sprawling mansion in Point Grey. The house seems empty as the bodyguard leads me down a long hallway. There are family photos along the walls, of Bernard Lam and a woman I've never seen before. His wife, probably. Some of his father and mother.

We go into a study at the end of the hall, where Edison Lam waits. He looks up from his papers when we enter. "Hello

NO GOING BACK     319

again," he says to me. "Kristof told me you got into some trouble while I've been away."

His glance passes from me to the bodyguard, who closes the study door and stands just inside of it.

I nod. "You could say that."

"Your friend, the man you were with when we visited your apartment—"

"Brazuca?"

"Odd, I thought he was your romantic partner. I was not aware that people are referring to their significant others by their surnames these days."

"I can't keep up with the trends, either." I decide not to tell him about smashing.

"Before he got into that unfortunate car accident, your Brazuca informed me of two potential lines of inquiry for the man who murdered my son."

"And you saw the video of the murder."

He looks away for a moment. If this man has a nervous tic, he would display it now. But of course he doesn't. "Yes."

"I'm sorry."

"You didn't kill him. But you were there. And you were kidnapped by those bikers who are associated with Dao. Not your friend Brazuca. You. Why is that?"

Kristof doesn't move, but I can feel his energy shift. Become laser-focused.

I unzip my jacket and slump on the couch. There's a moment

of tension as I debate whether or not to put my feet up, but I don't want to push my luck, which I can feel wearing thin.

Now that I'm comfortable, I tell them the truth, because I may not have liked Bernard Lam, but he didn't deserve to die the way he did. I'm in this mess because I'm trying to protect my child. Edison Lam is involved to understand the death of his own. Some people say children are a joy. Others believe them to be a burden, one that will suck the life right out of you. Whatever it is, there's no doubt that they steer the direction of your life.

Mr. Lam mulls over what I've just told him. "What you're saying is my son planned to give you over to Dao as an incentive to reveal information about these Three Phoenix people."

"He thought he might need me to get Dao's attention. A little trick up his sleeve. He thought Dao could be paid off."

"He underestimated Dao's hatred for you."

"Yes."

"I have a proposal for you, Ms. Watts."

I have a feeling I know what's coming. Since Bernard Lam's death, this has been inevitable.

"My son wanted to use you without your knowledge, which is why he insisted you weren't part of that meeting."

"Yes."

"And you went along that morning and tried to find Dao on your own because you didn't trust my son."

"No, I didn't. My purpose for being there was always to dig

up some dirt on Dao. Maybe get him to admit that he ordered my assassination. Find a way to put him in jail."

"He will go to jail," says Edison Lam. Then he sighs. "My son defied me at every turn. He was impossible to deal with. His mother spoiled him too much, I think. He was her only child. He wasn't good at reading situations, or people, properly. Some things you can't teach."

He lapses into a thoughtful silence. I'm ready to fall asleep on this couch. "We both want David Tao to face justice. We want him off the streets. He seems to be obsessed with you and, like my son, I want to use that. But we don't have time to waste with lies and deception. Do you understand what I'm saying?"

"You want to use me as bait."

"Yes. Will you consider it?"

"No need," I say. "You're right. He needs to face justice for what he's done. Let's finish this."

There's movement by the door as Kristof comes closer. "Jon Brazuca told us to look into those bikers and WIN Security."

I nod. "WIN had a connection to Ray Zhang, Dao's previous employer."

"WIN Security is a big operation in the Pacific Northwest. They've worked with almost all the major players in this region. Including Michael Acosta's Nebula Corporation."

"Who Dao used to work for—at least until he murdered your son," I say, looking at him.

"Yes," says Mr. Lam. "After the Indonesia video surfaced and authorities identified the same man in both that video and the report of violence against that mining protester, Michael Acosta is suddenly unavailable for comment. Neither he nor WIN will go anywhere near Dao. It's too dangerous. They'll disavow all knowledge of him moving forward and will hide behind carefully worded public statements."

"The bikers, then."

"No." Kristof shakes his head. "That pickup truck was set on fire. There were human remains found inside. They have just identified Curtis Parnell as the deceased. That was the man who rammed Brazuca's car and pulled you from the passenger seat."

"When I escaped, I shot him," I say. "I killed him."

"You grazed his thigh," says Kristof. "It was nothing serious. My people were watching and saw someone come by and pick Parnell up. He was later seen at that clubhouse walking on crutches."

"But someone killed him. Put him in that truck."

They exchange glances. "We think Dao must have."

I shake my head, let my hair down to ease the tightness of my scalp. "But that doesn't make any sense. He leaned on them because of their Three Phoenix connection. He needed them."

Edison Lam looks at me. "If you're right, and he's not in his right mind, it's possible his emotions got the better of him. From what you say, and from what I saw in that video, he's unstable. He didn't have to kill my son, but he did. He didn't have to kill this Parnell man—"

"*If* he did," I add.

Lam nods. "If he did, he didn't have to."

"But you think he flew into a rage? Where the hell is he, then?"

Nobody answers me. "What about Van Nguyen? We need to find him."

"We lost track of him," says Kristof. "He never went back to the house he kept you in. I think there must have been a camera setup that I missed."

I think about it for a moment. "Then we get to him through Peter Vidal." I tell them about Vidal's connection to Nguyen. "Problem is, he's a hard man to get ahold of."

Edison Lam rises from behind his son's desk. "We'll take care of that. If we find Nguyen, we'll find Dao."

I had said the same thing about Jimmy Fang. But this feels closer. The Fang case led us to Nguyen, which is more than we'd had before.

He nods to Kristof. Kristof nods back. I feel no pity for Peter Vidal.

But Vidal is one step ahead of us.

When we return to the marina, me and Kristof, and two other men from Kristof's team who have joined us in a separate vehicle, we find the yacht empty. Vidal isn't at his house in Point Grey, either. He's long gone.

# 61

KRISTOF BRINGS ME back to Simone's apartment. I don't invite him up, but he follows anyway. Simone is still awake, still tapping away at one of the computers in her office. When she hears me enter the apartment, she walks into the kitchen wearing a man's oversize button-down shirt that skims her thighs. There's a hint of black boxers peeking out from underneath the shirt.

Kristof keeps his eyes on her face, but she doesn't restrict herself in that way. She lets him know this is her home, her castle, and she'll send long, lingering glances to anyone she damn well pleases. She gives him a slow look up and down. Taking in his slim, strong physique, the air of strength, the gray eyes like a Vancouver day, and the cheekbones that belong on a fashion model.

"Nice, but not my type. Thanks anyway, Nora," she says.

When she goes, she leaves behind a sexually charged tension that neither Kristof nor I are in the mood for. We've both had a long day.

It's impossible to tell how Kristof feels about being nice but not nice enough. "The problem with using someone as bait is that if a person senses a trap, it's over," Kristof says.

"Is Kristof a first name or a last name?" I ask.

"It could be both, depending on a person's culture."

"What's it with you?"

He doesn't answer.

"Even if Dao senses a trap, he might still take a chance. He despises me, remember?"

"He doesn't know about this place? About this . . . friend?"

"No. He knows about another friend who I used to work for. Leo Krushnik. He has his own investigation operation on Hastings Street. The bikers watched Leo's apartment and his office, but I'm not sure their people will still be on the job if Dao killed Curtis Parnell."

"I'll have my team take a look at the place to see if anyone is keeping an eye on it." Kristof looks through me, toward the door. I think he only came in to see where I was staying, to enter another line of data into the report he has created for me.

"I'll be in touch tomorrow," he says.

When he leaves, Simone comes back in. "That man needs a little excitement in his life."

I begin to laugh, out of sheer exhaustion. I take off my jacket. "You're exciting."

"He should be so lucky. Who is he, anyway?" she asks, following me into the bedroom.

I fill her in.

"Everything is moving too fast. We're trying to figure out who Dao is, where he is. We're trying to keep up with the investigation to see if the authorities find him first. We're trying to keep you and Bonnie alive while we do it. It's too much. I've been looking into Van Nguyen, and since he doesn't live at his West Van house, I'm assuming he has another property, maybe purchased through a shell company. I'm still working on it. Also not much on his alleged girlfriend, the restaurant manager. She's still overseas, rumor has it in Dubai. Whoever these people are, they know how to lay low." She shakes her head. "Okay, maybe it's time to get Brazuca in here."

"No," I say quietly.

"Don't you think he'd want to know you're alive? And, more importantly, wouldn't he want to be involved?"

"I know he will. He always has before. But it's still too dangerous."

"Is my favorite misanthrope growing some kind of conscience? I'm shocked and delighted. Alright. Give me an hour and let me finish up some work. Then we'll go over everything we know about Van Nguyen."

Simone doesn't know what happened between Brazuca and me in Indonesia, and after. Or that I'll do anything to keep him from getting hurt worse than he already has been.

Time passes, I don't know how much. I fall asleep waiting for Simone to finish her work.

The smell of fresh coffee jolts me awake.

"You have to see this," Simone says. She's crouched in front of me with her open laptop, much too close. "They found him."

"What are you talking about?"

Her eyes are dark pools. There are currents of emotion flowing behind them. She's trying to explain something to me and keep her feelings in check all at once. Though I'm groggy and part of my brain is still asleep, I understand this with a glance. Then I see why when she speaks next. "Dao. I think they took him into custody last night."

# 62

I SIT UP. "How do you know? Did they release the information?"

"Nothing has been released. The police aren't saying any-thing. This was posted to the comment section of a news blog."

"Hard Facts?" It was infamous in certain circles for having a comment section that was used by criminals themselves. Seb used to work with the excellent journalist who ran it. Krista Dennings used to work with her, too. Calling it Hard Facts was a bit of an insider joke. The blog itself was solid, but the gold was all the useful speculation and shade in the comments.

She hands me the laptop. "That's the one. The Fugitive Squad or whatever they call themselves rolled up on a biker bar in Surrey. Apparently, it's the second time in a week they've been there. They found a man matching Dao's description and brought him in."

"Positive ID?"

"No. Apparently, he didn't speak—according to three sepa-rate comments. There was some horrific racial abuse on the part of the people commenting, saying that he wasn't speak-ing because he's an immigrant and doesn't know English. Nora? What's wrong? Please don't look at me like that. This is good—it could be him. Nora?"

I try to respond, want to respond, but it's like some kind of fever has gripped me. Since I survived that burning warehouse in Detroit, I've thought of nothing but finding Dao and finishing this. But they caught him. It's over. It just doesn't feel that way right now.

"Hey," says Simone. "Hey, you." She sets down her coffee mug and puts her arms around me.

Edison Lam's Point Grey mansion is a graveyard. All the lights are off, and Kristof is nowhere to be found. A little Chopin wouldn't be out of place here. I buzz at the gate. There's no answer on the intercom. The security cameras at the gate clock my every move, though.

A car turns onto the street. I step into the shadows, not bothering to get into the Corolla, which I parked at the curb. It's not even five a.m., and the sun hasn't yet made an appearance. It's too early for a house call, but Simone's news has changed my plans.

The car pulls into a driveway four mansions down.

I cross the street and keep walking. An early-morning stroll without my dog is anathema to me. It feels wrong. We should be on these pristine streets together watching the world wake up. But I won't go to her before I feel some kind of closure. Life is too precious.

After circling around the block, I find myself in front of Lam's house again. There's still no answer to my buzz on the intercom. But I can feel someone there. It's one of those rare moments I feel a certain level of sentience coming from an inanimate object. It's not just a camera. It's a window. There's someone on the other side, watching.

"Is it him? Is he the one they picked up last night?" I ask, speaking into the box. I turn to look directly at the camera mounted on the outer wall, the one closest to me. "Answer me, goddamn it! It feels too easy. Doesn't it feel too easy?"

The last question comes out as barely a whisper. I can't explain it any other way. I'm thinking of Dao, knowing he wouldn't go down without a fight.

Something isn't right.

My calls to Bonnie go unanswered. Lynn and Everett, too. I'm so desperate I try Adele's office, but it's Saturday and nobody answers the company line.

Then I do something out of character. I call the police, the Whistler RCMP. I tell them my neighbor's house has been broken into and give the cabin's address. I hang up and get into the Corolla.

There's one more call it occurs to me to make. "I'm going to Whistler," I say to Simone.

"Wait, Nora," she says. "They've got to make a statement soon. They've already said there's a suspect in the manhunt in custody. Let's just hang on for a bit, okay? The weather is terrible. There's another foot of snow coming our way. Don't drive in these conditions."

"I have to," I say. "I can't reach Bonnie or her parents. I've already called the police to take a look. I'm just . . . I have to check."

She's silent for a moment. Of all people, Simone realizes what it has taken for me to call the cops. "Fine, okay. What's the cabin address?"

I give it to her and hang up.

After starting the car, I run back to the intercom. "I'm going to Whistler." Once again, I give out the address. Just in case there's someone listening.

It's snowing, a light down that drifts more than falls. It's only until I get onto the highway that I remember I don't have winter tires.

There's traffic approaching Squamish. On the radio they say the road closure has just been lifted about an hour ago. In the dead of the night, when police were apprehending a suspect at a biker bar, a minivan crossed the center line and collided with an SUV. Two people were killed and two airlifted to a hospital in the Lower Mainland. No names are being released at this time, authorities say.

So it's not really my fault that I'm driving faster than I should, on a road so dangerous that two people were killed on it just hours ago. It occurs to me if I drive a little faster, I could solve the problem of my existence once and for all. I'm so tired, so strung out on adrenaline, that a swerve into a railway doesn't seem like such a bad idea. Bam. It would be over. But not until I make sure Bonnie is alright.

This drive, this treacherous road, it all seems to be leading to something inevitable. I just don't know what it is.

# 63

I FEEL OLD. It's entirely possible that I *am* old, but I keep hearing things like thirty is the new twenty, forty is the new thirty, and if you're not dead by fifty then maybe you should be. There have certainly been enough attempts on my life for me to consider my own mortality. I'm like a cat, though. A worn-out, mangy thing that is dragged through life kicking and hollering up a storm while she sharpens her nails.

I'm feeling mean like a cat, too, now that things are becoming clearer.

The aggressive holiday cheer does its best to distract me. As does the weather, which is holding steady below zero degrees Celsius. We're experiencing February-like temperatures and it's not even Christmas. People think because there's snow on the ground now, that there will be snow on December 25. Maybe it will happen. I'm not the person to ask. I'm not sure I'll live that long, but I'll do my best, if only for spite and vengeance.

I've had it with this tired old film. It needs to be over. But there was someone watching Bonnie. Someone who figured she's important to me, this daughter I'd given away.

This child I never wanted to be born.

How important, I never truly realized until I find the back

door of Adele's family cabin unlocked. I enter as quietly as possible.

It's too cold inside, even though the thermostat in the kitchen tells me the heat is on. A draft snakes its way through the house. The source, an open bedroom window. Bonnie's window.

The alarm has been disabled.

Nobody's home, but there are footprints going in and out from the unlocked back door. Not the front. The police haven't left a friendly note saying whether or not they've been by to check on an alleged burglary.

Bonnie's and Lynn's belongings are still here.

I sit at the kitchen table. It's snowing. Light flakes that drift down from above. The snow becomes heavier. Some of it has found its way inside through Bonnie's window and the back door, bringing the damp inside. Memories of the last time I sat here come flooding back. There's Lynn and her warning, of course. But there's also Bonnie telling me about her new girlfriend, flushed with the excitement of young love. There's me talking about Lebanon and Palestine, places I've never been to but are in my blood. About Winnipeg, where my father was born, and all the things I don't know about that, either. I explained to her my confusion about it all, so she'll know she's not alone in hers.

She told me about her abortion last year and how Lynn knows about it, but Everett doesn't. Then she asked why I didn't do one of those ancestry DNA tests and laughed at my suspicion of data harvesting. Then stopped laughing when her mind made the connection between blood harvesting—and the troubles she's been through in the past.

We talked all night while in the back of my mind I thought about Brazuca.

Because my defenses are already shattered by what I've found in this cabin, I think about him now. The inch of skin like a distant memory. The gray at his temples. The long fingers and his limp, which he stops trying to hide the more exhausted he becomes.

In this cold kitchen I think about all my actions that have led to this point. I'm shivering, so I get up to adjust the thermostat, an instinct I would have questioned in other circumstances, when I notice that the footprints outside lead not to the driveway where I parked but into the woods.

Three sets of footprints. Into the woods. Three unholy sets, one larger than the others.

Breadcrumbs. Leading away from the house.

Snow falls. A black cloud blankets the sky.

Something is waiting for me out there. It could be my daughter.

Please don't let it be her. Please.

The snow sends light up from below as I continue on.

# 64

THE LITTLE GUESTHOUSE looms up ahead. Nobody told me it was here, but it makes sense. Where are you supposed to stash in-laws and other unwanted guests but a place out of sight, hidden by the trees?

I follow the footprints right up to the door.

There's a drop of blood on the snow. Crimson on white.

The front of this guesthouse is protected by an overhang. This door, too, is unlocked. I push it open but don't enter right away. There are no sounds coming from inside. It's as cold in there as it is outside.

I can't move.

Two shapes are huddled in the entranceway. One body covering another. Protecting it, even in death.

It's Lynn and Bonnie, of course.

# 65

*THIS IS EVEN worse than Vancouver,* Dao thinks. Rain he could put up with, but snow isn't something he ever wanted to see again.

He's upset by what happened in the little cabin where he'd found the woman and the girl hiding. Their location was Nguyen's last gift to him. They must have seen his car from the street and ran to the second cabin just in case he came knocking. As if he wouldn't look. It had been snowing, too, so their footprints might have been masked—but they got it all wrong. There wasn't enough fresh snow.

Speaking of wrong, the cabin. Them running away from him. Him raising his gun. The woman, Nora, with the hood of her parka up. He only saw her from the back and his anger took over.

When she fell he saw the red hair.

It wasn't Nora.

His belly cramps up, almost doubling him over in pain. But it's a pain that he's become accustomed to. He goes back to his car, hidden farther along the street. That's when he sees someone pass him and pull into the driveway of the cabin he just left.

And he thinks he knows who it is.

# 66

LYNN'S DARK RED hair spills over Bonnie as she slumps over her, our daughter, soaking in the blood around them. She was trying to do the same thing I couldn't. It's a mother-daughter image I want to scrape from my brain.

The hands of the clock above their heads creep forward.

I hear music, but it's no Chopin. With a start, I realize the sound is coming from me. It's inside my head. It's all around me.

It's a voice behind me, shouting.

What's the voice saying?

I've slipped to my knees. When did that happen?

"Get your hands up!" the voice behind me shouts.

My hands go up.

They're yanked viciously behind me. I identify the RCMP officer by the yellow stripe running down the side of his black pants.

Why is there only one?

Then I remember the car accident. Death. Loss of life. More bodies and resources to the big bang-up on the Sea-to-Sky, the major crash. Nobody to investigate little burglary calls until now, when they send one lone officer.

It's cold, and he's not wearing gloves. Maybe that's why he

drops the cuffs. As he bends, he sees something and begins shouting at someone in the distance.

I know who it is before I look up.

Dao has killed yet again in a fit of rage and returned clearheaded to see the damage he's wrought. To see if I would come. And I have. I'm right here.

The officer has his weapon drawn, but he's too late.

Dao shoots him. Three bullets. Forehead and two body shots. A professional job because he's a professional.

I find my balance and stand.

"Why?" My voice doesn't sound like my own. It's a strangled, dying thing. I gesture to the house, to the scene just inside the door.

He stares at me. He doesn't look like the same man I'd remembered. He's aged a decade since the Indonesia video, stooped, obviously in pain. Wearing clothes that are far too small for him and bareheaded in this weather.

But when he speaks, it's the voice I remember from my past. "Jin died because of you. And my son . . . he died because of you, too."

"What are you talking about?" I look back at him, slackjawed, with absolute, mind-numbing horror.

Because I see. I see now, what this is all about.

# 67

AFTER SEEING BONNIE and Lynn in the cabin, it becomes all too real. I remember with crystal clarity snow-covered mountains almost two years ago. A ritzy chalet. In the reflection of a window, an erotically charged look passes between a man and a woman.

I followed the family to the wilderness of Ucluelet on Vancouver Island; I stood outside the Zhang residence and looked up. The waves of the Pacific Ocean crashed against the rocks, the surf coming far too close to my feet, but I was too arrested by what I saw to move.

A huge mansion, set along the rugged coastline, with glassed-in walls. In one of the upstairs bedrooms, Dao and Jia Zhang. The man and the woman in the window. They are naked, pressed against each other, in the throes of an affair I found shocking, though hardly anything shocked me anymore.

The baby who had cancer, the one they'd kidnapped Bonnie for, to see if she could be a bone marrow donor. But she wasn't. They were going to get rid of her because *she wasn't a match*.

To the world, the baby was Kai Zhang's son, but Dao treated it like it was his own. Jia's child was his own. After she died, that sick child didn't have a mother anymore.

He didn't stand a chance.

It makes sense now. Dao blames me for killing his family. He was always going to hurt mine for what he thinks I've taken from him. His whole world. A child's death is a black mark against humanity. Any child's death, but especially hers.

Jia's child.

On the boat, right before a whale breached, David Tao looked at Jia Zhang. A secret glance. A shine of something like love in his eyes.

Something like obsession.

Something like both.

# 68

DAO RAISES HIS gun. He blinks. His pupils are dilated.

He's so high he doesn't hear boots crunching the snow behind him, until it's too late. He whips around, weapon still raised, but this time he's too slow. Kristof has his weapon in hand, too, but he doesn't fire it, doesn't have time, because two shots ring out.

Dao falls.

I see Nate Marlowe in this moment, in that kitchen in Detroit. Bonnie's and Lynn's still bodies. I see their hair in a pool of blood.

The fallen officer's weapon slips from my hand. Whatever instinct drove me to grab it when Dao turned to face Kristof is now gone. I want nothing more to do with it.

Kristof is closer to Dao than I am. "Is he dead?" I ask, my voice sounding stronger than I ever imagined it could in these circumstances.

"Not yet, but he will be soon."

Kristof kicks Dao's weapon farther away from where it has landed. He takes the fallen officer's gun away from me, wipes it down, and puts it in the man's hand.

He looks behind me, into the cabin. He's silent as he assesses the scene. Then he collects himself. "David Tao went crazy in here, left, then you found the bodies. Shortly after, this poor officer stumbled on the scene of the crime. He was leading you away when David Tao returned. I heard the exchange of fire and came running, but I wasn't able to get here in time to save the officer from this madman. This hero in uniform was able to fire his weapon twice before he was shot dead. He deserves a medal for taking down a dangerous fugitive."

I don't say anything.

Kristof pulls out his cell phone. "I'll go wait for the authorities. You'll need to wash your hands. You were obviously near the officer's gun when it was fired. You two were in close proximity, so there will be residue on your clothing. But your hands are clean. You might be able to get away with this if you're lucky." He walks back to the main cabin.

He's wrong. My hands will never be clean again.

I'm alone again, so I move to Dao's side. Kneel in the snow beside him and watch the life leave his body.

"The baby couldn't have been yours," I say. I don't know where these words are coming from, only that I couldn't stop them even if I wanted to. Some part of me acknowledging that this man doesn't get to slip away quietly. "Bloodwork would have shown that. Jia would never have risked taking Bonnie if Kai wasn't the father. You were never her family, even in spirit. She was using you. It was just a fantasy she let you believe because it was convenient to her. All this, and for what?"

His eyes lock on to mine, but he can't move. Can't speak. He dies soon after, choking on his own blood.

It's not enough. There is no satisfaction. This is the part of me I was hiding from Bonnie when she asked about morality. What I have inside me, you wouldn't even believe.

It hurts so much to think of her now.

The silence returns, and it's both external with the hush brought by the snowfall and inside of me with the finality of death. So much death, and part of it feels like my own.

Snow falls heavily now, blanketing the trees. Because death is on my mind, I think of Seb Crow. He didn't read fiction, but there was one novel he kept on his shelf in the study where I saw him last. *Snow Falls on the Cedars*. No. *Snow Falling on Cedars*. But I never read it.

Why does this come to me now? I can't stay here any longer.

Back in the guesthouse I kneel beside my daughter and her mother.

I don't ever want them to be alone in here again.

It's then that I hear a sound, a rattle of a breath. A soft cry. Coming from Lynn—no. From underneath Lynn. From Bonnie.

My own breath lodges in my throat as desperate hope and panic take hold of me. My throat clears. Lungs open up as full as a singer who's been waiting for her encore. And I start to scream for help as loud as I can.

# 69

WHEN THE POLICE show up, they try to arrest me again even though Kristof explains to them that I had no part in the shootout.

They believe him eventually, because of his crisp appearance, his pale face shining out at them with confidence. He's arguing for me, and some part of me wants to be grateful, but it doesn't matter. Nothing matters anymore because they have whisked Bonnie away to the hospital and I can't focus on anything else.

I'm taken to an interview room. People speak to me, but I don't hear them. "Where's my daughter?"

"Can you tell me—" says a cop with the earnest face of a teenager.

"How is she?"

"Ms. Watts, this is a serious—"

"Bonnie. Her name is Bonnie. She's seventeen years old. Is she . . . did she survive?"

"Ma'am—"

"Is she alive? Tell me!"

"She's alive," the cop says eventually. "And she'll live. The bullet hit her arm, but it seems she was struck unconscious by the fall to the ground. Broke her nose something awful. Lost a lot of blood, too."

It's only then that I can breathe a sigh of relief and refuse to speak on principle. Firstly, because I'm not about to talk to the cops now that it's all over. More importantly, I guess I'm still in shock. Bonnie is alive, but Lynn is still as dead as she was when I found her in the cabin.

Edison Lam has sent me a legal representative. I'm not one to look a gift attorney in the mouth, so I let her do all the talking. Kristof does some speaking as well, though I don't know what exactly he says; I just observe him, how calm and cool he is. How unsurprised.

The lawyer gets me out of the interview quickly. I'm in shock, she says. The trauma of finding my daughter near death and her adoptive mother murdered—this is after fearing for my life and going into hiding. Why wasn't I taken to a hospital first? She hints at racial bias. This could be grounds for a suit. There must have been a fresh batch of sensitivity training, because these are the magic words. They let me go. I go to the hospital to look for my daughter, where I'm told by a nurse who must have once been an army general, with her rigid back and impassive face, that Bonnie has been transferred to a private hospital. The nurse won't tell me which one.

"Ma'am, if you don't leave, I'll be forced to call security."

In fact, she already has. Two security guards approach from

behind me and escort me out to the parking lot where I stand, confused and cold, wondering what to do now. I call Leo and ask him to bring Whisper over to Simone's place.

Edison Lam is waiting for me when I get there. Simone pulls me into a hug while I stand with my eyes empty and my arms by my side.

"You sent Kristof to finish the job if I didn't," I say to him. "You heard what I said through the intercom? The address I gave?"

"I'm sorry for your troubles," says Mr. Lam. "But what does any of that matter anymore?"

We are silent for a moment. There's nothing else to say, but he finds a way to persevere. "Please send your banking details to my Vancouver office." He puts a card on the counter. "We'd like to arrange payment for your assistance in the research into David Tao's background, the work you did when my son initially engaged your services. You'll be paid in full, of course."

He mentions some other things, about services rendered, but what he's really buying is my silence in his investigation of his son's death. Because he's now saying something about a nondisclosure agreement.

I stop listening. Is this how Brazuca felt when Bernard Lam started talking about money? I think about all the calls I made to Bonnie and Everett that went unanswered.

At some point Simone tells Edison Lam to get out.

# 70

EVERETT HITS ME at the funeral, in the parking lot after the service. A big swing at my jaw that makes me think of Brazuca as it connects.

It's an act of blatant misogyny.

If I were a man, he would have swung harder.

Whisper goes for Everett's throat, and Simone barely manages to pull her back. Everett is restrained by two people I've never seen before in my life while my daughter stands listlessly off to the side with bandages over her nose. She won't say a word to me. Won't even look in my direction. She's wearing a black parka over a long black dress. The wind sends her hair flying, and she's shivering with cold or rage. I can't tell. Maybe it's a little bit of both, but she won't bother to clarify. She's ignoring me the same way she's ignored all of my attempts to reach her. She rips the brass key from around her neck and drops it on the ground.

Someone calls the police on Everett, for the assault. I decline to press charges.

"It should have been you!" he shouts as the strangers drag him away, his face smeared with tears.

I nod. Yes, I know. It should have been me.

Bonnie and Lynn were both shot at as they tried to flee.

Two bullets in Lynn and one in Bonnie. Three bullets to take a life. Lynn died almost instantly. There's almost no comfort in that thought.

Everett finds none, either.

"Don't listen to him," Simone says, pulling me back to the Corolla. But I do, of course. It's the only thing that happened at the funeral that makes any sense. The Corolla refuses to start. It, too, gives up on me. Simone arranges for a boost from the funeral director.

Afterward, I stop by Brazuca's apartment and stare up at the window. A habit I can't kick. Then the memory of a shoulder, a square of sunburned skin.

A shadow crosses the window. As I watch, I listen to the messages he's been leaving me. Asking me to call him back. Asking for an explanation. Offering his condolences. Et cetera. There, on the spot, I delete the messages.

I don't send Edison Lam my banking information, so he mails a check to Simone's place. I didn't know they still had those. I burn it in Simone's sink. She calls him to ask for another one. Which she keeps for me.

Leo sends me an advanced copy of Seb's memoirs, to be published in several months. In the acknowledgments Seb has thanked me for being his caretaker and his friend. I burn the book, too, this evidence that I'm a good and worthy person.

People have been hurt because of me. Bonnie, Brazuca, and Nate.

People have died. Lynn. Mike Starling. Joe Nolan. The Zhangs, who may have deserved it. The baby, who didn't.

In a moment of weakness, I call Nate and apologize for what happened to him over voicemail. I don't hear anything back, and that's about what I deserve.

There are times when I think of my daughter and then all the strength bleeds out of me when I realize I will never have a relationship with her. There'd been days when I cursed her for the darkness she came out of, what she'd represented in my life. She was the best part of me and I had spent years trying to forget she was alive.

I try to burn the brass key as well, perhaps to see if brass can burn, but Simone pushes me away before it chars and saves it. She gets a brand-new leather strap for it.

The key sears into my chest every single moment of every single day. It's no less than what I deserve. It's like a Stradivarius violin. Rare, precious, a piece of history to hold in your hands. But take away the history and you have an inanimate object. A violin is only as good as the musician. A key is only good if the door it opens exists. If you can put it into a lock and, with a turn, enter a room you long to be in. But what if the room and the door aren't there anymore? Or, worse, they are but no one knows where to find it?

There's a lock in Palestine that opens with this key, but I don't know where it is. Some people sneer that Palestine doesn't exist anymore. That sounds about right. There's a group of people in Winnipeg who might share my father's bloodline, but he never found them.

These are my thoughts in the wake of Lynn's death.

Just before Christmas Leo sells the business to Stevie Warsame, who is upset he has to learn bookkeeping for an entire company. Leo leaves me rambling messages begging me to visit on Christmas Eve. He says I can stay for New Year's Eve also. I can stay as long as I like.

I delete the messages. He just wants my dog. I think she wants him, too, the whore. But she is content to go with me on my long walks, the drive-bys of Brazuca's place.

Two days before Christmas I pick up the phone and a man whose voice I used to know says, "Hey there, Trouble." As far as nicknames go, it's a little on the nose. But this man in particular has good reason to know just how much trouble I am.

"Hi, Nate," I reply, surprised at how clear my voice sounds.

The next day I put all my belongings into the Corolla, including Whisper, of course. We stop in front of Lorelei's house. It's the same as always, an East Van bungalow. There's a wreath on the door, the single holiday decoration.

"Should I go in?" I ask Whisper. She ignores me, riveted by the action across the road where some poor soul is stringing up lights on Christmas Eve and his chocolate lab pup is standing by the ladder for helpful encouragement.

I take one long, final look at my sister's house.

The lights are on, and there's movement inside. She's entertaining. At another time I would have been perverse enough to knock on the door and guilt her into letting me in. But I don't see the point of that anymore. I put the car in drive before I can second guess myself. Then head to Leo's apartment building. There's an open space in front just waiting for me. Something has finally gone right. I couldn't bear having to park around back, seeing the place where Brazuca's MINI got hit. Reliving the memory of Brazuca.

Leo comes down and opens the back door of the car. Whisper gets up, wags her tail, and licks the side of his face. He breaks out into a grin. "Come on," he says to her.

She stays in the car.

"Come on, girl. Uncle Leo bought you some new food. I hear it's delish."

Whisper isn't having any of it.

"Go ahead," I say to her.

She ignores me and plants her butt.

"She's not coming," Leo says.

I don't understand her hesitation. She'd left with him so easily before. "Go on, girl." I give her a little push. She growls at me. Actually growls.

Leo closes the door. He lingers outside of the car, and I know he has something to say to me. Now that I'm here, I wait. But he decides to keep whatever it is to himself. An act of mercy, perhaps, but for me or him, I'm not sure.

He gives me a little wave and goes back to the apartment. Across the street the Szechuan place is closed. A closer look tells me that half the storefronts on this block are going out of business. There's a sign up a few doors away, a community notice asking for input. Peter Vidal's Devi Group has bought up the block and wants to open an art gallery and cultural center.

I look up.

The neon pink lights of the Szechuan place are indeed off, permanently now. To make space for art and culture, I suppose. For community, or someone's idea of it anyway.

Whisper barks at me from the car. She's telling me to hurry up.

# 71

BRAZUCA DISMANTLES THE telescope and puts it in the carry bag it came in.

He opens the safe in his bedroom and takes out his documents, the gold watch his father had given him when he turned eighteen, and the engagement ring that once belonged to his mother. The one his ex-wife returned calmly before she asked him to leave. She was tranquil, growing increasingly more reasonable toward the end, as his addictions spiraled out of control.

"I've never been unfaithful," he said to her one night, after a particularly vicious argument about where he'd been. It had come out like a plea, but that wasn't what he meant. He guessed he meant he was at a bar, as usual. Drinking alone.

She'd given him a curious look. He remembers it to this day, how puzzled she was by his insistence that he wasn't all that bad. That there was still something to save. "What does that have to do with anything?" she asked.

He didn't know, but it had seemed to be an important point at the time.

She set her boundaries and said, "You can no longer cross this line with me. I've had enough. It's over. Good-bye."

He never understood how she could be so cold, until now. Until he's faced that coldness, yet again, from Nora. Who won't return his calls. He'd seen her at Lynn's funeral, from a distance. Something in him broke when Everett Walsh hit her. Her expression, the emptiness there . . . it's going to stay with him for the rest of his life.

Brazuca puts all his things in a small rolling suitcase, along with a few items of clothing that do the best job of hiding his gauntness. He closes the empty safe. There's one item missing. His handgun, the only weapon he owns, which was never recovered from the MINI after the crash.

He takes one last look at the apartment and leaves it behind without a moment of regret.

A week later, he watches the sun go down from his patio.

The seaside town in the Canary Islands is empty of everyone but locals, and the night is quiet. He adjusts the settings on his telescope while he waits for the stars to come out. The little apartment cost him next to nothing. He can live here for the rest of his life with what he's made from Bernard Lam. He might be comfortable doing exactly that.

He didn't get to Alberta, after all. But there are other places to go to see the Northern Lights.

To pass the time, he opens up his laptop and plays the video clip he's been watching on a loop. Nate Marlowe, a different kind of star, no less compelling, is doing a filmed acoustic session for a Seattle radio station. It's just him, another bass player, a woman at the keyboards, and a backup singer.

Nate starts playing. The intro is long, hypnotic. When he begins to sing, his voice is like sandpaper. The backup singer steps forward. She hasn't yet lost her tropical tan, so her skin is the color he's become used to seeing. She's dressed in jeans, a loose sweatshirt, and a baseball cap. She looks like she wandered in from the street until you notice the mic in her hand.

When she sings the second verse, it brings tears to his eyes. Every time. It has nothing to do with the lyrics of the song, nothing to do with the arrangement or the haunting chords Nate Marlowe is playing. It is the pure, unadulterated emotion that her voice wraps him up in.

He has known Nora for a long time, but watching her sing is when he begins to truly see her.

The first time he met her was during an AA meeting. There was a thunderstorm raging outside and the church basement was almost empty. Only a few stragglers came in, some more for warmth than for anything else, and Nora. Whisper was at her side, and when someone mentioned that all pets should be left outside, Nora slapped the woman with a stare so cool the woman turned away and didn't speak to anyone else for the rest of the meeting.

She holds so much of herself back, except when she's singing. Embracing this raw, striking talent of hers. He wishes she would have shared this side of herself with him.

On-screen, the last chord is still reverberating through the air when a look passes between the two singers and Nora slips out of the room.

Brazuca searches daily, but there are no more videos of Nate and Nora singing. It is the best version of the song, with seven times as many views as the studio recording. The number is in the millions. It climbs every day.

The video feels like an absolution between Nate and Nora. It swims with emotion. They are holding grief at bay, the both of them. It is so beautiful and raw it's uncomfortable.

When the song is done, Nora simply leaves without fanfare.

It's over.

Good-bye.

# 72

WHISPER AND I head farther away from the border, leaving the blues behind us as we go.

We don't look back.

Well, she does, but she's fickle like that.

It's early, the sunlight just breaking through the dim Pacific Northwest slate. An endless sheet of gray broken only by the shadowed mountain peaks that watch over this landscape. Weary sentinels that seem to have been there since the dawn of time.

I'm feeling poetic. I'm feeling not like myself.

Behind us, at the end of a treacherous highway, a mother sits in a kitchen with her daughter. While snow falls on trees beyond the window. They tell stories, slipping into each other's memories. What they are looking for they find in each other. Another woman enters the room, and the shimmering thing between them grows to include her. So domestic, so banal, this scene of three women in the kitchen together. Though one of them is not yet an adult, she's not a child, either. She is her own thing, coming into her skin more and more as the days pass. She is the best thing the world has to offer. Kind eyes, unlike any other pair the adults in the room have seen. A love of dance and art.

In that kitchen with a dog sleeping on a rug by the door, they are a family. Like something out of book on a shelf that no one has read. A memory like a secret.

# ACKNOWLEDGMENTS

I WOULD LIKE to acknowledge the indigenous territories upon which I live and work.

Thank you to Lyssa Keusch, Liate Stehlik, Kate Parkin, Katherine Armstrong, Kaitlin Harri, and Danielle Bartlett.

I'm grateful for the expertise of PH, Dave Pledger, Sunni Westbrook, and Josette Calleja. I would also like to thank Sam Wiebe, Lori Rader-Day, Alix Hawley, Lou Berney, Elizabeth Little, Steph Cha, and Linda Richards for their support, and my family for being the reason I'm able to do this at all.

# ABOUT THE AUTHOR

SHEENA KAMAL holds an HBA in political science from the University of Toronto, and was awarded a TD Canada Trust scholarship for community leadership and activism around the issue of homelessness. Kamal has also worked as a crime and investigative journalism researcher for the film and television industry. Her academic knowledge and experience inspired her debut novel, *The Lost Ones*. She lives in Vancouver, Canada.